Reality Check

Rachel Storm is a woman who has it all. A great job, an amazing apartment, a decent paycheck…and overbearing mother hell-bent on seeing her married before the next millennium. Rachel doesn't *want* to get married. She likes her life the way it is, but her mother won't let it rest.

When her sister announces her wedding, the little white lie Rachel told her family about her "fiancé" blows up in her face. Now she has to find a fiancé by the weekend or face the wrath of the wedding nazi.

Doug, the impossibly good looking gay guy from the office, seems like the obvious choice. There's just one little problem with her plan—Doug isn't gay. And he plans to spend the entire weekend trying to get Rachel into his bed.

Miss Independent

The last thing Amanda Storm needs is a man in her life—
but no matter where she goes, she can't seem to get rid of them.

After three marriages and a near-miss, Amanda decides to
wash her hands of men once and for all and try living life on her
own. She moves away from her family, buys a cottage and gets
a job waiting tables at a busy local bar to put herself through
college. But then she meets Joe, who appoints himself as her
savior, and everything goes downhill from there.

Joe Baker knows a woman in trouble when he sees one.
Amanda might be good at faking it, but she's in way over her
head. As her neighbor, he's willing to help her with whatever
she needs done around the old cottage, but she won't accept his
help. All he can do is sit back and watch things fall apart
around her, and try not to say I told you so when it happens.
Somewhere along the way, his protective feelings turn into
something more, but after three failed marriages, Amanda
wants nothing to do with commitment. Joe isn't a man to give
up, and he's determined to show her they're meant to be
together--no matter what it takes.

Heart of the Storm

Elisa Adams

A Samhain Publishing, Ltd. publication.

Samhain Publishing, Ltd.
512 Forest Lake Drive
Warner Robins, GA 31093
www.samhainpublishing.com

Heart of the Storm
Copyright © 2007 by Elisa Adams
Print ISBN: 1-59998-427-X

Reality Check Digital ISBN: 1-59998-006-1
Miss Independent Digital ISBN: 1-59998-153-X
Reality Check Editing by Ansley Velarde
Miss Independent Editing by Sasha Knight
Cover by Scott Carpenter

Reality Check electronic publication: January 2006
Miss Independent electronic publication: January 2007
First Samhain Publishing, Ltd. print publication: July 2007

Contents

Reality Check

Chapter One

Why did it seem like the rest of the world had gone mad and she was the only sane one left on the planet?

Rachel slapped her palm against her cheek. This had to be a twisted, stress-induced dream, because there was no way her mother had just told her that Amanda was getting married. *Again.*

"Rachel, are you there? You'll come home for Amanda's wedding, won't you?"

"Of course I will, Mom." She shifted the phone from one ear to the other and bit back a groan. "I wouldn't miss my only sister's wedding."

Even if it was her *fourth* one. In *eight* years.

Amanda changed husbands like most women changed their toothbrushes. Why attend this wedding when she could watch the videos of the other three?

"Why is this the first I'm hearing about a wedding?" A little warning would have been nice. Who planned a wedding in three days, anyway?

Only crazy people. And her family fit right into *that* category. They'd probably invented it.

"Amanda told us last week, but I know how busy you are and I didn't want to bug you with minute details until I absolutely had to."

Translation: advance notice would have given Rachel time to come up with a plausible excuse. They might be nuts, but they weren't fools.

"So can I assume we'll see you on Friday?" Miriam Storm continued in the sing-song tone that had made Rachel want to jump off a bridge during her teenage years. Of all times, why did family loyalty have to pick now to rear its ugly head?

She snorted. It wasn't loyalty wrapping its thick fingers around her throat. It was guilt. Years and years of guilt her mother had spoon-fed all her children. She'd been so clever about it that none of them realized what had happened until they'd moved out of the house. Years later, Rachel was still dealing with the residual effects.

"Friday. Um, hold on a second and let me check my schedule."

She gave her desktop calendar a quick glance, praying for some big, important meeting that would make it impossible to take off for an entire weekend. Her nails clicked on the gunmetal gray surface of her desk. Even a bikini wax would be preferable to the toothpicks-shoved-under-her-fingernails torture Amanda's nuptials were sure to be.

The little square marked with Friday's date mocked her with its glaring, undisturbed whiteness. Blank. Nada. Zip. Not even a deadline she couldn't miss. She dropped her forehead into her hand and resigned herself to her fate.

"Sure. Friday sounds good, Mom." About as good as a hangover, the flu, and PMS, on the same day.

"We'll be having a small dinner party, just family, that night, so make sure you and your fiancé arrive by seven o'clock."

"Yeah, no problem. I'll be there by—" *Fiancé* clicked in her mind and the words died in her throat. Her family didn't really expect her to bring *him*, did they?

She sank back into her leather chair and closed her eyes. Of course they did. Why wouldn't they? After years of borderline harassment from her mother on the state of her love life, Rachel had done the unthinkable and bragged about the wonderful man she planned to marry. Smart, funny, ambitious, handsome...

Nonexistent.

Now the teensy little fib had come back to bite her in the butt, and she hadn't had a tetanus shot in years.

"Well, I'm not so sure he'll be able to make it. He's really busy on the weekends, and he can't just drop everything on such short notice."

"Rachel Storm. Something is going on that you're not telling me about." Her mother clicked her tongue. "Are you two having problems? You haven't spoken much about him lately. What was his name again?"

Her small office seemed to close in around her, the beige-painted walls moving toward the center of the room, the navy blue carpet folding up at the edges. She sucked in a deep breath of industrial-cleaner-scented air, the pounding of her heart a hollow echo in her ears. Years of her father teaching her to respect her mother and never let her down all came flooding back. If anything went wrong with this wedding, she would be blamed. Being one of the few sane people in the family, she couldn't take that kind of weight on her shoulders.

"No, Mom. Nothing's wrong. We get along just fine." Not surprising, considering he didn't exist. She glanced toward the ceiling and muttered a soft curse. "I'll talk to him and see if I can get him to take a few days off, just this once."

And then she'd make a laughingstock of herself in front of her whole family by dragging her imaginary friend to Amanda's wedding.

The thought galvanized her into action. She bolted upright in her chair. A click of the mouse opened the address file in her computer and she started scrolling through the list of personal contacts.

Billy? Nope. Got married three weeks ago. Shane? No way. He'd spent most of last month in jail for check forging. Somehow, she doubted her parents would approve. Trey? Maybe. On second thought, no. He was pretty to look at, but he couldn't string four words together to make a coherent sentence--though that might go unnoticed with the way her mother monopolized any conversation held within twenty feet of her. Halfway through her short list of personal contacts Rachel came to a realization.

She needed to get some new friends.

A knock at the half-open office door provided a welcome distraction. Her gaze flew from the computer screen to the doorway and she found herself staring at the sexiest pair of golden-green eyes she'd ever seen. Her body reacted in uncharacteristic deer-in-the-headlight fashion, as it always did when *he* caught her with his gaze.

Doug Bennett.

He stood in the doorway, a friendly smile on his face, tapping a thick manila folder against his palm.

A little over six feet tall, broad shouldered and beautifully muscled. Light brown hair worn long enough on top to make a woman want to tangle her fingers in the silky strands. Firm lips, strong jaw, nose that looked like it had been broken a time or two. Thick eyelashes, and those eyes...they had the ability to make her wet with just the right glance.

She made a point not to show her emotions at work, but whenever he walked by she drooled on the inside. If she'd been looking for a relationship, he would have been at the top of her list. He was perfect. Exactly what she'd always wanted in a man but had never thought she'd find. Smart, sexy, and strong.

And gay.

Ironic that the one man she'd found in years who got an immediate reaction from certain feminine parts of her body had zero interest in any of those particular parts.

"I have the information you asked for. Is this a bad time? I can come back." His deep, smooth voice sent a quiver through the parts in question. It took her lust-hazed mind a few seconds to realize he'd spoken to her. About work. And he expected a response.

"Listen, Mom, I've got to go. Work emergency. See you on Friday." She dropped the receiver back into the cradle.

The fiancé-finding mission would have to wait.

"What can I do for you, Doug?"

"Here's the paperwork you asked for on the Myers property." He leaned forward to slide the file onto her desk. A stray lock of light brown hair fell over his forehead and her fingers itched to brush it away.

She sat on her hands. "Thanks. I'll have the brochures ready for you in a couple of days."

"Excellent. I appreciate it." He glanced to the seat of her chair. "Is everything okay? You look a little stressed."

"You have no idea. My sister's getting married, some last minute thing, and my mother's insisting..."

Her voice trailed off. Doug's gaze locked with hers, his eyes sparkling with amusement, and something clicked inside her head.

He'd be perfect. A giggle bubbled up in her throat. More than perfect. He *was* her imaginary man personified.

Every woman in the office had panted after him since he started working at Stellar Realty a few months ago. But gossip moved through the office at the speed of light, and within a few days one of the secretaries had made it known Doug was involved with someone named Brett. Bad news for the single women who'd been hoping for a date with the sexy real estate agent, but good news for Rachel. Long-term relationships made her stomach churn.

Her last three had been unmitigated disasters, thanks in part to the bad soap opera known as her family. Though she couldn't give them all the credit. Her deep-seated inability to commit had been the real culprit. By the time the relationships reached the meet-the-parents stage she'd been looking for an excuse to escape. Someone equally uninterested in anything more than acting all sappy and lovey-dovey would be just what she needed for the weekend.

"You wouldn't happen to be free this weekend, would you, Doug?"

"Why? Do you want to get together and go over the design for the brochures?"

No. She wanted to get together and go over every inch of his body. With her tongue.

"No, I had something else in mind. Why don't you sit down? I was kind of hoping for a small favor, a weekend of your time. I..." she paused, trying to put her situation into words that wouldn't have him running in the other direction. "I mentioned that my sister is getting married this weekend. I told my mother I would bring my fiancé, which creates a little problem for me."

Doug took a seat chair across from her desk, leaning forward and propping his elbows on his knees. The stripes in his tie matched his eyes. "What's the problem with your fiancé?"

She sucked in a gulp of air. *Calm and relaxed, Rachel. Don't get worked up about it. You can do this.* Of course she could do it. If she didn't look at him.

As the marketing director, she ran the entire marketing department of a large real estate company. If she couldn't sell Doug on her idea, she might as well retire now.

"I don't exactly have one." She rested her hands on top of her desk and pasted on her best professional smile. "I now need to find someone to feign, only for the weekend, to be my intended, otherwise it will ruin the whole event for my mother."

He frowned. "And telling her the truth never crossed your mind?"

If it were really that simple she never would have invented the fiancé in the first place. "You don't know my mother."

He offered her a tight smile, but didn't laugh or get up and leave. She took that as her cue to go forward with her plea. "This is where you come in."

"Let me get this straight. You want me to go with you to this wedding, for a whole weekend, and pretend to be your fiancé?"

"That about sums it up."

He laughed. The jerk. "You're serious about this?"

"Very serious. Think of it as a mini-vacation. It'll be a lot of fun." Her voice broke on the last word. "We get along great, and I think you'd be perfect to help me out with my...problem."

"How do you figure?"

Her face flamed. It was simple, really, but oh-so-complex at the same time. He hadn't grown up in her house. He wouldn't understand. Learning about her family's...quirks really had to be a hands-on experience.

"Neither one of us is interested in pursuing anything more than a weekend of pretend engagement. Don't worry about public displays of affection. My family knows that I'm against them, so you're safe in that respect. All you'll have to do is look good and make a little idle chitchat."

She sucked in another big gulp of air. Air filled with Doug's clean, spicy, masculine scent. A little while flag rose inside her head as she recognized his cologne. One that made her go weak in the knees when worn by a normal man. When worn by a demigod like him, it hit her a little higher than her knees, dampening her panties and making her wish she'd packed a vibrator in her briefcase.

And if she didn't get a grip, like five minutes ago, he might call the mental hospital and tell them he'd found their escaped mental patient.

She took a pen and a pad of paper from her desk drawer and set it in front of him, drawing inspiration from all the sales seminars she'd sat through. "Why don't you write down your address so I know where to pick you up? Is Friday at five-thirty good for you?"

He sat back in his chair and crossed his legs. His eyes darkened to a moss-green and seemed to bore right through her. Something low in her stomach trembled and her nipples peaked against the satin cups of her bra. After this meeting, she might have to go on blood pressure medication.

A hint of a smile danced at the corners of his lips. "You seem to be forgetting something. I haven't said yes yet."

"Huh?" Her hopes fell out of the sky and rocketed to the ground, dying a fiery death.

"I didn't say I'd go with you." The husky tone of his voice was enough to send her body into a lust-induced state of shock. Why did all the good ones have to be married or gay?

"Oh. Okay. The details are negotiable, I guess. Do you want something more in the way of compensation?"

A slow, dangerous smile spread across his face. And then he did the last thing she expected. He winked. If she wasn't worried about retaliation from some big guy named Brett, she might have jumped over her desk and attacked him.

"First of all, relax. You're getting ahead of yourself." He smoothed his tie down his chest. Her gaze followed the movement. "I don't care about compensation. This isn't some business deal, Rachel. It would be a favor, for a friend, on my own time. I don't mind helping my friends, as long as they ask properly."

She dragged her gaze away from his black dress shirt, and the hard lines of his chest underneath. "I'm not following."

"Ask me nicely."

His demanding tone pushed away the sensual fog in her brain. He had to be kidding. Ask nicely? What was this, kindergarten? "You want me to say please?"

"That would be the general idea."

She bit back a groan. She wanted a fiancé for the weekend, not a date with Miss Manners. "Doug, would you *please* do me the honor of being my fiancé for the weekend? It would mean so much to me, you being my *friend* and all."

"Thank you." Something that looked like—but could absolutely not be—lust passed across his gaze.

She squirmed in her seat. Why did he have to look at her like that? It was like dangling a piece of triple chocolate cake in front of a diabetic. She couldn't taste him, but right about now she'd give her left arm for a just little nibble.

Doug pushed himself up from the chair and leaned across her desk, his face inches from hers. Everything seemed to move in slow motion as her gaze fixed on his mouth. Her face lifted, her lips tingling in anticipation of the contact.

"Did you hear me, Rachel?" His quiet, smooth tone slid over her skin like melted butter, making her ache inside.

She ripped her gaze away and flopped back into her chair. Maybe this wasn't such a good idea. How was she supposed to get through a weekend when she couldn't manage ten minutes? "I'm sorry. I must have missed it. Would you mind repeating it?"

Way too much amusement lit his eyes. "Twelve Ocean Terrance Apartment 3C. Five on Friday. Don't be late."

He left the office without even a goodbye. As soon as the door closed behind him, she rested her forehead on the cool metal desk and prayed for the rest of the day to fly by so she could go home and take a cold shower. Or ten.

Brett was one lucky guy.

8003

Doug sat in the quiet sanctum of his office, his feet propped up on his desk, his mind reeling. What had he just agreed to? He was going to spend a whole weekend with Rachel Storm, pretending to be her fiancé. Part of him had wanted to jump up and punch his fist into the air when she'd asked him so nicely.

Please.

Just that one word slipping from those lush pink lips had been enough to get him instantly hard. He'd had to rush out of her office so she wouldn't notice the effect she had on him and change her mind.

It hadn't been right to make her beg like that, but it had been worth every second to watch the anger spark in her eyes and hear her voice get all soft and husky. Visions of her saying that word to him in bed, begging him to make her come, all that dark hair and alabaster skin against his black sheets, only added to his indecent state of arousal.

Rachel between his sheets, writhing and moaning, her legs wrapped around his hips, her nails clawing his back.

What an image *that* made.

In the two months he'd been with Stellar Realty, he'd been watching her. At first glance, the nickname the men had given her seemed well-earned. Ice princess. Not many of the men in the office had looked past her façade to see the woman underneath. Since Doug had been working with her, he'd done nothing but look.

She did her best to make the men who might be interested think the only heart she had was the one from a past lover she kept in a jar on her mantle. But a few inconsistencies had come to his attention. Ones that made him think she might not be as frosty as she wanted everyone to believe.

This afternoon she'd plowed ahead, barely even stopping to take a breath. Most might see it as cockiness, but he didn't. He saw it for what it was. Insecurity. A nervous tick that he found endearing and sexy at the same time. It had taken all his willpower not to lift up that navy blue conservative skirt, push her panties out of the way and slide his cock into her.

He pressed a palm to his groin. *Down, boy.*

For months he'd been trying to crack through her cool exterior, but had yet to find a foolproof way inside. And then she'd dropped the perfect opportunity right into his lap.

She wanted a pretend fiancé? He could do that. No problem. At the same time, he'd to get to know her even better than he had through two months of casual conversations. This weekend he'd dig down deep, find out what made her tick.

Find out what would make her climb into bed with him for an incredible night or two of sweaty, steamy sex.

She'd told him the terms were negotiable. Good. Because they would to have a little talk about those public displays of affection.

Chapter Two

By the time Rachel stood at Doug's front door on Friday evening, her hands shook and an odd feeling of dread had built in her stomach. He hadn't shown up for work. The quiet, dimly-lit hall around her only added to her anxiety. The entire third floor of his building seemed deserted. Not a soul in sight. She glanced around, half-expecting to see tumbleweeds blow past. What if he'd changed his mind? What if he'd decided he didn't want to go and was too chicken to tell her?

What if Brett had pitched some kind of a fit and planned to come after her with pick axe?

Her knees buckled. She might as well go and pick out a headstone now and save her family the trouble of doing it later. She'd never live this down. Not in a million years.

"Control yourself. Don't let anyone see you sweat. Whatever happens, do not lose your cool." Even as she muttered the words, she dug her fresh manicure into the leather strap of her purse. One of the tips snapped. So much for calm, cool, and collected.

Before she could do her nails any more damage, she knocked on the door. And waited.

No answer.

So not a good sign.

She'd just raised her fist to knock again when the door swung open. Doug stood across the threshold, one hand in the pocket of his jeans. His gaze snagged hers and held. She curled her hands into fists. A couple more nail tips cracked against her palms.

There had to be something wrong with her. She pressed the back of her hand to her forehead. No fever.

Men never had that effect on her. She didn't allow it. They'd proven time and time again that they weren't worth the effort of a relationship. But Doug, for some reason, seemed to get past all her barriers with just a look. *One look.*

It was the kind of cheesy stuff romance novels were written about. That fabled one person who could turn a woman inside out without doing anything at all.

She huffed a laugh. In order to get him to notice her as a potential partner, she'd have to have some pretty drastic surgery.

"A little early, dear?" Doug asked, his tone laced with humor. The smile on his lips had all the moisture rushing from her mouth to points further south. If he kept looking at her like that she'd need to borrow his bathroom to change her panties.

"You had me worried when you weren't at work today." She glanced past him into his apartment to cover her discomfort, which seemed to be multiplying by the second. A gay man who looked that good in a simple gray t-shirt and jeans ought to be banned from going out in public.

"Nice to see you, too, Rachel."

He expected pleasantries? He was lucky she was still breathing. "We need to be on the road within ten minutes in order to keep on schedule. Now if you'll just let me in, we can go over what you need to pack."

He raised an eyebrow. "You came over ten minutes early to help me pack?"

"Yep. Are you going to let me in?"

The slow shake of his head, coupled with the laughter in his eyes, settled a ball of something hot into the pit of her stomach. He was enjoying her discomfort, the masochist she'd suddenly become was enjoying his enjoyment.

"Look, this isn't a joke. It's late. We have to go." She tapped her watch face with her fingernail, one of the few she hadn't yet broken.

He cupped her chin in his big, warm palm and the hot ball in her stomach spread to all her extremities. She opened her mouth, but couldn't make a sound. His touch turned her brain to mush and made her body beg for things that made even her blush.

He ran his thumb across the seam of her lips before he dropped his hand. "I thought we had this discussion yesterday. You need to speak to me nicely. If we're going to play a happy couple, you're going to have to break down and act...*happy*."

"I *am* happy." Though she'd be a whole lot happier if he'd push her up against the wall and put her out of her misery.

"Oh, yeah. That's really obvious." He stepped back to let her inside. "Lighten up a little, Rachel. It isn't going to kill you to smile."

No, but if she let down her guard she might do something stupid like grope him. Being sued for sexual harassment wouldn't look good on her resume. "If I was looking for advice, I'd see a psychologist."

"Now there's an idea." A warm chuckle rumbled from his chest. "Though I have to say I kind of like this anxious side of you. It's sexy." He winked.

In order to keep from asking him where the nearest bed was, and if he'd like to join her in it, she pointed to a big black suit bag parked next to the door.

"Is that your luggage?" A matching duffel lay to one side of the suit bag, the top zipped neatly.

"Yep. Let me just grab it and we'll—"

"Hold that thought. I just want to make sure you packed the right things." She got down on her hands and knees and unzipped the suit bag to peruse the contents. "Don't you have a tie that matches better with these pants than the two you've packed?"

Or a tie that wasn't butt-ugly? Weren't gay guys supposed to have incredible fashion sense? He must have missed the boat on that one.

The door slamming shut drew her attention back to Doug. He stood over her with his arms across his chest, his foot tapping on the flagstone foyer. Her heart thumped against her ribcage. "What?"

"I think you missed your calling. You should really go into airport security." A small smile tugged at the corners of his lips. "When I have a woman in that position, I usually prefer her to be doing something else with her hands. And her mouth."

Omigod. Her hands clenched into fists around the silk ties. Her lips parted, just the thought of his suggestion sending a wave of tremors through her body.

"Jerk." What kind of a gay guy made comments like that, anyway? Wasn't it against the rules?

"I'm many things, honey, but a jerk isn't one of them," he told her, his gaze locked on her breasts. For a man who claimed not to be a jerk, he sure managed a dead-on impression of one. And he managed to make her like it. Which was a feat unto itself.

In a desperate attempt to focus her thoughts back on the situation at hand, she stood and cleared her throat. "Does Brett mind that you're doing this for me?"

His gaze snapped to her face, his eyes narrowing. All the humor fled from his expression. "How do you know about Brett?"

Touchy, aren't we? She dropped the ties into the bag, zipped it closed and stood. "It's not exactly a secret. No need to get upset about it. So you're unavailable. No big deal."

He gave her a stony glare before he turned his back to her. The muscles across his shoulder blades stretched tight and her fingers ached to smooth them. She stuffed her hands in her pockets. "I'm sorry if I said something wrong."

"I'd prefer to keep my private life private, if you don't mind. I told you I'd do a favor for you. As a friend only. But this isn't a high school sleepover. We aren't going to be sharing all our secrets."

He leaned down to pick up his bags, and her gaze drifted to his rear end. Very nice. Spectacular, even. Tight and firm, the perfect size to cup in the palms of her hands. She swiped at the drool gathering in the corners of her mouth.

"Brett's gone," he said as he stood and walked to the door. "So don't worry about that being a problem. We'd better get out of here or we're going to be late."

Well, excuse me. Talk about a hundred and eight degree turn. Okay, so talking about Brett was off-limits. Though she supposed she could understand why talking about his unconventional relationship would be a little uncomfortable. "I didn't mean to offend you."

"You didn't." He ushered her out the door and locked it behind them. "But we've got to draw the line somewhere. We need to leave as much of our personal lives out of this as possible."

"There's nothing wrong with your personal life." Her assurance earned her a particularly dark look. "There's no need to be ashamed of your lifestyle."

"Lifestyle?" He nearly choked on the word. "I have no idea what you're talking about."

She blinked. Was he still in the closet? So it wasn't just talking about Brett that made him angry. It was the whole gay thing in general. That was fine with her. It would be easier to pretend she was head-over-heels in love with him if her mind didn't plague her with constant reminders of his sexuality.

She shook her head as they stepped into the elevator. The only thing keeping her from sending Doug back to his apartment and forgetting the whole thing was the fact that she'd never live it down if she didn't show up for Amanda's wedding with her "fiancé" in tow. She'd never be able to face her family again. Though that didn't sound like such a horrible idea anymore at all.

৪০০৪

Twenty minutes—and at least a thousand sidelong glances at Doug—into the ride, and she'd had enough of the silence. He'd leaned back in the seat and closed his eyes as soon as she'd started the car. Her family would never buy it if they didn't at least talk to one another.

"Hey, Doug? We need to get to know each other. We have two hours in the car. We might as well spend it wisely."

He didn't even bother to open his eyes. "You're probably right."

There was no *probably* about it. Considering they'd been "engaged" for six months, they should at least know some basic facts. What kind of woman didn't take the time to get to know her future husband?

One whose future husband was a figment of her imagination.

"Tell me about yourself. What's your full name?"

"Douglas Aaron Bennett."

Okay. She felt like a contestant on one of those dating shows where they set up two completely incompatible people and followed them around all night to see how long it would take before they beat each other to a bloody pulp. The only things missing were the cameras and the obnoxious host, though someone in her family would surely fill that position.

At work they'd always had pleasant, if not vague, conversations. Why the silent treatment now? "How old are you?"

"Twenty-nine." He shifted in his seat, lifted his hand to his mouth and yawned.

She snorted. Not right now, buddy. We've got a lot of ground to cover if you're going to convince my parents that you're totally devoted to me. "When's your birthday?"

"Tomorrow."

"Good to know. Mine's—" Wait a second. Did he say *tomorrow*? "Your birthday is this Saturday?"

"Yep."

"Your thirtieth birthday is the day before my sister's wedding?"

"Looks that way."

His confession stunned her so much her hands slackened on the wheel. The car started to swerve into the neighboring lane. She yanked the wheel to right the vehicle, her heartbeat pounding in her ears. "Why didn't you say something?"

"I didn't think it really mattered. It's just another day."

"Why wouldn't it matter? Thirty is a milestone birthday."

He let out a noisy sigh. "What is it with you women? Why do you all get so worked up about aging? So I'll be a year older. Who really cares?"

"I would." Men had it so easy. They got sexier with age. Gray hair was distinguished. Women just aged. There was nothing distinguished or sexy about boobs that hung to one's knees. "Tell me about your family and your childhood. Give me something to work with here."

"My mom's name is Anna. My dad's is Riley. They had me later in life, when they were in their early forties. No brothers or sisters, no aunts or uncles, just me and my parents. I grew up in Providence. Moved to Massachusetts for college—BC, in case you need to know that too—and never left. Never married, no children, no ties, except to my job. Anything else you need to know, or is that sufficient, Ma'am?"

Sufficient? He had to be kidding. They'd just barely scratched the surface. And what was with that Ma'am crap? "I suppose that's a start. What about your favorite color? Favorite food? Life's ambition? These are all things my mother is going to ask, you know."

Knowing Miriam Storm, she'd probably ask for everything right down to his underwear size, but Rachel didn't want to scare him. And a small part of her was starting to want to see him squirm. Okay, maybe not so small.

"If you insist. My favorite color is green. I'll eat pretty much anything except for sushi and liver. I have my dream career right now, making great money. I like long walks on the beach at sunset, romantic dinners by candlelight, and cuddling in front of the fire on winter nights." He laughed, a deep, husky sound that made her stomach flutter. She liked it. A lot.

"Walks on the beach and candlelit dinners? Snuggling by the fireplace?" Yuck. Not really her thing. But hey, if that was what he and Brett enjoyed doing, more power to them.

"I was just kidding about those last three. I feel like I'm auditioning for some TV dating show."

She couldn't help but chuckle. Great minds thought alike. Or was that simple minds? "In a way, you're right. Think of it as reality TV, without the whole TV part."

"So this is just reality, huh? Bringing me along seems a little extreme."

The whole situation sounded dumb when he put it that way. "More like reality squared. Being with my family is like watching *The Brady Bunch* through a broken window. My family can be a little... well, for lack of a better description, nuts. One weekend with them and you're going to need a long vacation."

"Oh, come on, Rachel. They can't be that bad."

She'd make a believer out of him yet. "*Please.* Living with them was like being trapped in a soap opera. It wreaked havoc on my formative years."

"That explains a lot." He laughed again. "What's so terrible about them?"

She glanced at him as a car passed heading in the other direction. The headlights illuminated his face, casting an odd glow on his amused expression. He thought this was funny, huh? He'd see just how funny it was when Miriam got her hooks into him. "Okay. You asked for it. Just don't say I didn't warn you. Now it's my turn to fill you in on my life. My parents are Miriam and Earl. They've lived in the same house since they got married and started having us kids.

"There are five of us all together—Jake is thirty-one, Brian is twenty-nine, Amanda is twenty-eight, I'm twenty-six, and David is twenty-four. I went to state college, started working for Stellar three years ago. No marriages or children, either, and don't plan on them for a long while yet, if ever. My favorite color is red, and my favorite food is fried chicken, which I can't eat because it goes straight to my hips."

He glanced at her, a corner of his mouth lifting into a very sexy half-smile that caressed her skin like the heated touch of his hands. "I like my women a little rounded. Those skinny model types don't do anything for me."

Her stomach bottomed out. Lord, the man had a way with words. But there was one slight flaw with his supposed *confession*. Women as a whole didn't *do anything* for him. "Um, okay. If you say so."

She tossed him another glance and gulped at the blatant sensuality in his gaze. Uh, oh. A few more minutes of that and she'd be putty in his hands. Putty he wouldn't have a clue how to use.

She turned her focus back to her driving. It wouldn't be much longer and they'd be there. Good thing, too, since she'd nearly run them off the road just from being close to him.

"Oh, I do say so, Rachel." In the next second, his hand was on her, brushing her hair behind her ear. "I like your hair down. It's sexy this way. So much better than those old lady buns you wear at work. I didn't realize it was so long. Hair like this, it's fantasy-inspiring. Do you know what a guy thinks about when he sees hair like this on a beautiful woman?"

Ohmigod. She needed to pull the car over—*now*—before she got them both killed. Time for a new rule. "You can't touch me."

Doug chuckled. The sound did amazing things to her insides. His fingertip trailed down the side of her neck, leaving a line of goose bumps in its wake. "Why not? We're supposed to be engaged, right? Isn't your family going to get suspicious if I don't touch you once in a while?"

When his finger flicked across her collarbone, she jumped. And gasped. And involuntarily jerked the wheel.

The car swerved into the breakdown lane, coming an inch from hitting the guardrail before she got control and pulled the little sedan back onto the road. Her heart thumped in her throat and she couldn't quite catch her breath. The guy should come with a warning label like the ones on prescription drugs. *Do not take while driving.* Or better still, *do not take if you're sensitive to large amounts of testosterone in a very small space.*

He yanked his hand away as if he'd caught fire. "Okay, okay. Point taken. I can't touch you. At least not when we're in a car."

She imagined he'd have the same effect on her ability to walk. Not wanting to spend the weekend in the emergency room, she shook her head. "I told you before. My mom knows I'm not into public displays. All you have to do is stand there and nod every once in a while."

And look really, really sexy.

And smell great.

And smile that smile that makes me—

"Is it getting hot in here?" She flipped on the air conditioning, twisting the dial to full blast. Maybe that would cool her suddenly out-of-control hormones.

The only thing it did was make her nipples bead. Completely embarrassing.

Damn, damn, damn. They were *so* not off to a good start.

She kept her gaze trained on the darkening road, but Doug's stare burned into her all the same. "Are you attracted to me, Rachel?"

Oh, yeah, like she'd really admit that to him. That would give him too much power over her. The last thing Doug needed was a power trip. Or more ammunition to pick on her than he already had. "No. Of course not. Why would I be attracted to *you*? That's the craziest idea I've ever heard."

"Even crazier than asking me to fake being your fiancé for the weekend?"

Well, hell. "Um, no, not really. But still, I would never be attracted to you. Never. Not in a million—"

"Rachel?"

Just the way he said her name had her insides melting into a puddle of lust. She just hoped she'd be able to get the stains out of her seat. "Huh?"

"You're lying through your teeth."

&OG

Torture. That's what this car ride was. Doug turned it over and over in his mind, but couldn't come up with a more apt description. She was so close. So damned close and he couldn't touch her.

Could her car be any smaller? He'd had ride-on toys bigger than this as a child.

His left leg had fallen asleep an hour ago, and his right one had just woken up, cramping and tingling in protest. He needed to get out and stretch before he found himself with a permanent incapacitation.

"Are we nearly there?" He had to force himself not to look at her. If he looked, he'd want to touch. If he touched, she'd run them off the road. He'd prefer to live, and touch her later when they weren't in a vehicle traveling sixty-five miles per hour down a dark stretch of highway with metal guardrails on each side.

"About five more minutes."

The soft anxiety in her voice made him break his vow and look at her. She glanced at him out of the corner of her eye—something he'd caught her doing an awful lot of tonight. At least a lot for a woman who denied having any attraction to him.

He shook his head and shifted in the uncomfortable seat. If she had asked—and he'd been a little disappointed that she hadn't—he wouldn't have denied *his* attraction to *her*. She had to know. He'd done nothing to keep it a secret.

He couldn't wait to get her alone.

First they had to suffer through some kind of family party, but after that Rachel would be all his. Assuming they were even allowed to sleep in the same room. The thought of being kept away from her all night left him cold—and defeated his purpose for even coming on this little excursion.

"What are the sleeping arrangements this weekend?"

She slowed the car and turned down an exit ramp. "We'll have my old room. Don't worry, though, it has twin beds."

Twin beds? Didn't that just suck. At least they'd be in the same room. He'd just have to work with what he had. And twin beds could be very...cozy, given the right situation. "It must be nice to get to sleep in your old room."

She snorted. "It's like coming home again—but not in that sappy Hallmark way. More like wandering onto the set of the Jerry Springer show."

He laughed. She had to be exaggerating. No one's family could be that bad.

He hoped.

"My mother kept all our old bedrooms the way they were," she continued. "That way we'd have a place to sleep when we came home to visit. Except for Amanda's, since she's spent most of her adult life with various husbands. Amanda's room became the sewing room. My mother is a sewing freak. She used to make all our clothes."

"That doesn't sound like a bad thing."

"You've never had to wear polyester socks and linen underwear."

He burst out laughing, though he couldn't be sure that her deadpan crack had been a joke. "Amanda's the one who's getting married this weekend, right?"

"She is. Don't get too excited about it, though. She's just adding to her ex-husband collection. Her first was a car mechanic, her second an out-of-work musician, and her third a waiter at a local café. This new one owns his own business of some sort, so it looks like she may be moving up in the world."

"Are you for real? I mean, you're not exaggerating or anything, are you?"

"Um, no." She snorted again. The very unladylike sound seemed to fit her perfectly. "The sad thing is that my mom makes a huge deal out of it, every single time. She doesn't get it that Amanda's never going to stick with one guy long enough for her investments to pay off. Brace yourself. We're here."

She pulled up in front of a huge white Victorian-style house with an expansive, well landscaped lawn. "Are you ready?"

He caught a glimpse of movement from inside the house. A curtain pulled back in one of the front windows. Two older women stood there, their faces practically pressed to the glass. Doug smiled to himself. Time to start the fun, and give Rachel a weekend to remember. "Almost. There's something I need to do before we go inside."

She paused in the middle of opening the car door. The overhead light lit the interior in pale yellow and gave the women in the window a clear view right into the car.

She shifted in her seat to face him, her expression exasperated—and adorable. "What do you need to do now?"

"This." He cupped her face in his hands and kissed her.

Chapter Three

Rachel held her lips stiff against Doug's. *For all of two seconds.* Then she embarrassed herself by plastering her body against his—at least as plastered as her center console would allow—and kissed him back.

She felt his touch all over, when in reality his hands hadn't moved from her face. She dragged her own hands up his sides to his shoulders in a feeble, and totally false, attempt to push him away.

Who was she kidding? She'd wanted his lips on hers since he'd gotten into her car. This was like a dream come true.

Only, she had to be dreaming.

Because Doug was *not* interested in women.

The thought doused her lust with a bucket of icy cold reality. She shoved him away. "What do you think you're doing? I thought you agreed not to touch me."

He laughed, but his expression held the same glazed-over lust she knew he saw in hers.

What was up with that?

"I just thought we should give them a little show." He pointed his thumb toward the living room window, where her mother and grandmother stood staring out at them.

Wonderful.

"Do you know what you just did?"

"I just kissed my bride-to-be?"

"Very funny." She gave him a swat to the shoulder. "Good going, genius. Now they're going to expect it all the time."

"What's wrong with that? Isn't that what real fiancés do?"

"I wouldn't know. I've never had one." She climbed out of the car and opened the back door to pull out her suitcase. Doug followed her out and snatched her suitcase from her hand.

"Rachel, you've got some serious intimacy issues." He grabbed his own two bags and headed up the front walk.

"I can carry my own luggage, you know," she called after him. Either he didn't hear her, or he pretended he didn't. Considering he was a member of the male species, she leaned toward the latter.

She rushed up the walk and stepped in front of him, one hand propped on her hip. "Let's get one thing straight, Douglas Aaron Bennett. We are *not* involved. There is obviously no interest in a relationship, on your part or mine. Don't confuse this little act with something it's not."

He shook his head and let out a frustrated sigh. "Look, princess, I think you're the one who needs to get something straight. I'm doing a favor for you, simply out of the kindness of my heart. You want this to look convincing, right?"

She nodded.

"I'm a touchy-feely kind of guy. Deal with it, or take me home now."

She blinked up at him, not sure how to respond to his demands. And then something he'd said sunk in and she had to swallow against the lump that formed in her throat. "Did you just call me princess?"

"Yep." His smile didn't have any of the humor or lust she'd seen before. "As in *ice* princess. For a little while there I thought you might have a heart lurking somewhere under that bitchy exterior, but now I can definitely see how you earned the nickname. When someone tries to get close, you to cut him off at the knees."

"What nickname? *Ice princess?* Who calls me that?"

"Most of the guys in the office, and I think a few of the women, too." He rolled his eyes. "Oh, please. Like you had no idea."

She hadn't. And it hurt more than she cared to admit. Tears, of anger as well as hurt, welled in her eyes, but she refused to acknowledge them. "There's nothing wrong with wanting to keep my personal life separate from my work life."

"You're right. There isn't. But me coming with you this weekend has brought us into some very personal territory. I suggest you stop trying to treat me like some employee you can boss around and more like a friend. An equal."

She let out a breath of pent-up frustration, and a little emotional pain, and nodded. "I'll try."

"Not try, you'll do." He cocked his head to the side and his hard expression softened. "Are you crying?"

Yes, you big jerk, and it's all your fault. "Why would I do a stupid thing like that?"

"Geez, Rachel, you're so keyed up about all this you're ready to snap. Take it easy, okay? I'm sorry if I hurt you. Honestly, I thought you knew about the whole ice princess thing."

He brushed her tears away with the pad of his thumb—an act so intimate it sent a shiver through her. Part of her wanted to scream at him for daring to do something so personal, and another part of her wanted to lean into his touch.

Didn't multiple personality disorders run in her family?

"It's okay. And I'm sorry if I treated you badly."

"You didn't." He took her arm and led her up to the front door. "But I'm not going to give you the chance to start."

"Okay. I can handle that. But you need to stop being so overbearing, too."

"I'm on your side in this, honey. Stop shaking. It can't be that bad." He twined his fingers with hers and squeezed. A tingly feeling ran from the tips of her fingers straight up to her shoulder blade. She bit back a sappy grin.

"You're right. I'm probably exaggerating."

And then her mother flung open the door and threw herself at Rachel, hugging her so tight she could barely breathe. She hadn't exaggerated at all. Being away from her family made it so much easier to put up a mental block against their...eccentricities. "Mom, let go."

Grandma DeeDee stood behind Rachel's mother with her white hair in pink sponge rollers and some kind of hot pink, tent-like dress at least three sizes too big draped over her tiny frame. Rachel shot her a help-me glance, but Grandma DeeDee shook her head and laughed.

"You're late. Where have you been? We were all so worried about you," her mother said, her voice muffled by Rachel's hair.

It took Rachel three tries to lift her arm high enough to look at her watch. "Yeah, by five minutes."

Her mother pulled back and looked at Rachel, shaking her head and making a clicking sound with her tongue. "But you're always ten minutes early. I was about to start calling the hospitals."

Rachel threw Doug her best I-told-you-so glance, the one she'd been perfecting since grade school. He blinked back at her, his eyes wide, looking ready to run. She tightened her grip on his hand. "Mom, this is my fiancé, Doug."

To Rachel's sheer and utter embarrassment, her mother launched herself at Doug, practically jumping up into his arms. After a few seconds of the vice-grip hug, he started to cough.

"Omigod, Mom, stop it!"

Her mother released Doug and stepped back, looking at the two of them with a huge smile on her face. "Oh, Rachel, he's *gorgeous.*"

"I know. He's—hey, wait a second. Why do you sound surprised?"

Her mother shook her head, her brassy curls bouncing around her ears. She set her hands on her plump hips. "I never thought...well, we all just assumed...I don't know how to put this."

"She thought you were lying about being engaged," Grandma DeeDee piped in, as usual not wasting any time with sugarcoating. "She just assumed, since she'd never met the man, that there wasn't any man at all."

Rachel's jaw dropped so low she was surprised it didn't hit the porch floor. She needed to laugh. She needed to cry. She needed to scream. She'd put herself through all this worry for nothing? She looked at Doug and flinched at his darkening expression.

He was going to *kill* her.

He leaned in and, under the guise of planting a kiss on her ear, whispered, "We'll talk about this later." He turned to her mother. "Mrs. Storm, it's a pleasure to meet you. Rachel has told me so much about you."

"Only good things, I hope." Her mother smiled even as she threw Rachel a warning look. "Dan, this is my mother-in-law, DeeDee."

Dan? "Uh, Mom, it's Doug."

Her mother crinkled her nose. "Are you sure? I could have sworn you said his name was Dan."

"Yeah, Mom, I'm pretty sure I know my fiancé's name. It's Doug Bennett."

Doug chuckled. She jabbed him in the ribs with her elbow.

"Rachel Bennett," Grandma DeeDee murmured. "Oh, well. Could be worse. You could be marrying someone like your sister's man. Ronald Tandy. Imagine that. Mandy Tandy."

Mandy Tandy. It sounded like a porn star. Rachel couldn't resist mouthing "told you so" to Doug as they followed her mother and Grandma DeeDee inside.

ഉറ

"Jake! Bring your sister's and her guest's bags upstairs to your old room," Her mother called as they all walked through the front door.

Rachel froze. Jake's room? No. She must have heard wrong. Jake's room would be bad. Very, *very* bad. "Mom? What's wrong with my old room?"

"We've got a full house this weekend. Jake, David, and Brian are sharing your room. Grandma DeeDee has David's room, and Uncle Hal and Aunt Eleanor have Brian's room. I figured you wouldn't mind giving your room to the boys since there are two beds and a futon in there, and you and Dan can take Jake's double bed."

"Doug, Mom. It's *Doug*." She bit the inside of her cheek and counted to ten.

Her mother frowned. "That's what I said. Come with me, Dan. Let me introduce you to Rachel's brothers. Jake! David! Brian! Get over here!"

How her father could stand all the screeching, Rachel hadn't a clue. She'd only survived through high school by keeping earmuffs close by.

"Double bed, huh?" Doug whispered, his tone sending a shiver down Rachel's spine and planting a tiny seed of doubt in her mind.

He *was* gay, right?

If not, she would be in a heap of trouble, because there was no way she'd be able to keep her hands off him for the whole weekend.

"Jake, come and get these bags, will you?" her mother yelled again.

Jake looked up from what appeared to be an engrossing conversation with a man Rachel didn't recognize and headed toward them. Rachel's hands shook as Jake neared. She hoped he didn't get too overprotective. Having three large, fairly intimidating brothers had chased away more than a few of her dates over the years.

Damn those brothers, trying to make sure she didn't get hurt. Who did they think they were, anyway?

"Hey, Rach." Jake leaned in and kissed her cheek. "How are you?"

"Great." *Ready to pee my pants, I'm so nervous.* "Jake, this is my"—she choked on the word— "fiancé, Doug."

Once she started coughing, she couldn't seem to get it under control. Jake looked worried, but Doug patted her on the

back—a little too hard, she'd have to *thank* him for that later—
and she finally drew a cough-free breath.

"You okay, Rach?" Jake asked, shooting a look at their
mother. Her mother just shrugged, so Jake turned his attention
back to Doug. "Good to meet you. We all heard so much about
you last Christmas. So, you're what, a stockbroker?"

"Real estate agent. Mostly commercial. Rachel and I work
together."

"Oh, yeah?" Jake asked, one dark brow rising.

Rachel waited for him to call her on yet another lie, but he
didn't. She let out a sigh of relief. Three down, only a few more
to go. And her other siblings weren't nearly as intuitive as good
old Jake.

Rachel grabbed Doug's arm. "Let's go meet my dad."

"Your dad, huh?" Doug asked, stumbling after her across
the living room to where her father stood with her uncles,
drinking beer and laughing. "Which one is he?"

"The big guy with the blue shirt and the bottle of Sam
Adams in his hand." Given the hour, probably his *fifth* bottle of
Sam Adams—which could either work in their favor or send
Doug to the emergency room. She crossed her fingers that his
injuries wouldn't be too bad.

Doug's eyes widened. He scanned the room as if looking for
the nearest exit. "What did you say he does for a living again?"

"I don't think I did." She tightened her grip on his hand and
dragged him across the floor. "He's a police detective."

Doug stopped moving, and no amount of yanking on her
part could budge him. "Gee, Rachel, don't you think you should
have mentioned that sooner?"

"What's the problem?" She tried for wide-eyed innocence,
but the look on his face told her she hadn't managed it. At six-

four and two hundred and fifty pounds, her dad would frighten any man she brought home—especially one planning to lie to him about his intentions.

Doug would just have to deal with it. He'd agreed to help her, and she planned to see this thing through. Since she couldn't get him to move, she waved wildly. "Hi, Daddy!"

Doug let out a little snort. *"Daddy?"*

"Oh, shut up." She pasted on a sweet smile. *"Honey."*

"Whatever you say, *dear*," Doug said just as her father reached them.

He smiled at Doug and stuck out his hand. "Earl Storm. Good to finally meet you, Dan."

Rachel groaned. Not another one. *"Doug.* His name is Doug, Dad."

"Nice to meet you, Mr. Storm," Doug said, an odd expression on his face. She had a feeling he was trying to keep from laughing. She couldn't really blame him. She'd be laughing herself.

If this was happening to someone else.

ℰ⳼ℭ

"All in all, I think it went pretty well. My dad liked you— which is a huge plus, let me tell you—my brothers liked you, my mom and my grandma, too. And Amanda and Ronny. Everyone thinks you're great."

Doug watched Rachel's ass as she fished around in her suitcase. His cock stirred and he forced a laugh. "No, everyone thinks *Dan* is great. What'd you do, make this phony fiancé out to be some kind of Nobel prize-winning genius?"

Not that he minded being thought of as some kind of superhero. And he enjoyed seeing Rachel's face flame when she got flustered. The ice princess, fumbling for words? No one at work would believe him. It turned him on.

Big time.

"Very funny." She spun, her arms crossed over her chest and her lips pursed, but he saw right through her act. That's all the whole icy façade was. An act. A deterrent that wasn't working too well at the moment.

He'd seen her in her element tonight, seen her warm and caring nature with her family and friends. Seen the sweet side she kept hidden under all her pretenses.

Hidden even deeper, she had a side that was intense and passionate. It showed in the way she challenged everything he said and didn't let anyone push her around.

He planned to bring that passion to the surface. Soon.

Before they left at the end of the weekend, he would experience it firsthand.

"Your family is interesting," he told her. "They're nice."

She shook her head. "You're too kind. *Really.*"

"I grew up with no noise whatsoever. I always wanted a bunch of brothers and sisters, but my parents weren't interested in any more kids. Being here with all this activity is refreshing."

Rachel snorted. "Translation—strange beyond explanation. Total *Twilight Zone* material. You know what? I'm really tired. Why don't we get this over with and get into bed?"

That had to be the best idea he'd had all night. His cock wholeheartedly agreed, springing to attention.

He'd been a little disappointed when she'd changed into her sleeping clothes. An old t-shirt and a pair of men's flannel boxers. Her choice didn't suit the polished woman she seemed to be at the office. He'd hoped for some kind of slinky, expensive nightgown—red or black silk, maybe.

Or nothing.

Yeah, that would have been a dream outfit.

They'd work on the naked thing. One step at a time. But surprisingly, she looked cute standing across the bed with her rumpled clothes, messy hair, and smudged eye makeup. Not a beauty queen. Not an unattainable ice princess. A real woman. A real, sexy, soft woman he wanted to put his hands all over.

He pulled back the sheets of the double bed. "Getting in?"

She chewed on her bottom lip, making his arousal ratchet up another notch. What those lips would feel like wrapped around his cock, stroking him—

If he thought about it for another second, he'd explode. The naked, wrapped around him part would come. If he didn't push her too hard the first night. "Come on, Rachel. What are you waiting for?"

"Maybe I'll just sleep on the floor."

He barked a laugh. No way in hell was he going to let *that* happen. "Come on, Rachel. Give me a break. It's not like I'm going to attack you in your sleep or anything."

"I guess you're right." She climbed into the bed and he followed, pulling the covers up over them. She turned on her side, facing away from him, and yawned. "I don't have anything to worry about with you, do I."

It was a statement rather than a question, and it had him wondering. She'd said a couple of similar things on the ride up. Either she was blind, or just pretending to ignore the semi-erection he'd had since he'd stuffed himself into her little car and got a good whiff of her soft floral fragrance.

"No. Of course you have nothing to worry about with me. I'm as safe as they come."

Nothing could be further from the truth.

Chapter Four

She'd never had a dream quite so vivid.

A man—a hard, muscular one with *great* hands—lay in bed with her, his body wrapped around hers. One of his hands kneaded her breast while the other splayed over her bare stomach. Rachel felt his erection pressing into her rear and pushed back against it. "Mmm. You feel good."

"Yeah, you, too," he whispered in her ear. "I want you, Rachel."

She might as well play along with the fantasy. It wasn't every day a girl had a dream *this* good. "I want you, too. More than I've ever wanted anyone." Her panties dampened, her nipples beaded, and her heart raced. His lips brushed her neck, her earlobe, her shoulder, inciting little riots among her nerves. Pleasure zinged through her bloodstream and her breath hitched in her lungs.

Too bad it was only a dream. When she woke up, she'd be all alone again, as always. Except...

She hadn't gone to bed alone last night.

Doug.

Oh, shit.

She snapped her eyes open, too startled to move. Sometime during the night, he'd cuddled her against him and wrapped her in his arms. Or had *she* cuddled up to *him*? It really didn't matter. The end result was the same. His limbs tangled with hers, his hand resting on the bare flesh of her stomach because her shirt seemed to have ridden up to just below her ribcage. Just below her breasts. Breasts his fingers were scant inches from touching.

She held very still, afraid to even breathe. They'd both been dreaming, obviously, and gotten a little carried away. *Everything is fine. You can get out of this one. No problem. You've gotten out of worse in your life, Rachel, much worse. Just ease out of his arms so you don't wake—*

Halfway through her mental pep talk she panicked and jumped out of bed, practically pulling Doug to the floor in the process. Her heart raced and her mouth had long since gone dry.

"What are we doing?" she gasped, struggling to draw a breath. What would have happened if she hadn't gotten out of bed?

Doug flopped onto his back on the mattress and groaned. "Nothing yet."

Yet? What did he mean by that? And why did he sound so awake? "Please tell me you were sleeping, and you didn't know what you were doing."

He laughed. The deep, raspy tone made her traitorous knees go weak. "Do you want me to lie?" he asked, looking up at her with eyes entirely too alert for so early in the morning.

"Look, I don't know what you're trying to pull here, but we already had this conversation." She shook her head, trying to make sense of the situation. She felt like she'd just fallen down a rabbit hole and everything around her had changed. "Where you dreaming about Brett when you were...fondling me?"

She paced the room, tugging at a strand of her mussed hair and twirling it around her finger. Something wasn't right here. None of this made any sense.

"No, Rachel. I wasn't thinking about Brett. You're the only one that's been on my mind lately."

She stopped by the door and leaned against the wall, arms crossed over her chest, trying to make her stance look tough when she really felt ready to keel over. "Yeah. *Right.* What would Brett say if he found you making out with a woman?"

"She wouldn't care, since I told you already that she's gone." He shot up to a sitting position, his eyes in rapid blink mode and a flush rising in his cheeks. "Wait a second. Did you say 'he'?"

"Well, yeah," she whispered. Her mind was still trying to come to terms with the fact that he'd referred to Brett as a 'she'. What the hell?

Oh, this was not *so* good. She'd made a very big mistake here. *Huge.* She'd lied to her family and karma had come to bite her in the butt—in a big way.

"Um, Doug?"

"Yeah?"

"Brett *is* a man, right?"

His eyes widened and he jumped out of bed. "*What?* Are you out of your mind? *No,* Rachel. Brett is most certainly *not* a man. She's the woman I dated for the past year."

Woman.

Brett was a *woman.*

"Oh." The word came out as nothing more than a small sigh. She knew she should say something, but at the moment words were a little hard to come by. She racked her brain for something intelligent to say, but couldn't form much past "huh"?

"You thought I was gay." His tone was accusatory, his expression dark. "I can't believe you actually thought I was gay." He shook his head furiously before scrubbing a hand down his face. "This is nuts, Rachel. Crazy. I can't *believe* this. What would ever possess you to think that?"

She swallowed hard, her pulse racing. Doug liked women.

Doug liked *her*.

Or at least he had before. After their little misunderstanding, all bets were off.

"I'm sorry." Somehow, it sounded woefully inadequate. "I don't...I don't know what to say here."

She braced herself against the wall, waiting for him to start yelling and throwing things. But he didn't. He stood there, in the middle of the room, shaking his head back and forth and staring at her with an unreadable expression.

And then he did something unexpected, given the fact that she'd openly questioned the man's sexuality. He laughed. "You really thought I was gay?"

"Well, yeah," she tried to laugh with him, but still waiting for him to flip out, she couldn't quite manage the sound.

"Wow. Just...wow." He walked over to where she stood and crowded her body with his own.

It was then that she truly noticed his state of undress—and how amazing it looked on him. She licked her lips despite knowing it would give him the wrong idea...or maybe the right one.

"So you asked me to help you with your little problem because you thought I wouldn't hit on you?" he continued, his tone laced with a healthy dose of humor. "You figured you were safe with me, huh?"

She nodded, trying to gulp down the enormous lump in her throat. Her concentration had suddenly shifted from their major misunderstanding to the fact that Doug stood pressed up against her, wearing nothing more than a pair of cotton lounge pants that rode indecently low on his trim hips and did little to hide how much he enjoyed sharing a bed with her.

"Well, you've made a huge mistake, honey." He smiled down at her, giving her the impression of a wolf snaring its prey. "*Huge.*"

Huge. *Wow.*

"Why is that?" she asked, her voice threatening to crack.

"Because I had my own agenda when I agreed to accompany you this weekend." He pressed his hips harder against her, the *huge* mistake pressing against her belly.

She almost whimpered, but caught herself at the last second. "You did?"

"Uh huh." He leaned in still closer, so close that his breath feathered through her hair. Her stomach tightened and she had trouble drawing a full breath.

"I came here to seduce you, Rachel."

Her heart rate bumped up to warp speed and every nerve in her body tingled. Oh, she had *so* picked the wrong guy for this. And if she didn't get out of the room right that second she'd probably pass out.

"I...I have to go to the bathroom." She ducked out from under his grasp and ran out of the room before he could stop her.

Ten minutes later, she still stood in the bathroom, tears streaming down her cheeks, her butt propped against the vanity and her arms crossed, trying to decide on her best course of action. She could do the right thing and admit all her lies, and then be able to relax enough to enjoy her sister's wedding. Or she could grab Doug and run, skipping out on her family completely and avoiding the embarrassment of a full confession. Or—and out of the three this seemed to be the only workable option, really, considering the trouble she'd gone to with her stupid story—she could go through with the plan as she would have if she hadn't found out her fake fiancé was planning something very, very *bad* this weekend.

Something that sounded very, very *good* to her.

She groaned in frustration. Had her life been transformed into a soap opera when she wasn't looking? This kind of thing did *not* happen in real life.

"Rachel?" She heard Doug's soft whisper just outside the door. "Are you planning to come out sometime this morning or do I have to call in a search and rescue team?"

"Very funny," she snapped, still a little irritated about the whole Brett-being-a-woman thing. Here she thought she'd be safe with him and he wouldn't try to come on to her no matter how much she might want it. Now that he had, and she realized she wasn't nearly as safe as she'd thought, she didn't know how to handle it.

"Come on, Rachel. Let's talk about this."

"I don't want to talk. I just want to be alone, okay?" She rolled her eyes as she listened to herself. Why did coming back to this house bring out the teenager in her? She sounded like such a moron.

Well, she deserved it. She'd been *acting* like a moron. Now she had to deal with the consequences.

Before she had a chance to react, the doorknob turned and Doug scooted into the room, sliding the door shut behind him.

Oh, just friggin' wonderful. Hadn't she bugged her father for years to put locks on the bathroom doors?

"What the hell are you doing in here?" She glared at him as much as her embarrassed state would allow.

"Your mother was coming down the hall. I didn't think you'd want her to see me standing outside the door, begging you to come out."

Yeah, that might look bad. He'd made a good call. *If* he spoke the truth. "Thanks."

"None of this is my fault, you know," he told her as he leaned on the vanity next to her.

No, really? "Gee, thanks for pointing out the obvious. I might have missed it."

"I'll still go along with your plan. If you want me to."

"No, I'd rather—" She bit back a sarcastic reply, deciding, for the moment, to be nice to the guy. If she didn't, he might *slip* and tell everyone about her lies. "Thanks."

He brushed her hair out of her eyes and she batted away the tears she pretended hadn't been falling since she'd run out on him. Her face burned and she tried to push him away, but in the next second he'd moved her hair behind her shoulder and started kissing her neck.

What was he thinking?

She scooted a few inches down the vanity counter to get away from him, but he followed. When she turned to tell him to leave her alone, he kissed her full on the lips. She really should dispute his intimate actions. *But why?* The man had the most incredible mouth.

She did feel the need to protest, though, when Doug pulled her in front of him so that her legs straddled his and her upper body pressed against him. She needed to stop the whole crazy thing before they did something they'd regret. "Umm," she mumbled.

Hold on. That didn't sound like much of a protest. Let's try this again. One more time, Rach. "Mmmmm. Doug."

Oh, yeah, that was so much better. At least she'd managed his name this time.

She threaded her hands through his hair—was it fair that the man had softer, thicker hair than she did?—and pulled him closer. He knew right where to kiss her to make her melt, flicking his tongue over her collarbone and up the column of her throat. She tipped her head back and gave him better access, ready to kill him if he ever decided to stop.

"Can you two possibly take this to your room? I really need the bathroom."

At the sound of Amanda's voice in the now-open doorway, Rachel jumped back. Her face flamed and her legs wobbled so much she could barely stand up. "Sorry, Mandy. We'll get out of your way."

Doug, very obviously trying to control a fit of laughter, stood up and walked past Amanda out the door. "I'll meet you back in the bedroom, Rachel. We'll finish this up a little later. Don't be too long, though, okay?"

She and Amanda watched his retreating backside—cradled by the cut of the lounge pants—as he walked down the hall toward the bedroom.

"Nice," Amanda mumbled appreciatively. "Where did you find that guy, a strip club?"

"No. We work together."

Amanda shook her head. "I bet he's amazing in bed."

And if you don't stay away from him, tramp girl, I'll rip you limb from limb. "Me, too," she answered, still too caught up in a sensual fog to pay much attention to her choice of words.

Amanda snorted in disbelief. "You mean you haven't slept with the guy yet? No wonder he was practically taking you apart in the middle of the bathroom."

"No, no. I just meant..." What *did* she mean? She couldn't tell Amanda the truth, but if she lied, it would make both she and Doug look bad. What woman in her right mind would spend months with Doug and not take him to bed? And what man in the history of the world would let a woman get away with that? "I..."

"You've been with this guy for a long time, and you haven't even screwed him yet? Jesus, Rach, look at him," she said as Doug disappeared into the bedroom. "Are you out of your mind? What are you waiting for? The next millennium?"

"Oh, shut up. At least I take my time and don't rush into things like *some people* I know."

Amanda burst out laughing. "Look, sweetie, you've got to trust me on this. Rush it. The guy is amazing. I don't know how someone as, well...bitchy as you, landed such a hottie, but don't screw it up by making him wait. He's a man. He'll go elsewhere to find what he wants if you don't give it to him."

"Things are fine, thanks. I've got it under control." She left Amanda standing in the doorway and followed Doug's path back to the bedroom. A sliver of aggravation knifed her insides. Amanda's laughter echoed through the halls as Rachel closed the bedroom door behind her.

Doug had reclined on the bed, his arms behind his head and his ankles crossed. His erection strained against the fabric of his pants, and he did nothing to conceal it. She gulped. And licked her lips. *Wow.* In reality, it had been a few months since she'd last had sex, but looking at Doug made her feel like it had been years.

Maybe Amanda was right. She shouldn't wait. She should give him what he wanted before he dumped her for someone who would.

Back up, Rach. He couldn't dump her. They weren't even involved.

"You like what you see?" he asked, his tone tinged with humor but also laced with a heavy dose of lust.

"Uh huh," she mumbled, her mind threatening to go into sleep mode.

What had she just agreed to?

Doug cleared his throat. "You want to come back to bed and help me with this...uh, problem?"

Problem? What problem? What could he possibly need her to—oh, no! *Be strong, Rachel. You two have a ton of things to sort out before you jump into bed together.*

She shook her head furiously. "Are you out of your mind?"

A corner of his mouth tipped into a sexy smile. "Yeah. With lust. Come back to bed, sweetheart. I promise I'll make it worth your while. Several times."

"Um, *no.*" She snorted and rolled her eyes for effect, though she doubted he really bought the tough girl routine. She'd already given him enough ideas for the day. Now she needed to pull back before she did something infernally stupid. Like sleep with the guy. Though, if forced to admit the truth, that didn't sound like such a stupid idea anymore. "Doug, get dressed."

"What? You don't like me like this?"

"Oh, I like you like that all right." Maybe a little too much, considering the illicit thoughts running through her head as she tried to tear her eyes away from the bulge in his pants. "But I don't plan to do anything about it."

Doug laughed as he got off the bed and walked over to her. "I know you don't want to be involved in a relationship right now. I can respect that. I'm not looking, either. Brett and I just broke up last month, and I don't want to rush into anything. But I want you, Rachel, so badly it hurts. We could just have a little fun. No strings, no commitments."

She whimpered at the closeness between them. Her body screamed Yes, yes, yes! But her mind scolded No, no, no, you stupid child. You can't have a fling with him here and then work with him for the rest of your life. "Um, I don't think—"

"See, that's your problem. You think too much. Don't think about this. Just feel." He lifted a hand to her breasts and grazed his knuckles over her nipples. A jolt shot through her, straight to her crotch.

"Need to get dressed," she mumbled. "Have to go downstairs for breakfast. And coffee."

He laughed. "Okay, I'll let you off the hook. This time. I have to warn you, though, Rachel. I don't give up easily. We'd be great together."

She shook her head, denying what she knew to be the truth. Yes, they'd be good together. But if they were too good, she might get attached. And that was exactly what she was afraid of.

Chapter Five

"What took you so long?" her mother asked Rachel as she made her way down the stairs, still dazed from her strange encounter with Doug—*who wasn't gay*.

He was also damned hot, and she didn't think keeping her hands off him would be easy. How would she get through the rest of the weekend and not confuse the fictional world she'd created with reality?

"Overslept." Rachel stretched her arms out to the sides and yawned for effect. "It's so quiet here. I'm not used to that."

"Sure. That cute little man of yours probably kept you busy all night, didn't he?"

Cute? She blinked. Not the word she would have chosen. Cute described kittens and ponies and little children dressed for Easter. *Sexy* would have been a better choice. Or virile. Intense. Masculine.

Bossy.

That one came to mind unbidden and she had put her hand over her mouth to stifle a laugh. Yeah, Doug could be overbearing at times, but—in some delusional way—she found even that a little bit sexy—which confirmed her suspicion that she belonged in a mental hospital. What kind of woman liked being told what to do?

Apparently, she did, which surprised her. Normally she liked to be the one doing most of the bossing.

She glanced at her mom and realized she was still waiting for the answer to her question. "No, he didn't keep me awake. Doug and I slept pretty well last night, Mom."

Emphasis on the word "Mom". Even if she and Doug had done more than sleep, her mother didn't need to know that. When it came to sex, she'd prefer to pretend her mother didn't know anything about it.

"According to your sister—"

"She's lying." Rachel hurried past her mother to pour herself a cup of coffee. This was all too much, way, *way* too early.

Rachel rolled her eyes when her mother followed. "But she said the two of you were in the bathroom—"

"Mom, this is Amanda we're talking about. The girl who got out of a year's worth of high school gym classes by telling the teacher she had a congenital muscle defect and she couldn't run or her legs would lock."

Her mother frowned. "True."

Whew. Got out of that one easy enough.

"I think we need to have a talk."

Damn it. So close. "Um, okay."

"I know you and Doug are in love." Her mother crossed her arms over her chest and stared at Rachel, nodding her head almost imperceptibly. Oh, shit. It was *that* kind of talk. "And sometimes when you're in love, you can get careless."

Rachel covered her ears with her hands. "Okay, stop right there. I've heard enough."

"No, you haven't. Remember, no birth control is one hundred percent effective. You don't want to have children until after you're married. Making babies is a beautiful, wonderful thing, but only when you're married to the right man."

Rachel snorted, trying to hold back a laugh at that one. In order to make babies, one had to actually have sex. And why was it her mother could never come out and say the word "sex"? Was she allergic?

"You do know about protection, right, Rachel?" her mother continued, her tone slow and clear—like this was the first time they'd had this talk. Rachel had been hearing it every year since she'd turned sixteen.

"Yes, Mom. I know about protection." She had no problem buying condoms, but she didn't want to talk with her *mother* about it. It was just about as comfortable as watching douche commercials with a boyfriend. She took a swig of her coffee, needing the jolt of caffeine now more than ever. "Are we finished? Can I make myself something to eat now?"

"In a second. We're not done here. I just don't want to see you get into trouble before your wedding day."

"Then why did you put Doug and I in the same bed?"

"I assumed the both of you understand how to practice a little safe..."

Come on, Mom. Say it. S-E-X. Sex. "We do."

"Well, I'm glad to hear that." Her mother still didn't look too sure. "And when is the wedding, exactly, dear? Have the two of you set a date yet?"

"December."

They both turned at the sound of Doug's voice from the doorway. Rachel, standing behind her mother, shook her head furiously and made a cutting motion across her neck with her finger. Doug raised an eyebrow, and one corner of his mouth, before shaking his head. She was going to ring his neck as soon as she got him alone.

And then he made it worse by continuing, digging the hole even deeper for her. "We're not planning to have a big wedding, though. Just the two of us and a Justice of the Peace."

Why had she ever thought bringing him along would be a good idea? Telling her mother she didn't want a real wedding was like telling a five-year-old that Christmas had been cancelled.

"Or maybe Vegas. We'll have a quickie wedding, and then spend a week holed up in one of those posh hotels, getting to know each other a lot better." He winked at Rachel as he walked into the kitchen and draped his arm over her shoulder. "Morning, Babe," he said as he leaned in and kissed her. Hard. Right on the lips. *In front of her mother.* Hadn't she warned him about public displays? "Morning, Mrs. Storm."

"Please, Dan dear. Call me Miriam."

Rachel threw a quick glance at her mom. She looked red and ready to pass out after Doug's little speech. Rachel could forgive her for getting his name wrong this one time. They were lucky she was still standing.

He laughed. "I'll call you Miriam if you call me Doug."

Rachel's mother shook her head. "I'll never remember that. And you'd better not even think about taking my daughter to Vegas. She deserves a spectacular wedding. Don't you forget it."

"I don't want a big wedding, Mom." She didn't want a wedding at all, but no matter how many times she told her mother that, the woman refused to believe it.

"Of course, dear." Her mother's glazed-over expression told Rachel she'd hadn't listened to a word. "Oh, and don't get too busy. After breakfast I need you to try on your dress."

Dress? What dress? Why had no one told her about any dress? "What dress are you referring to?"

Her mother clicked her tongue. "The one I made you for the wedding. Didn't Amanda tell you that you're going to be her maid of honor?"

"Um, no. She didn't." Nice of them to ask her if she minded. Having been the maid of honor in Amanda's past three weddings as well, she was starting to give "always a bridesmaid" a new name.

"Well, you are," her mother told her with a finality Rachel knew better than to argue with. "The dress is upstairs in my sewing room. You can't miss it."

Was she paranoid, or did her mother's last sentence have a very ominous tone?

৪৩০৪

"Can't miss it," Rachel mimicked her mother as she stared at herself in the mirror. *Yellow?* What had she been thinking, picking this color? Rachel looked like an overgrown canary.

Well, it wasn't really that bad—just a little...puffy. She would have preferred to wear something a little more understated. Like jeans and a t-shirt.

She heard a knock on the door and promptly ignored it, not wanting anyone to see her in this getup. It was bad enough that she had to look at herself in the mirror. If one of her brothers saw it, she'd never live it down. It was bad enough that she'd have to wear it on Sunday for the wedding. She tugged at the zipper at the back of the dress, but it wouldn't budge.

The knock came again, and Rachel blew out a frustrated breath.

"Persistent, aren't we?" She pulled the door open, expecting to find her mother or Amanda. Instead, she found the last person she wanted to see her at the moment. Doug.

He blinked down at her, his chest rumbling with what might be silent laughter. "Your mom thought you might need a little help with the dress."

"Oh, that would be great." She pulled him into the room and closed the door. "Meet me in the living room after dark tonight. You light the fire and I'll stuff it into the fireplace."

He laughed. "Somehow I think she'd notice if you showed up not wearing it tomorrow."

Rachel lifted the fabric of the skirt out in front of her, flicking at the satin with the tip of her index finger. "Gee, what makes you say that? It's very tasteful. Modest, even." Yeah, maybe if you worked for the circus. "The zipper is stuck. Help me get it down so I can change into something more normal."

Doug laughed. "I kind of like you just the way you are."

She'd strangle him if he didn't help her. "Don't pull this. It's not funny. Come on, get me out of this thing."

"I've been dying to hear you say that to me." He shook his head as he stepped behind her and lowered the zipper. Very slowly. His fingers brushed her bare skin on the way down and her breath caught in her throat. "Um, Doug?" she asked when he slid his hand under the fabric to touch her bare waist.

"Yeah?"

Her heart beat double-time against the wall of her chest. "What are you doing?"

"Helping you get this dress off."

At this rate, she'd be a puddle of bright yellow satin on the floor before he reached the bottom of the zipper. She allowed herself one silent whimper before pulling away. She spun on him, hoping the look on her face conveyed annoyance instead of the lust stampeding through her bloodstream. "Don't even think about it, Romeo."

"Oh, come on, Rachel." He reached out and grasped a lock of her hair, giving it a tug. "I couldn't think of a better birthday present than seeing you naked."

Birthday?

Oh, shit.

"Doug, I'm so sorry. I totally forgot that it's your birthday. Um, happy birthday." She winced as she said it. Too little, too late. "What do you want? Is there something I can get you?"

"Besides seeing me naked?" she added when she saw the wicked gleam in his eyes.

"Can't think of a thing." He pushed the dress off one of her shoulders and kissed her skin. "Actually, I have something for you."

"You do? It's not my birthday."

"I know." His smile made her heart stop. A sigh escaped her lips before she could stop it. His eyes had darkened to near-black, the heat in them enough to melt the slippery fabric of the dress right off her body.

And exactly how would that be a bad thing?

"Sit," he told her, pointing to the worn pink loveseat in the corner.

"Excuse me?"

"Just do it. It's my birthday. Humor me, okay?"

She scoffed at the idea of obeying his commands, but guilt at forgetting his birthday had her walking across the room. She flopped down on the couch, the dress' many layers of satin and tulle floating around her. She batted at the fabric for what seemed like a full minute before she got it settled down.

"Lean back and close your eyes," Doug told her, his hands shoved into the pockets of his pants.

"Um, okay." What was that saying again? *Open your mouth and close your eyes...* "If you even think about sticking anything in my mouth, you're going to lose a body part."

When Doug laughed in response, she realized he'd walked up next to her. "Do you know what you need, Rachel?" he asked, his tone deep and husky.

"A mother with better fashion sense?"

"You need to relax. You're so uptight all the time."

This couldn't be heading in a good direction. "Uptight? Who are you to tell me what I am? I'm perfectly relaxed, thank you very much."

Yeah, right. At the moment, every cell in her body had tensed to the breaking point. She could only think about how her body reacted every time Doug touched her—and hope that he planned on touching her right now. *Lots.*

He laughed again, and she realized he'd changed positions yet another time. It sounded like he was on the floor in front of her. She started to open her eyes, but he clicked his tongue.

"Uh, uh. Do as I asked please. Close those eyes. Trust me."

Asking her to trust him was like asking her to trust a snake. Her suspicions were confirmed in the next second when she felt him—at lightning speed—shove the skirt out of the way and nudge her legs apart. She tried to pull them closed, but he wouldn't let her.

"What do you think you're doing?" she asked a little breathlessly. Well, okay, a lot breathlessly. Something hot curled low in her stomach and her inner muscles quivered. How could he get her so aroused without even touching her? She'd have to change her panties as soon as he let her up.

"Helping you relax. You'll never make it through the weekend unless you loosen up."

His tongue traced a line up the inside of her thigh and she shivered. She knew she should stop him, and she would. Later. Right now, this felt too good to pass up. Fighting him was pointless—she wanted him as much as he apparently wanted her.

When he moved her panties out of the way, she felt his hot breath on her sex. Okay, time to stop. Ha! Like she'd be able to stop him when he had her brain so scrambled she couldn't even form a full thought.

He traced her folds with the tip of his tongue, using his thumbs to spread her gently. In the next second, his mouth latched onto her clitoris, his tongue swirling in circles that drove her insane. One of her hands clenched in the copious fabric of her skirt while the other tangled in Doug's hair, keeping him in place in case he changed his mind and tried to move away too soon.

His thumbs played over her most sensitive parts while he plunged his tongue inside her. She arched her hips toward him and then pulled away, wanting more, needing less, aching for everything he could give her. His warm, wet tongue felt so good against her. Too quickly, she felt her body tightening in response, and before she could control it, she tumbled into a shattering orgasm. She snapped her eyes shut, wanting to savor every pulse and tremble that ran through her.

Doug moved away from her and smoothed down her skirt. She drew a deep breath before she opened her eyes, inhaling the rich, masculine scent of Doug mingled with the scent of sex in the air.

"Wow."

"Yeah, that pretty much sums it up, huh?" Doug scooted up and flopped onto the couch next to her. He tipped her chin up with his thumb and kissed her. When he finally broke away, she felt breathless all over again. Breathless and ready for more. But then he disappointed her by standing up.

"Where are you going?" she asked, trying not to sound too needy. After all, it was his birthday and so far she was the only one who'd gotten a gift.

"We're going into town. Go get dressed."

She could barely make sense of his words. "Town?"

"Yeah. The bakery is closed tomorrow, so I told Miriam we'd pick up the cake today. She asked me about it when you came up here."

Oh, wonderful. Now he'd started volunteering her for errands without even checking with her first.

And when did he get so friendly with her mother?

Chapter Six

"Am I the only one noticing a theme here?" Rachel lifted the lid of the bakery box and peeked inside at Amanda's wedding cake—if she could even call it that. The thing was little, round, and so yellow she needed sunglasses to look at it. It was shaped like a miniature sun, complete with frosting rays jutting out of the sides. "And how does my mother expect this cake to feed thirty people?"

Doug laughed. "The cake isn't being served for dessert. The caterer is serving white chocolate mousse after the meal."

"Then why bother with the cake?" She wrinkled her nose. "And how would you know what the caterer is serving?"

"Your mother and I had quite a talk while waiting for you to finish with the dress." He kissed the tip of her nose and winked at her. "And the cake is a wedding tradition. You can't have a wedding without at least some of the traditions."

"Please don't tell me you're starting to buy into my mother's warped way of thinking." What kind of a tradition made someone spend fifty dollars on a ridiculous-looking cake that no one would even get to eat? "I feel like we should drop this off at the homeless shelter on the way by. At least then it might go to some good use."

"Then what would Amanda and Ronny feed each other during the reception?"

Oh, yeah. Yet another useless wedding tradition. "Why not the mousse? It's messier. More fun."

"I'll keep that in mind. Maybe I'll save some and we can play with it after the ceremony."

Just like that, her panties dampened. Her fingertips tingled and she nearly dropped the cake. The thought of her and Doug alone with a couple of servings of mousse had her wanting to drag him back to her mother's and up to their bedroom. But when she looked at Doug, he smiled a way—too—innocent smile and turned back to the bakery case.

"Will there be anything else?" the woman behind the counter asked.

"Do you want anything?" Doug asked.

Yeah, but she wasn't thinking about food at the moment, not with his dessert comment fresh in her mind. "Do you want a birthday cake or anything?"

"Are you going to jump out of it?"

Amanda's cake almost met with the floor yet again. She sucked in a deep, fortifying breath. *Damn. "No."*

Doug laughed as he handed the woman the money for the cake. "We're all set. Thanks."

They left the bakery with Rachel still in shock over his bold statements. He opened the car door for her and she started to get in. "Just put the cake inside. Let's go for a walk."

"Okay, but somewhere public." Every time he got her alone, she forgot about her vow—and his—to not get involved. He made her want things she shouldn't want from a man she'd have to see every workday for years to come. "We could go over to the park across the street."

She'd be safe there. He'd never think about attacking her in such a public place...even though the idea did hold a lot more appeal than it should.

ꙮ

As they walked through the very public park—hand in hand, *just to keep up appearances*—Doug tried to get Rachel to open up to him a little more. She didn't make it effortless. Ha! What an understatement. He would have had an easier time trying to crack into a bank vault.

But he wouldn't have had nearly as much fun.

Rachel was incredible. Why she didn't seem to see it, he had no clue. He shuddered when he thought about her soft moans as she came. It had been a perfect moment, destined to go down in the history of his life as the best sex he'd ever had without actually having sex. To see the ice princess let go like that—he couldn't think of anything better.

Well, maybe *one* thing. A little mutual satisfaction wouldn't hurt things any. He sighed and scrubbed his free hand down his face. That would come in time. But not too much time. He was a patient man, but patience only went so far.

"What was it like growing up in Vermont?" he asked, gazing across the pond to the green trees on the other side of the shore.

"Lilton isn't a big place." She sighed and tightened her grip on his hand almost imperceptibly. "It was kind of boring. That's why I moved. I wanted to live somewhere where no one recognized me on the street. I wanted to blend."

Considering the amount of people who greeted them on their walk, he couldn't say he blamed her. "It seems quaint."

"Suffocating is more like it."

He wondered if the suffocating part had more to do with Miriam than the town itself. Her mother meant well—he could see that in her actions, but she was a tiny bit...eccentric. Amanda seemed to have followed in her footsteps, at least in some ways, but Rachel didn't fit the family at all.

"Your mom and dad were pretty controlling while you were growing up, weren't they?"

"Is it that obvious?"

He shrugged. "Yeah, I guess it is. I don't blame you for wanting to get away."

She stopped and turned to face him, her fingers still entwined with his. "Don't get me wrong. I love my family. Just in small doses."

"Yeah, I know you do. You wouldn't be trying so hard to please them if you didn't."

"What's that supposed to mean?" She glared at him and his groin tightened at the fire in her eyes. He loved it when she looked at him like that. He'd love it even more if she put some of that passion to better use. "I don't try to please anyone but myself."

"And that's why you made up the whole fake fiancé thing."

"I didn't..." she closed her mouth and the corners of her full lips pulled into a frown. "I just did it so my mother would stop hounding me to settle down. I want to do things my way, in my own time. Is that so wrong?"

He understood perfectly. Wanting his own way had been a big factor in his breakup with Brett, but not in the usual way. She'd been too passive—a trait he didn't find very attractive in a woman. She never expressed her opinion, never argued even if she knew she was right. She agreed to everything he said.

Always. "No. It's not wrong. But you don't have to pretend to be cold in order to do that."

"Speak for yourself." She snorted. "I spent all my childhood doing what other people told me to. When I grew up, I just wanted to be my own person. Not answer to anyone. I guess I take it a little overboard sometimes."

"A little doesn't earn you the title of ice princess among your colleagues."

She laughed, and he was surprised that she didn't take a swing at him. For that comment, he probably deserved it. "You're one to talk. You're so close-mouthed about your private life that everyone in the office thinks you're gay."

"Yeah, I—hey, wait a second. Everyone?"

She nodded. "I told you that."

His gut clenched into a painful knot, his heart lodged firmly in his throat. "No. You told me that *you* thought I was gay. You didn't say anything about the entire office."

"Oops." Her eyes widened and she tried to pull him back into their walk. He stood his ground.

"Tell me the whole story, Rachel."

She laughed, somewhat nervously, and tangled her free hand in her hair. "It's no big deal. Really."

"Rachel."

She drew a deep breath and let it out with excruciating slowness. She relented when he narrowed his eyes at her. "Okay. Fine. Just remember you asked for it. When you turned Marci Redmond down for a date, she got mad. When she heard you mention something about Brett, she assumed Brett was a man and told a couple of the women in the office that you were gay. You know how fast things get around that office."

He did, but he'd never expected any of this. He shook his head and let out a breath, trying to relieve some of the tightness in his stomach. No man liked to have his sexuality called into question. He tried to tell himself it hadn't been all bad. The rumors had kept all the office bimbos from hitting on him. Still, he couldn't help but feel the urge to prove to the world that he wasn't who they thought he was. And Rachel stood right next to him, looking cute in her little hip-hugger jeans and cropped t-shirt...

She squealed when he pulled her close and kissed her, adding to the constant state of excitement being near her kept him in.

He dipped his tongue into her mouth and her whimpering turned into a soft sigh. *Nice.* He liked the noises she made when he aroused her, liked them a lot.

He liked the ones she made when she came even more.

The fierce tightening in his groin made him pull away before he bent her over a park bench in full view of everyone. As enticing as the idea was at the moment, it would probably be his last time making love to her as well as the first. He ended the kiss and brushed his lips over her cheek. "You look adorable when you're indignant. Did you know that?"

She shook her head. "Is that why you're always baiting me?"

He laughed. When she asked so bluntly, how could he not admit the truth? "Yeah. Yeah, it is. I get off on seeing you aggravated, okay?"

Her eyes got huge before she narrowed them. "That's a crude thing to say. Jerk."

"Ooh, baby. Talk dirty to me."

"Doug! *Shut up.* We're in a public place."

And if she wasn't so uptight, he'd consider taking her right up against a tree. He laughed to himself. They'd have to work on that. One of these days, he'd have her right where he wanted her. "What's your point?"

She gaped at him. "You like it when we argue, you love to boss me around just to get a reaction out of me, you're into public sex...are you some kind of freak?"

Freak? Not hardly. He was willing to bet she had more than a few lurid fantasies of her own. Ones he'd love to act out with her.

"Do I need to remind you that you get just as turned on when we argue as I do?"

She flipped her hair over her shoulders and rolled her eyes. "Do not." He loved it.

"Do so." He smiled and leaned in close, brushing his lips over the shell of her ear. "Tell me you aren't wet right now."

"*What?*" She tried to back away, but he grasped her upper arms and held her close.

"Come on, Rachel. Tell me that your panties aren't damp."

Her lips parted on a sigh and she glanced up at him. "This is too strange. I don't get turned on by domineering jerks."

"Actually, you do." He flicked his tongue over her earlobe.

"No. I like to be in control."

He shook his head. "You like to be in control sometimes. Other times, you want someone else to take over."

"You're wrong."

If he was wrong about this, he'd eat her banana-yellow dress. He knew a kindred spirit when he saw one. "Nope. Sorry. I'm right, honey, and we both know it. Why don't you stop denying everything?"

"So you think I want to sit around playing the little woman while you dress me up and tell me what to do? I'm not into that."

"That's not what I want, either. I *like* that you're outspoken and demanding. I like that you speak your mind and put me in my place when I deserve it. I like it a lot, actually." Evident by the near-painful erection straining against his fly. "I think we could really have a good time together, Rachel. I would love to see you totally let go and enjoy yourself. I want to be the man to make you lose control. There are so many things I want to do to you. At least a hundred ways I want to take you. It's my birthday. Do you want to know what I really want?"

"Me?" she asked in a small voice. He was getting to her. Finally.

"Uh huh. But I want so much more than that. I want to strip you naked and blindfold you. Then I want to kiss you everywhere. I want to spread your legs and slide my fingers inside you, suckle your nipples too. Do you know how your other senses are heightened when your vision is impaired?"

"Oh, my God," she whispered so softly he had to strain to hear her.

"Are you game for that?" Say yes, Rachel. Please say yes.

"Doug," she breathed, and he knew he had her. Still, he couldn't resist turning it up yet another notch. Just for fun. "Or maybe this instead. I've been bad today, with all my teasing and goading. Maybe you'd rather punish me instead."

This time she gasped, flicking her tongue out to wet her lips. Her gaze, unsure and completely aroused, locked with his and he felt it like a sucker punch in the gut. Why did she mean so much to him, so quickly? Why did he trust her with his deepest, darkest fantasies when he hardly knew her? He had no answers. He just knew she affected him like no woman ever had. Another wave of lust washed over him, nearly taking him to the ground. "Have you ever played like that, Rachel?"

"No." She dropped her gaze to her feet.

"Look at me, Rachel." She dragged her gaze slowly back up to his. When she paused at his erect cock, he nearly groaned. Once her eyes met his, he continued. "Do you want to? Do you want to let go, let me take care of all your needs?"

"Doug, I—"

He shook his head to stop her from speaking. "Or would you rather be the one to take control, see to every aspect of my pleasure? Does that appeal to you?"

"Yes, but..."

He smiled. He knew what she wanted, even if she couldn't voice it yet. He saw it in her eyes, in the set of her jaw. His Rachel wanted to lose control. He didn't blame her. Spending so much time in ice princess mode had to be hard on a person. "I can give you what you want, Rachel. All of it. You just have to trust me enough to let me in. Do you trust me enough to let me take care of you?"

She started to nod. A car horn blared from the parking lot and she shook her head. The passion in her eyes faded, but it didn't disappear. "It's getting late. We need to head back before my mother thinks we made off with the cake."

He let out a rough sigh. She was probably right. But that didn't mean he had to like it. He wanted her in a way he could barely control, and every second he spent around her made it ten times worse. He'd let her out of the conversation—for now. Later, when they were alone in bed, he'd do his best to get back to where they'd been before the distraction.

And in the meantime, he'd have to walk very carefully or risk injury to a very important body part.

Chapter Seven

"Did she offer to pay you?"

"Excuse me?" Doug snapped his gaze to Rachel's brother, Jake, his face heating even as he spoke. Rachel had had some last minute shopping to do, and had asked Jake to drive Doug to the rehearsal dinner—a strange thing to call it since Amanda had insisted that they not bother rehearsing the wedding. Jake had been civil, friendly even, up until he'd blurted his question. "Did who offer to pay me?"

"Rachel." Jake glanced at Doug as he stopped for a red light. "Did she offer to pay you for this little charade?"

"I don't know what you're talking about."

"Sure you do." Jake's hard gaze bored into Doug's. The light turned green and he focused his attention back on the road, but Doug knew he wasn't finished. "Rachel's supposed fiancé's name is Dan, he's some kind of a stockbroker with blond hair and blue eyes, five foot ten and medium build. At least that's what she told us last Christmas. Unless you've undergone some pretty drastic changes, you aren't him."

Doug stayed silent, not wanting to incriminate Rachel—and himself—too soon. Thoughts flew through his mind so fast he couldn't grasp any single one. Why hadn't Rachel bothered to tell him he didn't fit the description she'd come up with for the fake fiancé?

Jake let out a breath, shaking his head. "Tell me, Doug, what did she do to convince you to play along? Did she hire you from a casting agency?"

Doug bit back a laugh at that one. He could easily have seen Rachel doing just that. And she might have, had he not walked into her office when he had. "No. We really do work together."

"Are you seeing each other?"

Depends on your version of "seeing". "Not exactly."

"Not exactly," Jake repeated softly. He glanced at Doug and laughed. "I guess she had this coming."

"What do you mean?"

"She's been pulling shit like this all her life. She manipulates and controls and bends the situation to suit her needs. I know she does it as a defense mechanism, but it can get annoying. Now I get the feeling she's not in as much control as she'd like to be. I'm sure it's killing her to not be able to tell anyone what you two are doing. It's good. She needs someone to show her she doesn't have to be the boss all the time."

Doug got that feeling, too. He still had to prove it to Rachel.

"I won't be too hard on her," he said, glancing out the window. He couldn't be. As much as he tried to fight it, he'd started to care about her too much.

Jake laughed even louder. "Don't be too easy on her, either. She needs to get over herself. And don't worry about me saying anything to my parents or Mandy. I'm getting a kick out of watching the whole thing."

Doug laughed this time. Easy didn't describe anything he wanted to do to Rachel.

Jake pulled his car into a parking space in the restaurant's lot. After he switched off the ignition, he turned to Doug, his expression serious. "Just don't hurt her. Don't lead her on. If you want more from her than just the weekend—which I get the feeling you do—great. I'm all for Rachel finding someone she can be with. Someone who gets her. If you don't want anything more than just this, be honest with her. It'll kill her if you drag her out of herself for nothing—and then I'll have to break your legs."

"I won't hurt her," Doug promised. He meant it. For the first time since agreeing to this charade, Jake's words made him think about his true feelings. He wanted Rachel for more than the weekend. He was afraid to admit it, having only really known her for a couple of days, but he'd hang on to her for as long as she'd have him. He just hoped she felt the same way.

ⅎ⅏

"First thing in the morning Lois from the flower shop will arrive to decorate the yard," her mother told Rachel as they walked into the restaurant for Amanda's rehearsal dinner—sans an actual rehearsal. *Well, when you've already done it three times, you probably don't need the practice.* Rachel blinked when she realized her mother was still speaking.

"And the caterer is scheduled to arrive at eleven. The Justice of the Peace will be there in time for the start of the ceremony at noon. Am I forgetting anything?"

Besides the fact that this whole thing is a giant waste of money since Amanda's going to get a divorce in another year? Not a thing. "Sounds like you've got it covered. What is the caterer serving for the meal? Macaroni and cheese with buttered corn and yellow potatoes on the side?"

She looked at Rachel like she had six heads. "Of course not. Don't be silly. Jules is preparing a light meal of lemon pepper chicken with golden rice pilaf and sautéed summer squash."

Absolutely nuts. "They make medication for that, you know."

"What was that, dear?"

"Nothing. Look. There's our table." Rachel steered her mother to the table where the rest of their family—and Doug—sat. Her stomach flip-flopped just looking at the guy. It didn't help that he gave her a smile filled with pure, unadulterated sensuality. She'd never make it through the meal in one piece. Never. She'd be better off dragging him home and into bed now, while she still had some semblance of control over the situation.

She took her seat next to Doug and kissed him on the cheek—for appearances only, of course. It had nothing to do with her growing attachment to him. Her mind still swam from what he'd said to her in the park. She'd been so turned on that she'd barely gotten back to her car without collapsing on the pavement.

He knew it, too. She saw it in the way he smiled, the way he rested his fingers on her shoulders. But did she want to do anything about it?

Of course she did.

She wasn't a complete moron. Doug could get her hot and wet without even touching her. And when he *did* touch her, well, she completely lost control. She couldn't have picked a better man to play her fiancé.

Emphasis on "play". This is all fake, Rach. It's a ruse you created to fool your family, and nothing more. She seemed to be forgetting that more and more. Did Doug have the same trouble making that distinction?

Doubtful. He was a man. Their minds didn't work the way women's did. Men just wanted sex, without giving much

81

thought to the consequences. He'd probably take whatever she offered, wherever and whenever she offered it. She didn't have a problem with that kind of behavior, usually, but nothing here could be described as usual.

"How was the ride here?" she asked him, knowing Jake probably gave him the third degree. Over and over. When they were kids Jake had appointed himself her personal protector, and that hadn't stopped now that they'd grown up.

"Interesting," Doug said softly. He shared with Jake—who sat next to him—as he said it, a look that made her eyebrows lift.

Had Doug told her brother about their agreement? She glanced around Doug to look at Jake, who confirmed her suspicion with a wink. Jake knew! Her stomach bottomed out. If he didn't keep his mouth shut, she'd strangle him.

She kicked Doug under the table. "What did you do?" she whispered furiously—though she didn't know why she bothered. With her mother screeching, her father and other brothers talking baseball scores, and Amanda and Ronny having a less-than-friendly discussion about their honeymoon itinerary, there was no possible way anyone could have heard her.

Doug winced. "He already knew. I don't think you gave the guy enough credit. He had the whole thing figured out."

She glared at Doug, and then her brother. "Don't either of you *dare* say a thing."

Grandma DeeDee leaned across the table, her wrinkled hand cupped to her ear. "Say a thing about what, dear? Speak up, I couldn't hear you."

An immediate silence fell over the table and all eyes turned toward Rachel and Doug.

"They're planning to elope," her mother answered after a full minute of silent gaping, much to Rachel's embarrassment. "I told them not to even think about it."

"Good for you," Grandma DeeDee chimed in. "Young people these days. They do the most unusual things."

Like roping a coworker into playing house for the weekend? "Yeah, Grandma. You're right. When Doug and I get married, we'll go all out. The church, the white dress and tux, the limo. Right *dear*?" she added through clenched teeth.

"Not if that isn't what you want, *sweetheart*. If eloping would make *you* happy, that's what we'll do." A muscle in Doug's jaw twitched while he spoke, but she had a feeling it was more from amusement than embarrassment.

She kicked him again, harder this time, and smiled when he grimaced. She mouthed "Don't screw with me," and gave him a too-sweet smile.

He leaned in and whispered in her ear. "Don't underestimate me, sweetheart. I plan to screw you thoroughly this weekend. And you're going to love every second."

Her breath caught in her throat at his bold words, a curl of arousal unfurling low in her belly. She shook her head, trying to get control of her thoughts, but all she could think about were Doug's words, and how he planned to act them out. It all went downhill from there.

Rachel, in a lust-induced haze not even the fabulous chocolate cake could break through, spent the remainder of the meal pushing her food around with her fork and fantasizing about what Doug had promised. Doug seemed intent on not letting her forget, rubbing his leg against hers and resting his hand on top of her thigh and making it even more impossible for her to concentrate on food. As for her family, well, she really didn't know. With the way Doug kept touching her, she'd forgotten they were there until the time came to leave.

When they stood up to leave, Doug placed a hand low on her back, just above her rump. He leaned in to her ear and blew a hot breath across her sensitive skin. "I think it's time for a little fun."

ॐ⃝

Rachel stood in the center of the bedroom, concentrating on a worn spot on the carpet. Funny that Doug had kept her in a state of constant arousal for the whole day, but now, when they finally had time alone, anxiety crept up inside her and made her hands shake.

"Is something wrong?" he asked as he switched off the light, bathing the room in the soft glow of the moon filtering in through the parted curtains.

"I'm really tired. Totally wiped out. I think I'll just go to bed." She started to pull back the covers, but he stopped her with his commanding tone.

"Don't."

"Doug, listen. We really shouldn't—"

"Stop it. Stop denying yourself what you know you really want."

She snorted. "Oh, and you're such an expert on what I really want?"

He shook his head, his expression a heady mix of pain and passion. "I know what you want, because I want the same thing just as much. Maybe more. This isn't easy for me, either. I know we're both in the middle of a strange situation, but I'm willing to give it a try."

"It? What exactly is *it*?"

"Us." He spoke so softly that at first she thought she'd misheard him. *Us?*

"You mean sex, right?" What else could he possibly mean?

"Yeah, that too." He stepped over to her and pulled her in for a kiss.

Chapter Eight

As Doug kissed her, Rachel tugged his shirt out of the waistband of his pants. She broke the kiss to lift the shirt over his head and off, but a jolt of wicked inspiration hit halfway through the action. Instead of divesting him of the shirt completely, she pulled the stretchy material over his head and behind his back, trapping his arms against his sides.

"What do you think you're doing?" he asked, his tone wary, but she didn't miss the hint of arousal behind the apprehension.

"Relax, Doug," she teased. "You're so tense. Uptight even. It's not good for you."

"Why don't you give me a little help with that? Take my shirt off and let me touch you."

She wasn't stupid enough to believe she'd really trapped him, but she loved the feeling of power it gave her to have a big, arrogant guy like Doug at her mercy.

She lifted palms to his chest and pushed him back until his legs hit the bed and he lost his balance. He sat hard on the mattress, his eyes darkening with his arousal.

"Rachel," he warned, his breathing ragged. "You've had me worked up since you asked me to come to your sister's wedding. I won't be able to last long. Stop playing around."

"Just give me a few minutes." She leaned in and flicked her tongue over his flat nipple. He sucked in a sharp breath as she blew a stream of hot air over the damp skin. The next time she brought her mouth to his chest, she nipped gently.

"*Jesus,*" he breathed. "Rachel, *don't tease.*"

"You love it and you know it." She traced circles on his chest with her fingernail, lightly scraping, running her fingers through the soft hair peppering his smooth skin. "Admit it."

"Okay. Fine. I love it. I can't get enough of it," he ground out, his eyes narrowing. "Now stop playing and help me relieve some of this tension."

"Not quite yet. Have a little patience, will you?" She got on her knees next to him on the bed and sealed her lips over his before he could protest further.

She traced the seam of his lips with the tip of her tongue, felt him shiver against her. He struggled against the cotton shirt holding him in place, a strangled groan rumbling in his chest when she rested her palm against his erection. His muscles tensed as she ran her hands down his arms, across his chest. She was driving him crazy—they both knew it, and she loved every second of it.

He tensed as she ran her nails down his back, a low growl escaping his lips. "You like that?" she asked when she broke the kiss.

"Oh, yeah." Doug's eyes had practically rolled back in his head and his voice sounded like he'd swallowed sandpaper. It made her shiver as she drew her tongue along the line of his jaw. She brought her hand up the inside of his thigh until she cupped his straining cock again in her palm. A gentle squeeze brought a groan to his lips.

He trembled now, visibly, and she decided to take pity on the poor guy. Soon. "Tell me what you want, Doug."

"You."

"That's a given." She nipped at his earlobe. "What do you really want?"

"Just you." He looked at her through half-closed eyes, the pure need in his expression making her insides melt.

She paused her teasing at the plea she heard in his voice. On a level she didn't want to acknowledge, she understood what he needed from her—and she understood that they were about to cross the line from just sex to something more. How much more, she couldn't really say. She couldn't even be sure if she was completely willing to take the chance. But just one look in Doug's eyes and she knew she had to. She needed this as much as he did.

She crawled behind him and freed his arms. As soon as his shirt hit the floor, he turned and lunged, knocking her onto her back on the mattress. His kiss was rough, possessive, and it dragged out some deep, unfamiliar emotion inside her.

Within minutes—and with a lot of shifting positions—he'd managed to strip off her clothes and had gone to work on the rest of his. He grabbed something out of his pants pocket—a condom, good thing he had one with him. She hadn't brought any, not expecting to need them. If he hadn't been thinking...she sighed. She might not have been in the right mind to stop him. She watched him intently as he tore open the package and rolled the protection on. When he came back to her, she licked her lips at the sight of his straining erection.

Doug flopped back on the bed, resting his head on the pillows. "It's still my birthday."

"Uh huh." She crawled up beside him and placed a kiss in the center of his chest. "Have you decided what you want yet?"

"Yeah. I want you to ride me."

His blatant request sent a tremor through her entire body. How could she refuse him anything?

"Whatever you want." She straddled his hips and, gripping his cock in her hand, guided him into her waiting sex. His hands came up to grip her hips, helping her set the pace, before moving up to cup her breasts.

"God, you're so beautiful," he told her, his voice barely above a whisper.

"Not cold and unfeeling?" she asked. "Not an ice princess?"

He frowned and shook his head. "No. Never. I know you better than to believe that."

A sliver of shock rushed through her middle at his words. He sounded...sincere. A tear welled in her eyes and fought to hold it back, knowing that would only complicate things further. If he knew how his words affected her, he might get the wrong idea and think their weekend would lead to something permanent. She snapped her eyes shut, concentrating instead on the incredible tingling sensations sliding up and down on his cock sent shimmering through her. It was the only way she'd make it through the weekend with her heart—and her sanity—intact.

"Rachel," Doug whispered softly, his fingers plucking at her distended nipples.

A moan rumbled from her as she willed her eyes to open. "Huh?" Low in her belly the tingling of her impending climax started and she increased her pace. Doug smiled, his eyes dark.

"Don't go anywhere. Stay right here, in the moment. With us."

He pulled her down for a kiss she'd almost call tender just as she felt her climax wash over her. In the midst of the blood-pounding rush she felt Doug tense under her and heard him cry out with his own release.

She settled against him, resting her cheek on his chest while she drew deep, shuddering breaths. Her heart swelled and her throat clenched, her body and mind shattered by what she felt for him. She couldn't let herself feel *anything* for the guy. This would all be over in a day. But she couldn't help but want more from him. He stood up to her, made her feel things she hadn't felt in what seemed like forever. She again found herself fighting tears as he stroked her back with his big, warm palm.

Doug kissed the top of her head. "I told you we'd be incredible. Why did it take you so long to believe me?"

She lifted her gaze to his. "You only told me that a day ago."

"Really? It feels like forever."

Didn't she know it. The idea left a giddy feeling around her heart even as a ball of dread settled in her stomach.

ဆောင်

Much later, Rachel laid awake in bed, listening to Doug's slow, steady breathing. And thinking. Just as she'd hoped to avoid.

She was in too deep, and she had no hope of digging herself out. Usually she avoided emotional attachment, but the situation invited all kinds of intimacy. She felt closer to Doug than she'd ever let herself get to any man. That could cause a major problem for either one of them.

He did things to her that no man had ever done. Things that had nothing to do with sex, or even physical contact, but emotions she'd have preferred to keep out of the entire weekend. She *liked* being independent. Liked taking care of herself. She'd been called a control freak on many occasions, and grudgingly admitted how true the statements were.

But Doug had let her take control—in a big way. That alone shook her to the core. For such a big, strong guy, he'd had no problem letting her be on top—literally as well as figuratively.

It would have been better for her if he hadn't. If he'd been a typical controlling and domineering man, they could have had great sex and walked away from each other after the weekend. How would she be able to let go now, when he made her care about him in a way she'd avoided caring about any man for...well, ever? *Great job, genius. You've really gotten yourself into a fix this time, haven't you?*

She needed to confess the truth to her family—cleanse her soul as Grandma DeeDee liked to say. She needed to pull away from Doug before she started imagining them being here, planning their own wedding. It wouldn't be so tough, with their...thing being so new.

Yeah, right.

Chapter Nine

When Doug woke up with Rachel in his arms, it took him a few minutes to come to terms with what had happened. She lay cuddled against him, her warm breath feathering across his chest and her hand splayed over his stomach. She looked so peaceful and beautiful that he couldn't help but lean in and kiss her soft hair.

And then reality hit and he pulled out of her arms.

Was he an idiot? A complete moron? He had to be, since he'd allowed the worst to happen. He'd gone and started caring about her. And not even just caring. It was...it was...it was too soon to put words to it. *Way* too damned soon. Like months too soon. Years, even. He jumped out of bed, feeling like the breath had been knocked from his lungs.

He scrubbed his hand down his face as he paced the room. He hadn't come with her to get involved. He'd just wanted to get her into bed, not into his heart. But last night had been about more than sex. Much more. And he hadn't been prepared. Now he had no clue how to fix it.

He checked the clock. Four a.m. No one else would be up yet. Good. He needed some alone time to think. He pulled on a pair of shorts, grabbed a change of clothes, and headed for the shower.

Rachel surprised him by joining him minutes later.

"What are you doing?" he asked. "Go back to bed."

She shook her head. "We need to talk."

"Yeah, well, as you can see this isn't exactly a good time."

She put her hands on her hips and glared at him. Most of the effect was lost on him, since she stood in front of him naked and half-soaked from the shower spray. "It's the perfect time. You're naked. Vulnerable. You won't try to skirt the subject. This is important, and I refuse to go away until we've talked this out. Do you have a problem with that?"

"Actually, I do." The fact that he was nude caused half the problem. The fact that she was, too, caused the other half. His cock, which had been semi-hard before she'd climbed into the shower, now throbbed painfully. He had to clear his throat twice before he could get sound to come out of his mouth. "What subject are you talking about?"

"This is just sex, right? You're not going to go and get all sappy about this, are you? Cause, you know, that would be bad." She grabbed the bar of soap and started washing up. He couldn't believe that she seemed so unaffected by what had happened the night before. She acted like this was some kind of business meeting.

He would have laughed, if he hadn't been so shaken. Why did he feel like she was trying to convince herself as well as him? Suddenly, watching her naked and soapy and sexy, he didn't care what either of their motivations were. He just had to have her. Right that second. Whether it was to prove to himself that he could keep his emotions out of the equation, or prove to her that he couldn't, he didn't know. He just knew he had to do something.

He pushed her back against the shower wall, pressing his thigh between her legs. "It's all about sex. We're playing here, not actually planning a wedding. The only thing I want from you is to be inside you. Other than that, I could care less." Even as he spoke the words, he saw them for the lies they were. He would have apologized, had he not seen the look in her eyes. She didn't believe him any more than he did.

He wrapped her legs around his waist and took her fast and hard. The impossibly slick, wet friction of skin on skin had him going at a frantic pace, bringing them both to orgasm in minutes.

A good thing, too, since his legs didn't seem to want to hold him up for much longer.

He helped her rinse, rinsed himself, and turned off the water. They climbed out of the tub and he dried her off, since she seemed even shakier than he felt. "Are you okay? I didn't hurt you, did I?"

She'd come to him trying to prove there was nothing between them but a little mutual satisfaction—she hadn't said it, but they both knew it. He had a feeling that they'd proven something completely different. Not that he'd admit it to her. He wasn't that big a fool. A woman like Rachel would tear him apart if she found out he'd done precisely what she had asked him not to do.

He'd gotten a lot more than he'd bargained for out of this weekend. They both had. He'd gone into their arrangement hoping to crack her icy façade. Now that he had, he wanted so much more.

Stupid, Doug. You just got dumped by the woman you thought was your soul mate. Why pick up with another so soon, especially one so contrary?

Because he'd started to realize that the woman he'd thought was his soul mate hadn't even been close.

He hadn't known what he really wanted until it had come up and smacked him upside the head. He wanted Rachel—not just in a sexual way. He wanted her in his life. Probably for good. Now he just had to find a way to convince her to give it a shot.

ഇരു

Rachel stood in the back yard as the sun came up, wondering for what seemed like the millionth time if her mother had gone off the deep end. Planning too many of Amanda's weddings must have turned her brain to mush.

When her mother had said the florist would be there to decorate "first thing", she hadn't imagined the woman had meant first *light*.

This was nuts. The whole thing. The rushed wedding, the *fourth* marriage, the bright and obnoxious yellow color scheme, the decorating by sunrise. She kept looking around for someone to pop out of the bushes and tell her she was on *Candid Camera*.

"There you are. I've been looking everywhere for you."

She turned to see Amanda walking across the yard, her hair in bright pink sponge rollers and an avocado-green mud mask on her face.

"What's up?" Rachel asked, trying her best not to laugh at her sister on her *special day*.

"I should be asking you the same thing. Where's Doug?"

Rachel shrugged. She'd assumed he went back to bed after their little tryst in the shower. To be honest, she would have followed had she not had to meet the florist outside since her mother had to make last-minute adjustments to Amanda's gown.

She'd gone into the shower to talk to him. *Honest.* But her plans had all dissolved into the steam when he'd touched her.

It would be so easy to fall in love with him. Hell, she was already halfway there. Maybe more. He understood her better than anyone in her life ever had, and she'd barely even spoken to him until this weekend. That had to say something.

Yeah. You need medication. You're hallucinating.

She couldn't have him, not for good, no matter how much she thought she wanted him. He'd told her he was just in it for the sex. But was he really? She had said the same to him, but somewhere along the way had changed her mind.

She'd tried to be impersonal, she really had, but she was getting too old for mindless flings. Now she wanted more. But could she convince Doug of that? He seemed so set on keeping things out of emotional territory.

No, he didn't. That was just another one of her stupid excuses. She'd seen a spark of something in his eyes, something that told her he suffered the same emotional turmoil.

"Hello? Rachel? Where are you?" She came back from her self-analysis session to Amanda waving her hand inches from her face. "I asked you a question."

"What was it again?"

"Do you think Mom is going overboard with all of this?"

"Well, duh." Rachel sighed and pushed a hand through her hair. "I think you all belong in a mental institution. *All* of you. Especially your fiancé for wanting to marry you with your track record."

"Yeah. I've been thinking about that."

"You have?"

Amanda nodded. "I don't want to be alone, Rachel."

"That doesn't sound like a very good reason to get married."

"It's not," Amanda said quietly. "But I can't let Mom down. Or Ronny. He seems so happy about this."

"How long have you known the guy?"

"We first met three years ago, but we got close when my marriage ended last year, and we've been seeing each other since. But...I don't know. I guess the love will come in time."

Um, excuse me? Isn't love supposed to come before marriage? "You're not in love with him?"

Amanda shook her head. "No. I love him, but only as a friend."

A psychologist could make a mint off this family. Heck, forget the family. Amanda alone was worth a small fortune. "Then why did you agree to marry him?"

"I hate the thought of not having someone to come home to at night. He proposed, and I got caught up in the moment and accepted."

"Amanda, you cannot marry this guy."

"What am I supposed to do? It's a little late to break up with him."

"No, it's not. You need to, or you're not being fair to him."

Amanda sighed. "I guess you're right. Now I just need to talk to him. When you met Doug, did you feel that spark right away?"

"Yeah, I did." The answer came out before she could stop it, but she realized it was the truth. Taking it back would be a lie.

"You're lucky. I'm still looking. I probably will be forever."

Rachel watched Amanda walk away, and couldn't help but feel bad for her sister. With all the marriages, she'd only been trying to find someone to love her. Rachel saw her sister in a way she'd never seen her before, and all the animosity she'd felt for her dissolved. She was looking for the same things Rachel was.

At least Amanda had the courage to admit it.

೮ೞ

Hours later Rachel stood at the flowery alter in the back yard. Ronny stood across from her, shifting from foot to foot and looking ready to pass out. Rachel's heart went out to him. He really did seem like a good guy. He didn't deserve what Amanda was about to put him through. But she couldn't say anything to him, could she? That would be overstepping her bounds.

The Wedding March started, a tinny rendition playing from her mother's portable tape player, and Rachel had to suppress a laugh. Why go all out with everything else and use music that sounded like it was being played from inside a soda can? When it came to this family, logic had taken an extended vacation.

After what seemed like an eternity, Amanda, looking just as nervous as Ronny, practically ran down the aisle. When she stopped next to him, she turned to the Justice of the Peace. "Let's do this quickly, okay?"

Hold on a sec. Isn't this the same woman who didn't want to get married at all this morning? Rachel opened her mouth to speak, knowing she couldn't let them go through with this, but snapped it shut at Amanda's warning look.

"Amanda has instructed me to keep the ceremony simple and short," The Justice of the Peace informed the small crowd of family and a few close friends. "Before I begin, does anyone have any objections to these two young people being joined as man and wife?"

Rachel's breath caught in her throat. She waited for Amanda to say something—anything—to end this insanity.

"I can't do this."

Rachel let out a breath as she heard the words. But they didn't come from Amanda.

Ronny had spoken.

"What do you mean?" Amanda asked, sounding panicked.

He let out a deep sigh. "We've always been friends, Mandy. But I can't pretend we're more than that when we're really not. I'm so sorry."

For all of five seconds, Amanda looked like she was going to cry. And then she smiled and wrapped her arms around Ronny's neck. "You have no idea what a relief this is."

"You feel the same way?" Ronny asked, pulling back to look at Amanda.

"I do."

I do? Jesus. That was so totally the wrong time to say those words. This was like a Jerry Springer episode.

Frustrated and relieved at the same time, Rachel tossed her bouquet over her head and walked back down the aisle to where the caterer had begun setting up the meal. Someone had to notify the guy that his services were no longer needed, since Amanda had finally, after three and a half tries, come to her senses.

"I caught it!" she heard someone yell. She turned to see her cousin Janice clutching to her chest the bouquet Rachel just thrown. "I'm next! I'm next!"

Next to *what*? Be a bridesmaid at an aborted wedding? "You guys know you're supposed to catch the *Bride's* bouquet, right?" The women all looked at her, their eyes glazed over and their lips parted. "And it's supposed to be *after* the wedding happens. You know—oh, never mind." She shook her head and kept walking.

Hopeless. The lot of them.

Her mother caught her arm as she walked toward the caterer. "What just happened here?"

"Amanda finally grew a backbone."

"I spent all this time planning. I wanted everything to be perfect. Do you think there was too much yellow? Should I have chosen blue instead?"

Oh, yeah. *That* would have made all the difference. Rachel fingered her bright lemon-colored skirt. "Well, yeah, blue probably would have been a better choice, but that's not the point. She and Ronny are *not* in love. I think Amanda's finally realizing she doesn't need to be married to validate herself."

"But the flowers, the food..." Her mother's voice trailed off, her expression stricken.

Not wanting to see her mother cry, Rachel mentioned the only solution she could think of. "You know, yesterday was Doug's birthday."

She hiccupped and swiped at her eyes. "I didn't know that."

"He didn't want to say anything. He didn't want to overshadow Amanda's big day."

And then finally, her mother smiled. Doug would probably want to kill her for planting such an idea in her mother's head. She'd never live it down.

Perfect.

She smiled to herself. She'd be in big trouble later, and she had a feeling she was going to love every second of it.

Chapter Ten

All in all, the day had passed with relative smoothness. Despite the fact that no wedding had taken place, Rachel had enjoyed herself around her family for the first time in as long as she could remember. She'd even eaten a piece of the sunshine cake—and had liked even more shoving a slice in Doug's face when he hadn't been paying attention.

He had yet to pay her back for that one.

She shivered at the thought, remembering the seductive promise he'd whispered into her ear.

Doug walked up behind her, leaning his body against hers. "What are you doing out here all alone?"

"Getting a little fresh air. It's hot inside."

"I'm glad you got out of that dress."

She barely had. The zipper had stuck again, and she'd had to take a pair of scissors to it. The positive side was that she'd put the thing out of commission and no other woman would be subjected to wearing the monstrosity again. "Yeah, pretty terrible, wasn't it?"

"Nah, it wasn't so bad." He playfully nipped the side of her neck. "But every time I looked at you I thought about when you tried it on, and I wanted to do that again."

She went all hot and fuzzy inside. "Oh, yeah?"

He laughed. "*Yeah.* Listen, Rachel, I think we need to talk."

"I'm really sorry I told my mother about your birthday. I really didn't think it would bother you that she turned the reception into a birthday dinner."

"It didn't upset me," he assured her. "Though I doubt I'll ever look at yellow the same again. We need to talk about something more serious."

"What?" she asked, even though she already knew the answer.

"Us."

Us. She swallowed hard against the lump forming in her throat. "Okay."

"I went into this with every intention of proving you weren't the cold witch everyone believed," he told her. She tensed, and he laughed in response. "*I* knew you weren't, right from day one. I didn't want anything lasting to come out of this, and I know you didn't either, but I can't help the way I feel. I want more. When we go back home, I want to continue seeing you."

"You do?" Her heart cheered, her nerves jumped for joy, and her brain—the party pooper, as usual—questioned everything. "I thought you didn't want any kind of serious relationship."

"Yeah, that's what I thought, too." He gazed out across the yard toward the setting sun. "I changed my mind."

She smiled, but said nothing for fear that she'd chicken out, push him away, and ruin a perfectly wonderful moment.

"So, ah...what do you think?" he asked after a moment of silence.

She laughed. "I think we can work something out."

෨෬

Doug lounged in the passenger seat on the ride home, much like he had when they'd driven up to Vermont on Friday. But now, everything had changed. He'd gone up to have a good time, but he'd come back with a woman he hoped he could spend the rest of his life with.

Her family was a little nuts, but he'd had the time of his life. Even when Rachel had shoved that yellow-frosted cake in his face, he'd had fun. In fact, he could imagine rubbing that frosting all over her body—and licking it off. Inch by excruciating inch. He'd have her screaming his name by the time he finished, and once she came he'd do it all over again.

He cleared his throat, his body suddenly hard and aching. The two hour drive inside Rachel's tuna-can-on-wheels wasn't the time for such thoughts. They'd only lead to a lot of discomfort, in more ways than one.

Rachel glanced over at him. "Is everything okay?"

"Yeah. I'm just thinking."

"About what?"

He loved everything about her. Her imperfections made her the perfect woman for him. They fit. He couldn't describe it any other way. He wanted to spend a long time with this woman. Maybe even forever. "I could fall in love with you."

Rachel sucked in a sharp breath, her grip on the wheel tightening to the point of white knuckles. And then she smiled. "So what's stopping you?"

Not a blessed thing.

Epilogue

Doug stopped in front of the jewelry store window, pulling Rachel up alongside him. The mid-December night was clear and cold, the streets lined with holiday decorations. Snowflakes fluttered through the air, dancing like tiny fairies in the night, some landing on her eyelashes and her bangs. She batted the frozen wetness away.

She pulled her coat closer around her to ward off the chill. Doug draped his arm over her shoulder. The man was amazing. He always knew what she needed—even if he did give her a hard time on occasion. In the months they'd been together, they'd had their fair share of disagreements—especially since she'd moved into his apartment in September—but they made up as well as they argued. Maybe even better.

"What do you think of that one?" he asked.

She leaned closer and peered at the jewelry displayed in the window. "The bracelet? It's cute." Gorgeous, actually. If he planned to buy it for her, she wouldn't object.

"Not the bracelet, silly. Next to it."

She shifted her gaze from the fabulous bracelet to the—*the ring?* The *diamond* ring? Her breath caught in her throat, but she refused to let herself get excited yet. He couldn't be thinking what she hoped he was thinking. He had to be talking about something else. Maybe his mother wanted diamonds for Christmas.

"It's very nice," she told him noncommittally.

"Nice, huh? Is there one you like more?"

More? What was he hinting at? She swallowed past the lump forming in her throat. "That's an engagement ring, Doug."

"Yep. It sure is." He moved behind her and wrapped his arms around her waist, his chin on her shoulder. "So, do you like it or not?"

A chill skittered down her spine and butterflies burst to life in her stomach. She wet her lips with the tip of her tongue. "Usually you start looking at those when you plan to propose."

"Right again. Wow, you're sharp tonight." She felt his chuckle more than heard it as his chest vibrated against her back.

"What are we doing here?"

"I just want to pick out the right one. I know how particular you can be when you feel like you don't have control over the situation."

If it wasn't for his teasing tone—or the fact that he had her looking at engagement rings—she would have elbowed him in the ribs. "Ha, ha. You're a regular laugh a minute."

She felt his smile against her cheek. He brushed a kiss over her jaw. "I love you, Rach."

Her heart swelled at the words, just as it always did. What had she ever done to deserve something as perfect as Doug? "I love you, too."

"So what do you think? Do you like that one, or should we look somewhere else?"

"Doug?"

"Yeah?"

"Are you planning on proposing?" She held her breath for his answer.

"Actually, I am."

"Really? Sometime soon?" Like for the holidays, maybe? She couldn't hold back the giddy smile at the thought.

He paused so long she'd begun to wonder if he'd changed his mind. When he finally spoke, his voice had taken on a husky, thick quality. "How about now?"

Now? He planned to propose now? Oh, my. Well, she wasn't stupid enough to pass up this chance. She nodded vigorously. "Now works for me."

"Good. Rachel Storm, will you run off to Vegas with me to get married this weekend?"

She nearly passed out. "*What?*" Vegas? A wedding, alone, no friends and annoying family? *This weekend?*

"Well, I promised your Mom Vegas in December. I wouldn't want to disappoint."

She laughed. It sounded like the best idea she'd heard in a long time. Well, since last night when he'd tied her arms to the bedposts and—*stay in the moment here, Rach.*

"Then it's a date." He stepped back and turned her around, kissing her hard on the lips. "You are going to take my last name, right?"

Absolutely. "I don't know. I'll think about it."

Doug shook his head. "Well, at least I know I'll never be bored."

She'd see to that personally. Every day for the rest of her life.

Miss Independent

Chapter One

Being a professional wife definitely had its bonuses. Bonuses Amanda Storm missed on days like today. She swiped a hand through her sweat-drenched hair and muttered a curse. Why had she wanted to do the work on the property herself instead of hiring a handyman like her mother had suggested?

Oh, yeah. Because she'd wanted to be *independent,* though at the moment, the reason why she'd been so insistent on gaining that status eluded her. Home ownership had its advantages, the real-estate agent she'd contacted a month ago about renting properties had told her, but the man had failed to mention the downfalls.

"Stupid railing," she mumbled, narrowing her eyes at the warped wood like her glare would make a difference. It wouldn't. She'd learned *that* early on in the game of household repairs. If she'd been born mechanically inclined like her brothers or even her younger sister, Rachel, the thing would have been fixed on the first try, but, like independence, mechanical aptitude came with a pretty big learning curve. Though, she had to admit, she was doing pretty well for a twenty-eight-year-old woman who was living well and truly alone for the first time in her life.

"Just remember, you asked for it," she whispered to herself, the beginnings of a smile curling her lips. Yeah, she'd asked for it, and despite the problems, she wouldn't trade it for anything in the world. Stupid railing and all.

She didn't regret the snap decision to buy the little cottage—how could she when she'd gotten the fixer-upper at such a steal?—but it might have been easier if she'd hired someone to do the work on the place before moving her stuff in. Less than twelve hours into unpacking her car and bringing her possessions inside, she'd managed to find a hundred different things just waiting to be done. A week later, she'd only scratched a handful of things off her list.

Sweat dripped down her face and stung her eyes. Mosquitoes buzzed around her head, ignoring the ineffective repellant she'd purchased at the local pharmacy. At this rate, she'd look like she'd come down with chicken pox by morning, but she had no right to complain. She was a home owner now. Just the thought made her smile, despite the heat and the mile-long list of chores she had yet to make a dent in. The place was hers, and if *that* didn't scream of independence nothing else did.

Oh, yeah. Definitely a reason to smile. One of the few she'd had in the past year or two.

In all her time moving from husband to husband, what being alone really meant had never occurred to her. She knew the feeling now, better than she ever had, as she stood on the front porch of the tiny cottage baking in the nearly one hundred degree New England afternoon. She'd expected to feel lost, out of her element, and in a way, she was, but exhilaration raced through her bloodstream like a flash fire. For the first time in her life, she didn't have to share a damned thing, and she intended to keep it that way for a long time to come.

Yes, being a wife had its bonuses, but being a home owner had more.

Satisfied she'd done all she could to secure the rail on a temporary basis, she promised herself to call a professional first thing Monday morning and set the hammer down on the porch next to the glass she'd long ago drained of ice water. Slumping onto the step and drawing in a big breath of pine-scented air, she glanced around the tree-strewn land for what had to be the thousandth time in the week since she'd moved in. Her land. Her trees. Her shrubs, overgrown as they were. Her beach on the lake a few dozen yards away from the cottage.

Well, not entirely hers. She had to share the beach with the neighbor she had yet to meet. The real-estate agent assured her someone lived in the big house on the hill, but she had yet to see any signs of life. Not that she minded. She'd prefer to have the small beach to herself for as long as she could get it. She might be new to the whole living-alone thing, but she was already loving nearly every second of it.

Grabbing the empty glass, she stood and headed for the front door. Her parched throat practically screamed for a refill on the water, and a cool shower and a little afternoon TV time would be just what she needed after a long day of playing handyman. The boards creaked under her feet and she grimaced. The home inspector had said the porch—and the rest of the property—was structurally sound, but by next summer she wanted to replace the old, worn-out boards with new ones. A bigger, covered porch where she could hang a swing from the roof and enjoy the moon and stars on warm summer nights.

With one last glance over her shoulder at the lake, Amanda reached for the doorknob and gave it a turn. The door swung open on groaning hinges and she walked inside.

Her situation could have been a lot worse. The cabin was small—just three rooms and a bath—but the furniture she'd chosen was comfortable and sturdy, if not a bit plain. The price on the place had been right, too, thanks to the little building's fixer-upper status. What she would pay here monthly for mortgage wasn't much more than what she'd been paying for the hotel room she'd rented in town her first few weeks in Ludlow, while she'd been looking around for a place of her own and then waiting impatiently to sign the papers on her new place and move in. It wasn't much more than she would have paid for any of the apartments in town, either, and none of them had the privacy the cabin had—or the stacked washer and dryer in a closet in a corner of the kitchen.

So it needed a coat of paint and a decent amount of TLC. It wasn't anything she couldn't handle, either by doing the work herself or hiring someone to come out and do it for her. The payoff would be worth it in the end. She now had a place to call her own.

A place she didn't have to share with family or the latest man in her life, and that alone made it worth so much more than the asking price.

Her cell phone chimed and she snatched it off the counter, flipping it open and sparing a quick glance at the caller ID screen. A sigh caught in her throat. She'd been avoiding this call long enough, and it was time to face her demons. With a silent prayer that the call would go smoothly—and quickly—she brought it to her ear. "Hi, Mom."

"How did you know it was me?" The disappointment in Miriam Storm's voice had Amanda biting back a laugh.

"Caller ID." And the funny feeling she got in her stomach whenever her mother called. Amanda loved the woman with all her heart, but sometimes her mother went a little overboard. *I'm not sick anymore, Mom. Haven't been for years and years. No need to worry about me like you did when I was five.*

"Rachel told me you moved into your new place at the beginning of the week," her mother said, referring to Amanda's younger sister. She spoke in an accusatory tone usually reserved for special occasions, like when she bombarded them all with questions as to why none of her five offspring had managed to produce grandchildren yet. "I figured you would be trying to get unpacked."

Amanda nearly sighed at the prospect. What little she'd brought with her had been unpacked on the first day. Clothes, mostly, and some personal items and mementos. The furniture had been bought new from a nearby discount store and delivered on moving day, and she'd stocked the kitchen at the same time.

"I'm finished with all that, believe it or not, but I have a feeling you called about something else. What's up, Mom?" Amanda walked into the kitchen and opened the cabinets. Everything she needed was here. Plates, glasses, flatware and pans. She would have to make a trip into town later for some groceries since she had yet to buy more than a gallon of milk, some bottles of water and various cans of ready-to-heat meals, but even that would be pretty simple. Cooking for one didn't involve a lot of effort or ingredients. For Amanda, at least, it rarely involved more than a can opener and a microwave. "Is something wrong?"

"I just wanted to make sure you were settled okay."

Amanda rolled her eyes. That, and her mother wanted to lay on the guilt since Amanda hadn't called home the day she'd moved out of the hotel and into her new place. She hadn't even mentioned buying the house to her mother until after she'd signed the papers. Miriam would have tried to talk her out of it, convinced her to rent for a while instead of taking such a big step, and before she'd seen the place Amanda would have agreed. But one look and as crazy as it sounded, she'd known it was home. Or it would be, once the work was finished.

"I'm as settled as I can be for having just moved in. I'm fine. I promise. If I wasn't, you'd be the first one to know. You can stop worrying so much about me now."

"I'm worried about you for good reason, Mandy. You packed up and moved away without giving it much thought. Now you've bought a house, for God's sake, and gotten a job. Are you sure you're all right?"

Amanda shook her head. Her mother said the word "job" like that was a *bad* thing. As for being *all right*, she wasn't sure. The only thing she knew was that she felt better than she had in a long time. *If I can't take care of myself now, we have a serious problem.* "I think I'm okay. Really. I feel great, and I'm going to go with that feeling."

"You really shouldn't leave the door open here," a masculine voice spoke from behind her. "You'll get bugs. Or maybe something small and furry."

Amanda jumped and spun around, the phone clutched to her ear, and found herself face-to-face with a set of the bluest eyes she'd ever seen. Blue eyes set into a handsome, sculpted face framed by thick blond hair. Her breath caught in her throat and her heart hammered against her rib cage. He had to be the sexiest man she'd laid eyes on in a long time.

He was also a stranger, and she was out in the middle of nowhere with him. Her hand tightened around the handle of a frying pan in the dry rack next to the sink. "You scared me."

"Sorry. I thought you heard me come in." His lips tilted in a sheepish smile and he raised his hands in front of him, palms up. He glanced toward the counter. "You want to let go of the pan? I'm not here to hurt you. I just wanted to stop by and introduce myself on the way into town."

She loosened her grip on the handle, but only marginally. "Who are you?"

"Joe Baker. I live next door."

The breath left her lungs in a whoosh. So he wasn't some murdering psychopath. He was just the absentee neighbor. If she'd made him a little nervous by grabbing the pan, it was his fault for walking into her house without even knocking. Okay, he hadn't walked in, exactly, since he was standing in the doorway, but he should have stayed out on the front porch and knocked on the doorframe rather than just making himself at home in someone else's house.

She gave the stranger—Joe—a quick once-over and blinked. Yeah, his manners might need some work, but he had a nice face. A body to die for, too, clad in a pair of denim shorts and a T-shirt stretching across broad shoulders. She'd always been a sucker for a killer body and a cute face, and he had both in spades.

She swallowed hard. Why now, that she'd officially sworn off men, did this guy have to show up at her front door?

It was a sign. It had to be.

"I have to go, Mom. I'll call you later." Before her mother could protest, Amanda snapped the phone closed and set it on the counter. She could only deal with one problem at a time, and the one standing a few feet away took precedence. "Can I do something for you?"

"Like I said, I just wanted to stop by and introduce myself." He stepped into the cottage, his hand extended. "If you need anything, let me know."

She took his hand and shook it, and the unsettled feeling swirling in her stomach grew by leaps and bounds. The warmth of his fingers encircling hers sent a shock through her. She'd be lucky if drool wasn't dripping down her chin. He was the kind of guy Rachel would call a hottie, all tanned skin and muscled pecs and a spark of something in his eyes that told her there was a lot more to the man than what he seemed willing to let on with his friendly smile and goading tone.

And she was still holding his hand.

She released her death grip on the poor guy and took a step back. Suddenly, a little distance seemed like a very good idea.

"Anyway," Joe said, his gaze wary but bordering on amusement. "If you need anything, feel free to call. I'll give you my numbers, home and cell."

He reached into the front pocket of his shorts and took out a small, white card, thrusting it in her direction. Amanda forced a smile and grasped the corner of the card between her forefinger and thumb. She gave it a tug, pulled it from his fingers and dropped it onto the counter.

"Thanks. I appreciate it." If she touched him again, she might not want to stop. Her new neighbor would probably take issue with that, given she'd known the guy for a total of two minutes.

Then again, if the interested look in his eyes meant something, he may not. Yep, definitely a sign. Now she just had to figure out if it was a good one or a bad one.

She glanced away, busying herself with putting the clean dishes into the cabinet. He couldn't be as good-looking as she'd first thought. It had to be a trick of her imagination.

"You know where to find me if you have any problems," he continued, a hint of laughter in his voice. "And if you need help fixing the place up, give me a call."

Amanda narrowed her eyes. If she didn't know any better, she'd think her mother sent this guy out here to be her personal savior. *Guess what? The last thing I need right now is saving.*

She pasted her best cordial expression on her face and swung her gaze back to his. "Thanks anyway, but I don't mind doing a lot of the work myself."

He blinked, shock registering in his expression a second before doubt replaced it. "Okay, if you say so. Just keep what I said in mind. I'm a contractor, so I can handle pretty much any job, though I have to say the place looks like it needs a complete overhaul."

She followed his gaze around the room, but didn't see what he saw. Where he probably saw yellowed linoleum and peeling paint, old windows and torn screens, Amanda noticed something different. Potential. Lots of it. She could live with the lack of updates for a while, since a picture of the finished product had already formed in her head.

"What do you charge?" she asked, grasping for a way to keep things professional between them.

He shrugged. "Depends on the job. We could work something out."

Did he think she was destitute or something? So she drove a run-down car and lived in what he probably thought of as a shanty. She wasn't poor, though the down payment on the cottage had eaten a good chunk of her savings. She was a lot like the cottage. A work in progress. The repairs would come, in time. So would a newer-model car. But between the money she made working at a busy local bar and the remainder of her savings, she was by no means needy.

"Thanks. I'll keep that in mind when I'm ready to start repairs."

"Or even before that, if you need help with the porch railing."

He winked, and Amanda's face flamed. So he'd seen her half-assed attempt at wielding a hammer and pretending she knew what she was doing. If the floor would just swallow her up, she might be able to salvage what little dignity she had left.

She squared her shoulders and drew a fortifying breath before responding to his veiled rib. "I handled the railing fine."

His raised eyebrows told her he didn't believe her. One corner of his mouth lifted in a slow, sexy half-smile that had her heart thumping. She licked her dry lips and leaned back against the counter for support. The amusement dancing in his blue eyes only added to his appeal, despite the fact that he was laughing at her. She couldn't bring herself to be too upset with him. If she'd been him, she would have chuckled a little, too. He'd seen her at her worst, fighting with an inanimate object.

"I'm sure you did. I'm just putting the offer on the table in case you change your mind down the road. And if you ever want to have coffee or anything..." He stopped and shook his head. "Never mind. Forget I asked."

Amanda frowned. Had he really just asked her out? She'd just met the guy and already he wanted to have coffee with her.

She was an idiot for even considering the offer.

For a long time they stood there, neither of them saying anything, and Amanda had to shake off the sudden urge to get closer to him. If she was looking for a man right now, he would be at the top of her list.

Stupid, Amanda. Really stupid.

She swallowed hard. The old Amanda would have jumped at the chance to get to know him better, but the old Amanda had ended up married and divorced three times before she'd hit twenty-seven. Not exactly a poster girl for healthy relationships. She crossed her arms over her chest, hoping to steady her breath. What was it about this one particular man that made her react so strongly? So what if he looked good. She'd met plenty of handsome men in her life. What made him different?

She didn't know, but if she didn't get rid of him soon, her curiosity would get the better of her and she might take him up on his offer for coffee. Not a good prospect, given that she tended to fall in love at the drop of a hat, and out of it just as quickly.

"Well, thanks, Joe. I appreciate it, but I'm going to be fine." If she spent time with him, even during the course of repairs, there would be problems. She needed to stay as far away from him as possible if she wanted to keep her sanity intact. "I can handle the little stuff around here all by myself."

"I never thought you couldn't. I just figured I'd make the offer." He started backing out the door, the half-smile morphing into a full one filled with way too much amusement. "Keep the door closed, though, or you're just inviting problems I'm sure you don't need on top of all the other things you're planning to deal with."

Yeah, problems like a hunky neighbor with what seemed to be a white-knight complex. She definitely didn't need that kind of trouble.

"Thanks. I'll remember that." She closed and locked the door behind him, rested against the scarred wood and slid down until her butt hit the floor. Her face felt flushed and her heart was still beating a little too fast. Looking at him had a decidedly bad effect on her. Standing a few feet away, in the middle of nowhere with no one else around, the effect turned devastating.

Why him, of all people? He was the last man she wanted as a neighbor, simply because he was the first man she wanted in her bed since fiancé number four had left her at the altar—and she'd just met the guy.

෴

Well. That was…interesting.

Somehow Joe's brain had managed to shut down at the sight of her and turn him into a complete moron. What had he been thinking, asking her out not even five minutes into meeting her? The woman probably thought he was some kind of psycho. Or she thought he was desperate. He was neither, he'd just taken one look at her and lost control of his mouth.

He glanced over his shoulder at the cottage and shook his head. She was nothing like he'd expected. After the fight she had with the railing, he thought she would have jumped at his offer to help. Instead she'd all but sent him packing, and damned if her behavior didn't intrigue him. No matter what she'd said, the look in her eyes had spoken volumes. There'd been attraction there, but he'd also caught a glimpse of a different emotion. Anxiety. Fear, maybe. He recognized a woman on the run when he saw one. He didn't know yet whether she was running away from her ex-husband or something else, but it didn't really matter. He'd always been a sucker for a woman in need. His new neighbor might talk a good game, but the incident he'd witnessed on the porch just after getting back from his trip told a different story.

He'd gone to meet her solely to offer help. Since he'd finished renovations on his own house, weekends often found him bored and restless. A side project or two would go a long way toward fixing that. But then he'd touched her. She'd held his grip a little too long, and he would have laughed had the feel of her hand in his not warmed him all over. And he hadn't even asked her name.

Another quick look back at the cottage showed him he wasn't the only interested party. His new neighbor stood on her front porch, hammer in hand, head cocked to the side. When his gaze caught hers, she hurried inside. The slam of her front door echoed through the silence. She was interested, but she didn't want to be.

He could say the same thing about himself.

He turned back toward his house and started walking again. He'd been away for a little more than a week dealing with some problems at an out-of-state job, and it showed. The grass needed to be cut, and newspapers had piled up on the wraparound front porch. The gardens were all but begging to be tended. Probably had since before he left. He had his own problems to deal with, but for some reason, he couldn't stop thinking about his neighbor and the many things needed to be done around her small piece of land.

He stepped into his house and closed the door behind him. When Barry had told Joe he'd sold the cottage to a divorcee who'd moved to town, his friend had forgotten to mention the woman was beautiful. And young. Even wearing a ratty T-shirt and cut-offs, her brown hair hanging damp around her shoulders, she looked good. The confidence in her big brown eyes was a huge turn-on, and those full lips... He wouldn't even go there. He'd just met the woman.

He ambled into the kitchen, grabbed a beer from the fridge and opened it. Knocked back half the bottle before he set it on the counter with a thump.

"Not gonna happen, Joe," he muttered to himself. For whatever reason, his neighbor had decided to pretend she wasn't interested. He had to respect that. After his last disaster of a relationship—the one that, even now, refused to end—he wasn't looking for anyone, either. And that was why it killed him that he found himself not wanting to look away.

Curiosity getting the better of him, he picked up the phone and dialed Barry's number.

"Tyler Real Estate," Barry answered in the professional tone that, even now, made Joe grin. He remembered Barry from high school, when the two of them had gotten into so much trouble Barry's mother had threatened military school. Times had certainly changed.

"How's it going?"

"Hey, Joe. When did you get back into town?"

He glanced at the suitcases piled near the front door and shook his head. He'd get around to unpacking them. Eventually. When he ran out of things to wear and realized it was either unpack or do laundry. "A little while ago."

"Have you met your new neighbor yet?"

"Briefly. She's...interesting."

"Interesting," Barry repeated, his tone laced with humor. "Not how I'd put it. She's cute. Smart, too, to buy the cottage at the price Mrs. Krause was asking. Once she gets the place fixed up, it's going to be worth triple what she paid for it, easy."

"Yeah," Joe agreed half-heartedly, glancing through a window toward the cottage to see if he could get another glimpse of her. He couldn't. "She's...young. What's her name, anyway?"

"Amanda. She works at Maggie's with my nephew, Alex. She's twenty-eight, by the way, in case you were wondering."

Okay, so not young enough to be his daughter, but pretty damned close. "I didn't ask her age."

"You didn't have to. I know you." Barry laughed even harder this time. "Relax, Joe. She's well over eighteen. Hell, she's almost thirty, and you're not exactly an old man. There's nothing wrong with being interested."

"Even if I was interested, and I'm not admitting to anything here, she's made it clear she's not." And didn't that just kill him? The first woman to really intrigue him since the divorce, and she acted like she wanted nothing to do with him.

He took his beer onto the deck off the kitchen and settled into one of the Adirondack chairs overlooking the lake. The peacefulness of the scene usually calmed his nerves, but today it just made him more edgy. The trip had been stressful and he had yet to completely get rid of the headache that had been dogging him for the last few days. The messages Claudia had left on his machine while he'd been gone—all twenty of them—didn't help matters. Of course he'd gravitate toward the new neighbor. Amanda. Helping her would be a distraction from the chaos his life had become since his assistant had walked out on him three weeks ago with practically no notice.

"This one's right up your alley," Barry continued, as if reading Joe's mind. "She thinks she can do everything on her own, but look at her. She's a little piece of fluff who's going to fall apart the second she realizes there's no one around to help her. She needs you. She just doesn't know it yet."

Joe nodded in agreement. The woman needed someone. She'd never be able to do it all herself. He'd meant what he said. He was willing to help, as soon as she was willing to ask for it. She knew how to reach him. He wouldn't make the offer again, though. At least not for a while. No sense pushing her and having her resent him.

"I really need to take a break from women in need," he said instead of agreeing with Barry. After Claudia and the disaster that relationship had become, he'd promised himself to do just that, but one touch of Amanda's hand against his—a touch that had lasted, at most, ten seconds—and he was already willing to trash that promise in favor of spending more time with the woman.

"Despite what it might look like, I talked with her a lot during the week I took her out looking for houses. She's got a good head on her shoulders, even if she does have some sort of independence complex. I bet the two of you will become really great friends."

"You want me to make friends with her." Joe crossed his ankles on the deck railing and dropped his head back against the chair. He could just about hear the wheels turning in Barry's head. No matter what his friend might think, Joe didn't need to be set up, especially not with a woman he'd have to see on a daily basis, even once things went south—as all the relationships in his lifetime had eventually done.

Barry was silent for a long time before he spoke, and when he did, his voice took on a serious tone. "Listen, Joe. I know you. You say you're happy casually dating, but you're the kind of guy who needs to be settled down to be happy. You need to get on with your life. What Laura did was terrible. I won't deny that. But it doesn't mean your life is over. It's okay to get serious again. It's been five years."

Joe bristled at the mention of Laura's name. He was over his ex-wife, but he wasn't over what she'd done to him. Fifteen years of marriage, and she hadn't even had the guts to tell him the truth. Hadn't had the guts to leave him, either, until he'd found out about her affair.

"I've been dating."

"Is that what you call it?"

"I was dating Claudia for nearly six months, and you know that."

It wasn't a complete lie. His liaison with Claudia had begun as something casual, a mutual need to scratch an itch, as she'd first put it, but a few months into it she'd started talking about things getting more serious and he'd never corrected her opinion. She'd wanted to lean on him and he'd been more than willing to let her, but he hadn't loved her.

"What's her middle name?"

Joe swallowed. "I don't know."

"See? You know nothing about her. That's not dating. She's not even your type, and I think you know it. I understand being gun-shy after the divorce, but enough is enough. You deserve to be happy."

"I'm happy by myself."

"You just keep telling yourself that, and maybe someday you'll start to believe it. I've got an appointment. I have to get going before I'm late. Why don't we meet up later for drinks at Maggie's? Seven o'clock?"

Joe almost declined, but then changed his mind. What harm would it do to unwind after a long business trip? "Yeah. Okay. I'll see you later."

Odd that he found himself wondering if Amanda was working tonight. And wondering why he suddenly couldn't wait to see her again.

Chapter Two

Amanda stepped from the employee area into the dimly lit barroom, tying her apron around her waist. Pencil clenched between her teeth, she twisted her hair into a loose bun at the back of her head and secured it with an elastic. A quick scan of the room told her the place was jam-packed tonight. Good. The busier, the better. The shifts passed so much faster when she was constantly moving, and though she'd stumble out dog-tired after her shift and practically fall into bed the second she got home, the tips were a welcome addition to the moderate weekly paycheck.

The manager, Alex, stepped up behind her and tapped her on the shoulder. "The table in the back corner is all yours. Big tippers. They won't give you a hard time, either. At least not with me here."

She took the pencil out of her mouth and slipped it into the apron pocket next to the small pad of paper she used to record the orders. Most of the longtime wait staff could commit what the customers wanted to memory rather than writing it down, but it would be a good long while before Amanda could manage to keep all those orders straight. "Friends of yours?"

"My uncle and a buddy of his."

"Barry? The real-estate agent?"

Alex nodded, his dark hair falling across his forehead as he did. Amanda had to clench her hands into fists to keep from pushing the lock away from his eyes in a maternal gesture. Though the man was her boss, he was seven years her junior and looked even younger.

"Yep. And I'm sure he'll want to know how everything is with the new digs." He smiled, showing off the dimple in his right cheek. "How is it going, by the way? Is everything okay with the house?"

"It's great. Couldn't be better." She narrowed her eyes, squinting through the semi-darkness to see the two men sitting at the table Alex had indicated, and her breath caught in her throat. "The man your uncle is with is my neighbor."

"Joe's a great guy. He's dating Claudia Marshall, the niece of the woman who sold you the cottage."

Was everyone around here connected to everyone else? Despite the fact that Ludlow, New Hampshire was a college town, the locals seemed to outnumber the outsiders by a huge margin. When school started in the fall, the numbers would change, but for now, Amanda sometimes felt like she was standing outside a window, looking in. She supposed anyone who'd moved to her hometown of Lilton, Vermont, would feel the same way, but having lived there for her whole life, she'd sort of become part of the scenery.

Here she stood out. People noticed her. Asked her why she'd moved to town, and when she told them, asked what she planned to study at the college and if she planned to stick around town after she graduated. Having always been a private person, the questions seemed a little too close to an invasion of privacy, but if she didn't answer them, the gossip would start. Being fodder for all the wagging tongues in town didn't hold a hell of a lot of appeal.

"He's dating someone?" Funny, he hadn't mentioned a girlfriend when he was looking at Amanda like he wanted to eat her alive. When he'd asked her out for coffee. She shook her head. Men. They were all the same. Husbands two and three had had wandering eyes. Number three cheated on her with the same woman for nearly a year before he'd come clean and she'd filed the divorce papers. Her low-life radar must be defective, since she was always attracted to the wrong men. It seemed like her new neighbor was no exception.

Men were dogs. Even the ones who acted like they weren't. Joe's little omission clarified that for her better than anything else had in a good long while.

"You okay?" Alex asked, his brows knitting into a frown.

"Yeah, I'm fine." Now that she had her priorities straight. She wouldn't let them get skewed again, at least not for a man she didn't even know anything about.

Resolve firmly intact, she headed for the table, a smile plastered across her face when she really wanted to sneer at the jerk.

"Hey, guys," she said when she stopped at the table, focusing her attention on Barry and ignoring Joe. "What can I get for you tonight?"

"A couple of beers would be great." Barry mentioned a popular domestic variety.

"No problem. Be right back." Without even a glance at Joe, she spun on her heel and walked away from the table.

৪০৫৪

"What was that all about?" Barry asked once Amanda was out of earshot. Joe just shrugged.

"I guess she's ignoring me." Because she seemed insistent on pretending she wanted nothing to do with him.

Barry laughed. "What did you do to her?"

"What makes you think I did anything?"

"I've been married for long enough to understand when a woman's pissed. She's *pissed*, Joe. She ignored you on purpose."

"Impossible. I just met her this morning."

"And apparently you managed to strike out already." Barry laughed again, this time longer and louder. He clapped his hand down on the tabletop and shook his head. "It figures. You, Mr. Nice Guy, struck out with a woman you have to see every day."

"I didn't strike out." Not yet. He just had to figure out what it was she thought he did and try to fix it. If she was like all the other women who'd ever been in his life, figuring out the problem would take nothing short of a small miracle. "I went over to the cottage this morning and introduced myself. I was there for two minutes. I didn't do anything to offend her."

Except walking into the place without knocking first, but she'd left the door wide open. That was inviting trouble. If it scared her, good. Maybe next time she'd think twice about doing it.

Asking her out couldn't have offended her. At least he hoped not. She hadn't turned him down because she wasn't interested. And she hadn't given him any reason to give up.

"The woman's perfect for you," Barry continued, ignoring what Joe told him. "A lost cause. I couldn't think of a better neighbor for you."

"You think she's a lost cause?" Joe asked, frowning. He hadn't picked up that vibe from Amanda at all. She wasn't lost.

She was running away from something. Or someone. The fact only intrigued him more. Getting to know her, to learn what made her tick, had suddenly become top priority on his list. "She's not."

"Are you sure about that?"

"Yeah."

She needed help, though, and sooner or later he was going to find out what her problem was so he could try to find a way to fix it.

৪০৫৪

Amanda checked her watch and shifted on the edge of the curb just outside the bar parking lot. It had only been fifteen minutes since she'd called the auto club, and yet it felt like three hours.

Humidity still clung to the air despite the late hour—a little after midnight—and she swiped the back of her hand across her forehead. Of all the nights, and all the times, for her car to break down, it had to be now, when she was exhausted after a long night at work. Her feet hurt, her legs ached and she could barely keep her eyes open. The operator at the auto club told her a tow truck would be right out to help her, but even Amanda understood it would take a lot longer than a few minutes for someone to show up.

"Is everything okay?"

She glanced up to see Joe standing over her, hands in the pockets of his denim shorts. She sighed. A neighbor who wanted to "help". Yet another thing she had no use for—but relief flooded her anyway. "It's fine, thanks."

"Is there a specific reason why you're sitting on the sidewalk?"

"Other than the fact my car won't start? Nope."

"Want me to take a look at it?"

"Thanks, but I'm all set. The guy from the auto club will be here any minute now."

She expected Joe to walk away, but instead he propped his hip against the side of her car. "What's wrong with it?"

Other than it being well past its prime and ready to fall apart at the seams? She had no clue. "If I knew that, I wouldn't be sitting here right now."

"Does the engine turn over?"

"No. But it's really not your concern. They're going to tow it to the garage and the mechanic will take a look at it in the morning." And how she'd get to work until she had her vehicle back, she had no idea. She had enough to deal with tonight. She could worry about transportation to work later, when she'd had some sleep.

Joe crossed his arms over his chest. "How are you going to get home after that?"

She hadn't thought that far yet. *Thank you, Joe, for giving me yet another thing to worry about.* "I'll call a cab."

"Good luck getting one at this time of night."

She frowned. "What do you mean?"

"The only cab company in town has two cars, and the same number of employees. The cabs don't usually run past eleven."

She groaned. Just lovely.

"I'll stick around until the tow truck gets here. Then I'll give you a ride home."

She started to protest, but Joe held up his hand. "Don't. Unless you're planning on walking home or staying in town, you don't have many options. I don't mind giving you a ride. Your place is on the way to mine."

She had to admit he was telling the truth. Staying in town for the night held little appeal, and walking wasn't even an option. It would take her all night to get home. What would be the harm in taking a ride from her new neighbor? If he was friends with Barry and had Alex to vouch for him, he couldn't be that bad.

"You're not a serial killer or anything, are you?"

"Not hardly. You?"

What was it about him that put her at ease, yet made her all edgy at the same time? She might have seen herself becoming friends with him—if she wasn't so attracted to the man. She couldn't be friends with a man she wanted. Especially a man who was currently unavailable. Those were the ones she always ended up marrying. And divorcing.

"Where are you from?" Joe asked, his tone casual. He glanced up and down the street before returning his gaze to her.

"Vermont."

"What made you decide to move out here?" This question was less casual and a lot more probing than she was ready to deal with.

She shrugged, ready to give him the answer she gave anyone else in town who asked. The easy answer, and half of the truth. "I'm starting school at the college in the fall."

"Not many college students buy houses within a month after moving to town."

She was willing to wager not many college students were three-time divorcees, either, but she didn't point that out to him. "I like it here. Always have. My family used to vacation on the lake when I was growing up. I figured it would be a good place to settle down."

"Do you have family or friends here?"

"Isn't that kind of a personal question?"

He smiled. "I don't know. Is it?"

"Yes, it is." She swiped her hand across her forehead again and tucked a stray lock of hair behind her ear. "And no, I don't."

The lack of family in the area was the reason she'd chosen it. The place was familiar enough that she could make her way around town without getting lost, yet there was no one there to smother her with good intentions.

At least there hadn't been, until her sexy neighbor had pushed his way into her life.

"So you're all alone out here, no support system?"

"For someone who says he isn't a serial killer, you sure are starting to sound like one."

The smile widened. He raised his hands in the air, palms up, in a gesture of surrender. "Trust me. I'm safe. I'm just curious about you, that's all. Call it a fault, but I'm curious about people in general, especially women who seem to be running away from something."

"I'm not running away from anything." Except maybe herself. Leaving Lilton had been a necessity. A matter of survival. If she'd stayed, she would have continued on the same path of falling in love with and marrying the wrong men just to keep from being alone. Letting everyone around her take care of her instead of accepting responsibility for her own life. Back before she'd moved, she hadn't known it, but coming to Ludlow had shown her being alone wasn't the worst thing in the world. In fact, she'd quickly learned she liked it. *Loved* it, even.

"No?" He cocked his head to the side, brows knit together, and studied her for what felt like an eternity. Her face flamed under his scrutiny and she swallowed hard, dropping her gaze to the ground.

"What are you studying in school?" he finally asked.

Grateful for the change in subject, Amanda let out the breath she hadn't even realized she'd been holding. "Nursing."

"That's a tough program. Some long hours, from what I've heard."

"I don't mind. I've always been interested in the medical field. Since I was little, and I..." Her voice trailed off. She didn't even know the guy. What was she doing giving him her life story when he hadn't even asked?

"What happened when you were little?"

"I was in and out of the hospital a few times." *Just a slight exaggeration there.* "I got to know some of the nurses. I always thought it would be a fun job."

She held her breath, expecting him to question her further, but he seemed to realize it was time to back off. "What did you do before you moved here?"

"I was a secretary at a real-estate office." And things had started to get weird when Ronny, her ex-fiancé, had gotten serious with another woman. Amanda harbored no ill feelings for him despite the way he'd left her at the altar, but it had been a strain on the friendship they'd developed for her to see him with someone else. So they'd agreed it was time for her to move on. Registering for college had been a huge step—one she'd almost reconsidered at least twice a week since she'd signed up for the nursing program—but when she graduated with her RN in two years it would be one step closer to total independence.

"And you didn't like working as a secretary?"

"It was okay." Toward the end, there had been days she'd woken up dreading going to work, but she'd never told anyone that. It hadn't been anger, or frustration, that had caused the feelings. It had been...apathy. She just hadn't cared, and the lack of emotion had spurred her into making some pretty drastic changes in her life.

They sat in silence for a little while longer, only the sounds of crickets and the occasional bark of a dog echoing through the darkness, before Joe spoke again. "What made you decide to buy a house?"

"I talked to Barry about renting an apartment, and I did look at a few, but then he showed me the cottage and I decided to go for it."

Impulse control had always been an issue for her. Once she decided to do something she jumped in with both feet. Luckily, purchasing the cottage had been a smart decision.

"What about you?" she asked when he said nothing. "How long have you lived here?"

"All my life." His gaze swung toward her, a smile in his eyes. "I know just about every square foot of this town. Since you haven't been around long, maybe I could give you a tour sometime."

Her eyebrows shot up. It sounded like he was asking her out on a date...and she didn't date attached men. "You didn't mention earlier that you're dating someone."

"I'm not." He frowned, but soon understanding passed across his features and he shook his head. "You've been talking to Claudia, haven't you?"

"No. Someone else mentioned you were seeing her, though."

"I *was* dating her," he continued. "Past tense. We split up a little while before I went on my business trip."

Hope flared inside her and she quickly stomped it out. It really wasn't any of her business if he was dating the woman or not. Amanda was *so* not interested.

Okay, maybe a little bit interested, but she had no plans to act on that interest. She'd made a promise to herself—no more men in her life, no more dead-end relationships—and she intended to keep that promise.

"You change your mind about that coffee?" he asked, his tone as hopeful as the feelings inside her.

She didn't get a chance to answer. The tow truck pulled up and she jumped off the curb to meet the operator, glad for the distraction from what could have become a very uncomfortable situation.

ଅଓଷ

Amanda hadn't said more than two words since she'd ignored his question about coffee, and Joe was starting to get worried. Was Barry right? Had he done something to scare the woman off?

"Are you okay?" he asked her, sliding a sidelong glance to where she sat in the passenger seat of his truck, gaze focused on some point out the windshield. "You're really quiet."

"Yeah, I'm fine." She offered him a wavering smile, but didn't glance his way. "Just tired. It was a busy shift tonight."

Tired, and uncomfortable too, judging by the way she had a death grip on the door handle. Okay, so the woman didn't want to go out with him. Why couldn't he just take no for an answer?

Because she was lying. He'd seen it in her eyes tonight when he'd asked. She'd wanted to say yes, had been on the verge of doing so, but something was stopping her. And then the tow truck had shown up and she'd run toward the driver like she'd been stranded in the desert for months and he was carrying a gallon jug of water.

"When did you get divorced?" he asked, determined to get to the bottom of her reasons for turning him down despite the mutual attraction.

"Two years ago."

Okay, so maybe it wasn't a broken heart holding her back. Though he knew from experience broken hearts didn't have a time limit. It could be years before they healed completely.

"But that's not the reason I said no to the coffee," she continued, glancing at him with a wary expression on her face. "I'm not dating right now. I've had some bad relationships, and I need a break. Sorry, Joe."

"I can respect that." But he didn't have to like it. He turned his attention back to the road. So Barry was right. He'd struck out with Amanda. What was the big deal, anyway? It wasn't like she was the last available woman in town.

Ten minutes later, he pulled up in front of her house and got out of the car. Before he could get to the passenger-side door, Amanda had already opened it and was sliding off the seat onto the gravel.

He frowned. "I would have opened the door for you."

"I'm really not into the whole chivalry thing," she told him, heading up the pathway toward her front porch before he even had a chance to round the side of the truck. "But thanks. Thanks for the ride, too. I really appreciate it."

She lifted her hand to wave, stumbled and almost fell to the ground. She teetered a second before catching herself, but not before her purse flew out of her hand and landed a few feet away on the path, strewing its contents everywhere.

Laughing at the soft curse she muttered, Joe rushed over and started helping her pick the stuff up. Studiously avoiding the more feminine items, he scooped up her wallet and handed it to her. She took it and then he realized they were very close together. So close their lips just about touched.

For an endless second, neither of them moved. Neither said anything, and Joe's breath caught in his throat. Amanda blinked those big eyes, licked her lips, and he nearly came apart right there. The woman was too sexy for her own good, and she didn't even know what she was doing to him.

A dog barking somewhere in the distance broke the spell and Amanda stood, running her free hand down her thigh. She dug through the repacked purse and pulled out a set of keys. "Like I said, thanks for the ride. I do appreciate it."

He stood, trying to ignore the disappointment welling in his gut. "No problem. Anytime. If you need a ride to or from work until your car gets fixed, let me know."

"I have the next two days off, so I'm hoping I won't. But thanks. I'll keep that in mind." She left him standing there like an idiot, watching after her as she ran into the house and slammed the door behind her.

Chapter Three

Okay, so the situation could have been worse—but admittedly, not much. Amanda slumped down, her fingers burrowing in the dirt in the garden, and let out a shaky sigh. She'd heard from the mechanic at the garage earlier in the morning. Her car needed a new alternator. Not a huge problem as far as expenses went, but enough that her bank account would take a hit. Given that she'd used a good chunk of her savings to put a down payment on the house, she didn't relish the idea of using more to fix a car that was more than likely on its last legs. Not having a choice in the matter since she had to be able to get to and from work and, once fall came, to school, she'd told him to go ahead and fix it. She'd just have to tighten her budget a little more. In another month or so, she'd need to start buying school books.

And then there was Joe. Another worry she just didn't need. He'd almost kissed her last night.

She'd almost let him.

She'd spent the first twenty minutes after slamming her front door trying to convince herself she hadn't wanted him to, but in the end she'd had to admit the truth. She'd wanted it all right, and the fact settled in the pit of her stomach like a ball of lead.

She *so* didn't need the complications of having Joe as her neighbor. Even now, as she knelt outside trying to weed the overgrown mess that had at one time been called a garden, she couldn't stop throwing glances toward his yard.

He was splitting logs, of all things, in the middle of the summer. The log splitter he was using probably helped with the work, but given the sheen of sweat glistening on that rock-hard chest, the work wasn't easy. Manual labor suited him.

He looked up, saw her watching and waved a gloved hand. Yelled something she couldn't quite understand over the dull roar of the machine's motor. Her face flushing, she glanced back down at the garden and started ripping weeds out of the soil moist from an early morning rain shower. She swiped the back of her hand across her cheek to wipe off some of the sweat that seemed to be pouring off her face. It was hot today—and not entirely due to the weather. His barely clad presence created a good deal of heat. Man, he was something to look at. No woman in her right mind would be able to keep her eyes off a body like that.

He wasn't alone, either. There was a young guy with him who looked similar. A brother, maybe. It had to be—though from this distance he looked to be a good fifteen years or so younger than Joe. Tall, blond and handsome, the both of them. But Joe...he was filled out, and she'd been right about his body. She would have licked her lips, had they not been covered in nearly as much dirt as her hands.

With a frustrated sigh, she turned back to the garden—yet again—and started yanking weeds out of the ground with a vengeance. Stubborn weeds. Gave her such a hard time coming out. Why did she even bother, anyway?

Because she wanted to prove to everyone, and even to herself, that she could do it all on her own. When Barry had sold her the place, he'd given her the name of a landscaper in the area, but she got a lot of pleasure out of doing it herself. Yeah, the work was difficult and time-consuming, but at the end of the day she had something to be proud of. Her own place, slowly taking shape and starting to look like a home. Once the outside was painted, she had plans to put in some window boxes and fill them with flowers. Another month, maybe two at the outside, and it would be ready for her parents to come and visit. She could show them, once and for all, that the last thing she needed was a babysitter.

"If you won't take my help, at least use these."

Startled by the sound of his voice so close, Amanda jumped and swung her gaze over her shoulder. Joe stood behind her, his eyebrows raised as he studied the progress she'd made in the garden. In his outstretched hand he held a pair of worn leather work gloves. "They're a little big, I'm sure, but they'll do. They'll keep your hands from getting dirty."

Amanda rocked back on her heels, held her hands up in front of her face and shook her head, trying not to laugh. "I think it's a little too late for that."

"There are bugs in that dirt, you know. Lots of them."

As if a few worms and beetles would bother her. Did he think she was some prissy girl who was afraid of a little dirt? "Thanks, but I'm fine. Really."

"Well, take them anyway. You might need them for something else later."

"What about you? You need them now, with the work you're doing up the hill."

"I've got plenty. I work with my hands, remember? These are extra. Just take them, okay?" He dropped them onto the ground beside her, and she left them where they fell. If she needed gloves, she was perfectly capable of buying them herself.

But she didn't need to be rude, either. The man was just trying to be nice. It wasn't his fault she had an unwanted hormone surge every time he got within ten feet of her. "Thanks."

"It's nothing. Really." He lifted one bronzed shoulder in a shrug. "Did you hear from the garage?"

"Yeah." She told him what the mechanic had relayed to her. "He's got the part available and thinks it'll be ready tomorrow afternoon."

"I can take you to town to pick it up tomorrow when I get home from work."

"That would be great," she said through gritted teeth. She appreciated the fact that he wanted to help, but at the same time, a tiny twinge of resentment tightened her stomach. Once she had her car back, she'd feel better.

"Is there anything else you need?" Joe asked.

She squinted through the sun to get a better look at his face. As far as she could tell, the guy had no ulterior motives for offering her his help. He was just a nice guy wanting to do what he thought was the right thing. He'd accepted her rejection last night like a gentleman, and seemed to have no interest in holding it against her. Funny, but up until this point her life had seriously been lacking nice guys. Why couldn't she have met him years ago, before the first disaster of a marriage?

"No, thanks. I think I'm okay."

He shrugged and turned to walk away, but she called him back, struck with the sudden urge to return the favor and make a peace offering, albeit a small one. "Hey, Joe?"

He stopped, glancing at her over his shoulder. "Yeah?"

"I have a couple bottles of water in the fridge. You and your friend look like you could use a drink. Want me to get them for you?"

He started to shake his head, but then nodded and smiled. "That would be great if you don't mind."

"Don't mind at all." It was the least she could do, after he'd stayed with her last night while she waited for the tow truck, and then given her a ride home—and it would also show him that she had as much to offer him as he did for her. He wasn't the only one willing to lend a hand. She raced into the house and grabbed three bottles. Once back outside, she handed two to Joe. He thanked her and headed back up to his log-splitting machine, and only then did she sink onto the front steps, open her bottle and take a deep swig of the cool liquid.

Unfortunately, it did nothing to ease the burning in her gut. There was only one thing that would quench that, and it had nothing to do with water.

ଈଓ

A little while after Joe and Scott finished for the day, Joe walked down to the lake and dove into the water. Scott joined him for a quick dip to cool off before he headed back to town to meet up with his girlfriend.

"How's Monica?" Joe asked in as close as he could come to a conversational tone. There was still a hint of worry in his voice, no matter how much he fought to keep it out. Scott and Monica had been seeing each other for a few years now, and Joe was worried that it was starting to get really serious. Too serious for a twenty-year-old to be.

Scott rolled his eyes. "She's great. And Dad, don't start."

Elisa Adams

"I just don't want to see you tie yourself down to someone while you're so young."

"Like you did with Mom?"

Joe sighed. It always came down to that. Whenever he wanted to have a serious talk with his son about the woman in his life, Scott threw what had happened between him and Laura in his face. "That's not what I meant."

"Sure it is."

"Not like you think. Your mother and I were barely eighteen when you were born. Just out of high school. Definitely not ready for marriage, let alone children. It was a hard lesson to learn, and I hate to think you and your sister suffered because of it."

"We didn't, so don't worry. And I'm not thinking marriage with Monica yet. Geez. I haven't even hit twenty-one yet. Let me at least get through college first." He splashed water on his face and shook his head, spraying droplets into the air around him. "It looks like your new neighbor is watching again. Do you have something going on with her?"

"Are you trying to change the subject?"

"Is it working?" Scott asked, his tone hopeful.

Joe would allow him the distraction, since most of their talks lately surrounded his relationship and his age, and Joe didn't want to risk pushing him away. At twenty, Scott should be old enough to make his own decisions. It wasn't that Joe didn't trust him to do the right thing, he just knew what he'd been thinking at that age and hated to see Scott tie himself down when he still had so much life to live and so many things to accomplish.

"That depends. Is she really looking?"

144

Scott laughed again before stepping out of the water and grabbing a towel. He dried his shaggy hair and glanced up the yard to where Amanda knelt in front of the overgrown garden. "Yeah, she's really looking."

Joe swung his gaze toward where the cottage sat a few hundred feet away from the beach and saw she was, indeed, looking in their direction. It wasn't long before she turned her attention back to the garden she was pretending to weed. He smiled to himself.

That was the tenth time he'd caught her staring today alone, or at least it seemed like it. For a woman who sent out signals that she wasn't attracted, she was doing a terrible job of standing by that. Her silent perusal when she thought he wasn't aware made him want to get to know her even more. To find out what made her tick, and why he couldn't seem to get her out of his head.

"She's cute," Scott continued. "What's her name?"

"Her name is Amanda, and she's not interested in anything I have to offer."

"Did she tell you that?"

"Sure did." He shrugged. "She said she's not dating right now."

And then she'd almost let him kiss her. Not the actions of a woman who wasn't interested.

"Then why does she keep staring?"

That was what he was trying to figure out. "She needs help, but she won't admit it."

"Then she's the perfect woman for you. I know how you like to help people. Especially women."

Why did everyone act like it was a character flaw to be nice? He got out of the water, shook the excess drops from his hair and grabbed the second towel he'd brought down from the house. "Yeah, that's me. A regular Boy Scout."

"That's not what I mean, and you know it. I just think, if she's interested enough to spend her whole day staring at you when she thinks you're not looking, maybe it wouldn't be a bad idea to take her out. Or if you're not interested in dating, she does live right down the yard from you. You wouldn't even have to *take* her anywhere." Scott waggled his brows and broke down into a fit of laughter, collapsing into one of the lawn chairs on the beach.

"I'm not discussing this with you."

"Why not? Like I have no clue that you have sex? And believe me, if I wasn't seeing someone, I might consider asking your tenant out for a drink or two."

"You're not old enough to drink yet."

"Yeah, but she is."

"She's not much older than you. Twenty-eight."

"Good. Perfect for you. At least she looks a lot nicer than that witch Claudia Marshall."

"Scott..." Joe warned through gritted teeth.

"What? She is. Even Mom says so."

As if he really cared what Laura thought. He wouldn't say it in front of his children, but she'd screwed him over worse than any other woman ever had. Though he hadn't been *in* love with her like she'd needed, he'd loved her. Cared about her, and she'd cheated on him. Even after he'd found out the truth, it had been a few months before she stopped denying what she'd been doing. He'd washed his hands of the woman a long time ago, but the emotional wound had yet to heal. Mostly it pissed him off that he hadn't known what was going on until she was on her way out the door.

"Don't get like that," Scott continued. "I didn't bring Mom up to get you upset. I'm just saying that Kelly and I want to see you happy too. You deserve the happiness even more than Mom does."

Yet another discussion he didn't want to get into with his son. He loved his children, and even though he wasn't with their mother anymore, he wouldn't badmouth her. She hadn't badmouthed him to the kids, and he figured she at least deserved the same courtesy. He'd spent the past five years showing her a lot more courtesy than the woman deserved. Someone had to be the adult in the situation. Lord knew, it hadn't been her.

"We're not going there," Joe said.

Scott started to speak again, but Joe held up his hand. "I mean it. I do date. I *am* happy. You don't have to worry about me."

"Claudia doesn't count. She was nice, before, but lately she's been a bitch. You deserve someone better."

Joe nodded in silent agreement. Too bad the woman he wanted to spend more time with was so intent on avoiding him. She could say she wasn't interested, but another few days of this and he'd have to break down and ask her out again anyway. He couldn't stand her looking at him and not having at least said he'd taken the chance. Plus he was intrigued. Why was she so adamant about not taking his help? She had to be running away from something, even though she'd told him she wasn't. Everything about her told him she was lying.

He'd noticed it earlier, when she'd reluctantly thanked him for the gloves. For some reason, she was resistant to his help, but she was curious. And attracted. Hell, he'd seen that the morning before, when he'd stopped by to introduce himself. He had no plans for the following weekend. If he could convince her to join him for dinner—not a date, since she didn't want that—he could find out a little more about the woman behind the façade.

"I've got to head out," Scott said, breaking into Joe's thoughts. "Monica is waiting. You...just talk to Amanda, okay? You're acting like a couple of teenagers. I'll see you at the job site on Monday."

With a clap on his father's shoulder, Scott walked to his car, gave Amanda a quick wave before climbing inside, and took off down the street, leaving Joe to think about what he said.

And to curse himself for his indecision.

Chapter Four

Two weeks. It had been two weeks since Amanda had moved into the cottage, and though she loved it, living in isolation had taken some getting used to. Being so far away from town had been a problem at first, but now she'd gotten used to the twenty-minute drive and it wasn't so bad. Her proximity to Joe wasn't something that could be solved so easily. There were other properties nestled along the lake, but the area was fairly undeveloped so she had no other neighbors nearly as close as Joe. And his closeness bothered her in more ways than it should.

He'd asked her out again the day he'd taken her into town to pick up her car. Sure, he'd sworn it was just a friendly gesture, but she'd seen it for what it was. A veiled attempt at getting her to go out to dinner with him after she'd rejected his earlier offer for a cup of coffee. Given the way her heart sped up whenever she was within ten feet of him, turning him down hadn't been an easy thing to do.

She often found herself staring up at his house, seeing lights on at all hours of the night and wondering what he was doing. Wondering if he was alone, or if the woman he said he wasn't dating—the one Alex had told her about—was keeping him company. A sliver of unwarranted jealousy raced through her at the thought, though she had no claim to the man.

"Amanda?"

Amanda sighed. She'd forgotten she was even on the phone until her mother's voice had prompted a response.

"I swear, Mom, I really am okay," she said into the handset, holding the phone to her ear with one hand while trying to paint the trim around the windows with the other. "I told you before, I have a nice place. I have a job. I'd come out for the weekend, but I'm just too busy."

A good excuse if she'd ever heard one. She hadn't been home since she'd left, and in all honesty, had no plans to go back there until Thanksgiving. Maybe even Christmas. She loved her family, but they tended to go a little overboard sometimes. Her siblings would argue that she was the craziest of the bunch with her multiple marriages, but she did have a reason. It might not have been a good one, but it was there and she'd cling to it for as long as she could.

"We always have a family cookout in July," her mother continued. "You've never missed it before."

She'd never had a job to worry about before. Now things were different. She had real responsibilities.

"I'm sorry. I wish I could, but I can't get the time off from work." Satisfied that she'd done as well as she could with the trim given the shape it was in, she stepped back and leaned against the railing.

The railing she had just painted.

With a groan, she pulled away and glanced over her shoulder to survey the damage she'd done. Her white shorts now had a nice stripe of yellow across the middle of her rear, and the freshly painted railing didn't look so fresh anymore.

Of course this would happen now, when she was starting to make headway.

"Is everything okay?"

"Yeah, I just learned that I really shouldn't try to multitask when I've had about three hours of sleep."

"Making a new fashion statement?" Joe's voice came from the bottom of the stairs, making her jump. How did he always manage to sneak up on her? And why did he seem to get such a kick out of it?

"Who is that, Mandy?" her mother asked, and she could already hear the wheels turning in the older woman's head. "A new friend?"

Yeah, a friend. That was what he was. *Not.*

"My neighbor. Again." No one important. No one she should even be talking to since she couldn't seem to control her reactions whenever he was around. For the past week, she'd been doing all she could to stay away from him. If he kept asking, she might accept a date one of these days. "Very funny, Joe. Is there something you need?"

"Just to talk to you for a second."

"I've got to go, Mom. Sorry about the cookout. I'll make it up to you around the holidays." *Though I haven't decided yet which ones.* She hung up the phone, set it down on the top step and turned to Joe. "Yes, it's a fashion statement. It's all the rage in New York. Want me to do the same thing to your shorts?"

"Sure." He shrugged, trying for casual when she could see he was barely holding back a chuckle. "Why not. I could use a little excitement. It's been so quiet around here lately."

She blushed at the thought of having to touch his butt to paint the stripe across it, so instead she turned her back on him and started cleaning up her painting supplies. Now that he'd made the suggestion, her fingers itched to do just that.

"Seriously, Joe. What is it you need?"

"It looks like you're the one who needs help, not me."

"I don't need help. I can handle doing a little painting myself just fine."

"From the looks of things, you've done a lot more than just painting. The flowers you planted in front of the place look great."

"No big deal. It needed to be done, so I did it. That's one good thing about working the evening shift. I have plenty of time during the day to work around the house. Now if you don't mind, I really need to get inside to take a shower."

The second the words were out of her mouth she realized her mistake. Thinking about taking a shower, thinking about Joe in the shower with her...she leaned her head against the side of the house and groaned. For a woman who didn't want to get involved, she was really failing. Miserably.

"You look tired. Maybe you should take a break. Had dinner yet?" he asked, his tone laced with amusement.

Dinner? Had she eaten? No. She'd been so busy with the trim she'd forgotten everything else. She started to shake her head, but her stomach chose that moment to growl.

"I guess not. Can you take a little time off from home improvements? I brought in a pizza from town a few minutes ago, and it's too much food for me to eat all by myself."

The thought of a fresh, hot pizza brought a smile to her face. For the past few weeks, she'd lived mostly on canned soup, sandwiches and salads. The pizza place in town didn't deliver, and she'd never been able to justify a forty-minute drive round-trip just to get a meal. Her stomach growled again, not giving her the chance to turn him down. Instead she gave in. "Okay. Give me five minutes to change into some clean shorts."

And run a brush through her hair. And put on some makeup. And...she glanced his way and had to swallow hard. If he was looking at her like that without any primping, maybe she should skip the hair and makeup. Wouldn't want to give the guy any added encouragement.

Then again, maybe she would.

No. She couldn't think that way. If she did, she'd end up in another doomed relationship and that was the last place she wanted to be. Still, what could a couple slices of pizza hurt? Since she'd been keeping to herself, she had yet to make any real friends in town. She could be friends with the guy without the friendship turning into something else, right?

One look in his eyes and she realized it would be easier said than done.

ঃ০৩

A half hour later, seated on the deck overlooking Joe's backyard, Amanda was at peace with the man for the first time since he'd walked into her cottage warning her about the unwanted visitors she'd get if she left the door hanging open. Joe was...fun. He had a relaxed manner that had put her at ease almost immediately. They'd eaten and talked, and she'd learned there was a lot more to him than she'd first thought. The man was anything but simple, and it only made her want to get to know him better.

That couldn't be good for anyone.

Her loser radar had broken long ago, and she no longer trusted herself to be able to tell the difference between a good guy and a scum in sheep's clothing.

Joe wasn't like the other ones. He was real. He wasn't a bum, and would have no problem supporting a woman emotionally instead of leaving her on her own to take care of herself. If she was looking, he would be the perfect choice, which was why she really should stay away from him.

The more she learned, the more she wanted to learn, and it was a vicious cycle she had no hope of breaking out of anytime soon. He was what she needed, and everything she needed to stay away from. But how could she when he made her feel so comfortable? When he made a simple pizza and iced tea meal feel like something from a four-star restaurant?

Not to mention his house. The place was freakin' gorgeous. Open-concept with exposed beams, granite countertops in the roomy kitchen, and dark hardwood floors. It was like looking at her cottage, but all grown up.

When she'd stepped through the front door, she'd realized she was standing in the middle of her dream house, the one she'd wanted since she was a little girl. It looked so much like a place her family used to rent across the lake—and exactly like a place she'd always wanted to live. The sight had stunned her nearly speechless and still held her captivated even now.

"You're so quiet. Is everything okay?" he asked.

She looked up just in time to catch the concerned expression on his face. The evening breeze whipped a lock of his hair across his eyes, and she had the sudden urge to reach across the table and push it away with her fingers. "I'm fine. Just tired."

"Working too many hours on your feet down at Maggie's."

"It's not so bad. Besides, I really do need the job."

"Can you type?"

She narrowed her eyes. "Yeah. Why?"

"I have a job opening, if you're interested."

"Doing what?"

"My assistant left almost a month ago. I haven't found anyone to replace her on a full-time basis yet."

Okay, *so* not a good idea. Couldn't he see that? If she worked for him, she'd have to see him more, and she wanted to see him less. Seeing him more often would be dangerous to her mental health. The man wanted to *help* her, and help was the last thing she needed.

"Why did she leave?"

The look in his eyes darkened and he let out a harsh sigh. He glanced toward the lake, and it seemed like forever before he turned his attention back to her. "Another company offered her more money."

His tone made her regret asking. She leaned forward and placed her hand over his. "I'm really sorry. I didn't mean to upset you."

"You didn't." His expression softened marginally. "She made her choice, and I have to live with it. I just wish she'd given me time to find a replacement before she jumped ship."

Something told her there was more to the story, but she didn't push it. She didn't know him well enough to pry, and even though she was curious, she couldn't say she wanted to dig any deeper into his life. Everything she learned about the man made her want to get to know him better. Asking more about his assistant would edge them too far into personal territory.

The thought made her pull her hand back, and she folded it together with the other one in her lap. For a woman who didn't want to get involved with any man, ever, she was having a hard time remembering why she'd sworn them off in the first place.

Instead of sitting around dissecting her feelings and talking herself out of her original plan, Amanda jumped to her feet and started gathering plates and napkins off the table. "I should help you clean up. It looks like it might rain."

She rushed into the house, leaving Joe out on the deck staring up at setting sun.

&&CB

Joe shook his head, grabbed the pizza box and headed inside.

"Rain, my ass," he mumbled. For a little while there, she'd relaxed and allowed herself to just enjoy the company. It hadn't lasted long.

Something had spooked her, but he had yet to figure out what he'd said this time to scare her off. Could have been the job offer. Miss Independent wouldn't want her sense of freedom threatened by someone who actually cared what happened to her. She'd rather struggle, working for tips as a waitress in a dark little bar, than admit there might be something else for her out there. It would be two years before she finished nursing school, and he couldn't imagine her staying at Maggie's all that time. The shifts were late, and the crowds terrible and raucous sometimes. He could give her a better job, but he should have realized she wouldn't take what he offered.

She was working herself to the bone, and Joe hated to see anyone in that sort of situation. Especially someone like Amanda. Someone who made his gut clench and all his blood rush south with nothing more than a smile.

He stuffed the half-full pizza box into the fridge, walked over to the sink where she was washing dishes and switched the water off.

Her gaze flew to his. "What are you doing?"

"I was just going to ask you the same thing." He lifted a checkered dish towel off the stove handle and tossed it to her. "Dry your hands and have a seat. My house, my dishes. You need to relax."

"And you need to stop." She dried her hands on the towel and tossed it back.

"Stop what?"

"Stop trying to help so damned much. I'm a grown woman, Joe. I can take care of myself." Her eyes narrowed, flashing fire.

"Why do you have such an extreme need to prove that to me?"

"I'm not trying to prove it to *you*," she said through clenched teeth, a flush rising up her neck to stain her cheeks. "I'm trying to prove it to everyone else."

The last words were spoken so quietly he had to strain to hear them. She slumped against the counter, arms crossing over her chest. Her head dipped and her hair brushed the exposed skin just above the low neckline of her tank top. Suddenly, she didn't look so obstinate anymore. She looked...defeated, and he couldn't help the guilt that clogged his throat when he thought he was the one who'd caused her misery.

He walked over to her and reached a hesitant hand out, placing it on her shoulder after a few seconds of mental debate. Yeah, she'd probably shove him away and tell him where he could stuff his pity, but if a woman ever needed a friend, Amanda did right now.

Surprisingly, she didn't push him away. If anything, she leaned into the touch. He waited for the telltale sniffle of tears, and considered himself a lucky man when he didn't hear anything. He hated to see a woman cry, but he had a feeling

Amanda wouldn't appreciate any more comfort than she was allowing at the moment.

"It's not your fault," she told him, her gaze still glued to the floor. "I'm sorry I got upset. You didn't deserve that."

"Why do you reject me every time I try to help you?"

Now she looked at him, and the pain he saw in her eyes nearly undid him. He fought the strong urge to pull her into his arms, to stroke her hair and tell her everything would be all right.

"It's okay to lean on someone else sometimes," he continued when she stayed silent.

"Not for me it's not." She said the words on a sigh, straightened her shoulders and put some distance between them. Her expression hardened into the familiar stubborn one he'd seen so many times when he'd offered her help, and he knew it was a lost cause. Forget getting her to open up to him tonight.

He raised his eyebrows. "Want to explain that comment?"

"When I was little..." Her voice trailed off and she turned toward the slider, gazing outside. She pressed her hand to the doorframe and leaned closer to the glass. "Everyone took care of me then. They didn't stop babying me as I got older, even after...and I let them. It took me until last year to realize what a mistake that was."

"It's not a mistake to have friends."

"It wasn't about having friends. It was about everyone thinking I was fragile and couldn't do anything for myself."

With that, she spun around and paced back to where he stood, stopping right in front of him. She lifted her chin and glared at him. "I'm perfectly capable of taking care of myself, Joe."

"Believe me, I know you are."

"I'm an adult," she continued, her tone even more harsh than before.

"Another thing I've noticed." And man, had he noticed. Thoughts of her body, and what it would feel like under his, had kept him awake for many a night since she'd moved into the little cottage down the hill. The only reason he hadn't done anything about his attraction was because she'd been sending out so many signals telling him not to. If he caught one inkling of interest that wasn't countered with a stay-away sign, he might not be able to stop himself from kissing her.

In the end, she took the choice away from him when she stood on tiptoes, wrapped her hand around the back of his neck and drew him down for a kiss.

Joe held himself still for as long as he could, allowing her the chance to be in control and explore. If he pulled her closer, she'd probably run away, and at the moment that was the last thing he wanted. His whole body tightened, his muscles bunching and his hands clenching into fists at his sides.

He wouldn't take advantage of her vulnerability. Rushing things, in this case, would only lead to trouble. Talking with her over dinner, spending time with her in a relaxed state, had made him realize he wanted to get to know her, to take her out on the town, to give her everything she wanted and show her she didn't need to run away from anything anymore.

And damn, he was in some pretty deep shit.

He broke the kiss, extricated himself from her hold and pressed his lips to her forehead.

"What's wrong?" she asked, sounding as shaky as he felt.

"Nothing. I just don't want to rush you."

"You weren't. We could have stopped at any time."

He let out a laugh tinged with bitterness. *Easier said than done, Amanda.* "Stopping would have been really difficult for me a few minutes down the road. I think we should call it a night now, before we get carried away. I wouldn't want you to have any regrets in the morning."

He backed up, and she brushed her hands down her sides. She gave him an uncertain smile. "If you're really not attracted to me, it's okay to tell me that."

He crossed his arms over his chest and stared at her. How could she think that? She had to have felt his cock pressed against her. Had to know how being that close to her affected him. "You know that's not the problem, so don't pretend like it is."

"Then what is it?"

"You seem so intent on pushing me away. I'm not going to give you another reason. I'm still trying to figure out why you kissed me in the first place."

She opened her mouth to speak, but he silenced her with a hand in the air. "If we rush, you'll use it as an excuse to ignore me tomorrow. I'm not going to let that happen."

"I don't feel rushed."

The woman was something else. One minute telling him she didn't want to be involved, the next telling him she hadn't wanted him to stop kissing her. And as for the kiss...there had been a hint of desperation in her touch that bothered him. She'd kissed him for the wrong reasons. It wouldn't happen again until her reasons were the right ones.

He leaned in close and pressed a fast kiss to her lips. "Trust me, Amanda. I'm a sure thing. You just have to say the word. But I'm not going to take any less than everything. I don't want you going into this on impulse and regretting it the next morning."

She opened her mouth, closed it again and shook her head. A few seconds later, she started for the door.

"Thanks for dinner," she said over her shoulder as she stepped outside. "And...just thanks. I mean it. I really appreciate it."

It took a few seconds after the door closed behind her for Joe to be able to breathe again.

Chapter Five

Amanda's shopping bag hit the floor with a thump as soon as she walked through the front door. A swift kick sent the door slamming shut and she made her way to the fridge for something cold to drink. First thing she did when she got her next paycheck would be to buy the air conditioner she'd promised herself when she'd first moved in. Other expenses had taken precedence so far, but now she had no more excuses. Summer had hit full blast, bringing in a heat wave that didn't want to quit. New England summers tended to come quickly and be brutally humid, and this one was no exception.

Her hair hung in damp waves around her face and her T-shirt had been plastered to her back since she'd left town. The air conditioning in her car had gone on the fritz a few days before the vehicle had broken down all together, and for the first time in her life, she had to deal with those kinds of problems on her own. The thought didn't thrill her, though she kept trying to convince herself that it should. She was on her own. Just how she'd told herself she wanted to be.

So why didn't it hold so much appeal as it had earlier, when she'd first moved away from home?

Because she was tired. Tired and...frustrated. In the three days since Joe had all but kicked her out of his house after that scorching kiss, she'd done nothing but think about kissing him again. She'd lost too much sleep over it, and every other aspect of her life was beginning to suffer. According to Joe, all she had to do was say the word.

Well, what the hell was she waiting for?

She grabbed a glass and filled it with cool water from the tap before lifting the glass to her lips and draining most of it in a few sips. She was waiting for some kind of sign that starting something with Joe was the right thing to do. She'd been going over and over the situation in her head, and so far she'd been able to come up with a con to match every pro. He'd been right. She wasn't sure what she wanted. The one thing she was sure of was that she didn't want to get involved, at least not in another failure of a long-term relationship, so he'd saved her a lot of trouble by sending her away before things had gone further—and gotten even more confusing.

She looked out the window toward the lake and smiled. Between work and fixing up the cottage, she hadn't spent nearly enough time in the water. She could always go for a swim a little later. That was guaranteed to cool her off, and she needed cooling today. In more ways than one.

Her gaze snagged on something moving out in the lake and she blinked. Joe. He was walking toward the shore, running a hand through his hair. His swim trunks rode low enough on his hips that she got a good glimpse of the muscles there. She swallowed hard. The man was pure perfection, and in his own words, a sure thing. She pressed a hand to her belly. Too bad she'd sworn off all men less than three months ago. His offer was proving too difficult to resist. He'd probably known, when he'd made the offer, what it would do to her. It had made her think—almost nonstop since she'd walked out of his house. Maybe, just maybe, she wasn't as sure of what she wanted as she'd first thought.

Joe suddenly stopped walking and smiled, and she realized she'd been caught. He lifted one hand and beckoned to her, but she sank down along the counter until her butt hit the floor.

"Oh, my God." Of course, now he'd catch her watching. Why not? Was there anything else she could do to embarrass herself in front of the man? She still had yet to figure out why he'd want someone as neurotic and unstable as she must seem.

Yeah, the man probably thought she was a total headcase, and she wouldn't blame him if he did. She refused his help even though she needed it, she all but ignored him whenever he came in to the restaurant, and then she had to do something as stupid as kissing him. Definitely not the behavior of a sane woman. The fact that he was interested at all should have told her something about his own mental state, because up to this point she'd been sending him so many mixed signals his head should have been spinning.

A knock sounded on the door, but she ignored it. He'd want to gloat, and seeing him laugh at her didn't hold a lot of appeal right about now. After a few minutes of sitting silent on the floor, the knock didn't come again and she let out a relieved breath.

She should have realized it couldn't be that easy. The knob turned, the door swung open, and he stepped inside, a cocky grin on his face.

She slumped down even lower and propped her elbows on her bent knees. "By all means, Joe, come on in."

He shook his head, spraying droplets of water across the walls and floor. "You're the one who left the door unlocked."

"This is the middle of nowhere. Besides, I don't have anything of value. If someone wants my stuff that badly, have at it."

"Is the couch not comfortable enough for you?"

"It's fine. Why?"

"Well, you're sitting on the floor. Or is that because you didn't want me to see you watching me?"

Her face flamed and she swallowed down the lump of embarrassment forming in her throat. The guy was bold. A little too bold, sometimes, for his own good. And if she wanted to save herself any further embarrassment, all she could do was lie to his face. "I wasn't watching you."

"Oh, really?"

"Really. I was watching the lake. It's hot and I was thinking of going for a swim."

"So what's stopping you?"

"Oh, I don't know. There's something big and bulky blocking my front door, dripping water all over my house."

"Sorry." He took a step back, going out onto the porch. His deep laughter reached her from across the room and she narrowed her eyes at him. Exactly what, in this impossible situation, did he find funny? From where she was sitting, it seemed like one big, honking embarrassment after another.

"Come for a swim with me, Amanda," he continued, his stance casual and his expression anything but. "It'll be fun. We haven't had a chance to talk in a few days."

Not since he'd told her he was a sure thing. She shivered at the memory of those words. She was a sure thing, too, which was why she'd decided to stay away from him. If she got any closer, she might forget about swearing off men and take him up on the hard-to-resist offer she wished he'd never made.

Swimming with him was *so* not a good idea for way too many reasons, half of which eluded her now, with him standing so close and wearing so little. She shook her head. "I can't right now. I just walked in from shopping a few minutes ago. I have clothes and a few groceries to put away, not to mention a shower to take, before I have to be to work tonight."

His eyebrows rose and the expression on his face told her he didn't buy into her excuses for a second. "What time do you have to work?"

"Seven."

"It's only a little past two. You have plenty of time. You really look like you could use a swim to cool off." Mischief glinted in his eyes and his smile widened, full of challenge.

She should say no, but for some reason, she couldn't make herself turn him down. She really did need to find a way to cool off. Besides, she could swim with the guy without wanting to kiss him again, couldn't she? Maybe not, but she could pretend with the best of them. "Okay. For a little while. Give me a few minutes to put my swimsuit on."

She pushed herself up off the floor and walked toward the bedroom, needing to put a bit of distance between them while she still could. If she was going to spend the afternoon with the guy, she'd need to psych herself up for it first. If there was ever a time for a mental pep talk, it was now. "Go ahead and go back down to the water. I'll meet you there after I change."

∞

Joe headed back down to the lake, all but whistling as he walked. A stupid smile tickled his lips and refused to go away. After that kiss the other night, she might want to shut him out, but no way in hell would he let that happen. Yeah, she could say she wasn't interested until she was blue in the face, but her body language told a different story. So did the fact that he'd caught her watching—and it wasn't the first time, either. Since she'd moved in, there had been many times he'd glanced her way to see her standing in the window.

The smile spread over his face and he looked back over his shoulder. No one in the window this time, and he wondered if she'd really join him in the water like she'd said. At this point, he figured it was a toss-up. Once she was done wrestling with herself over what she really wanted, she would either come and find him or lock her door and not answer it if he knocked. His stomach sank a little when he realized the woman was probably leaning toward the latter, but maybe then she'd actually surprise him. She'd surprised the hell out of him the other night when she'd kissed him. If he wasn't mistaken, he had a feeling she'd surprised herself nearly as much.

Before he swung his gaze back toward the lake, he caught a glimpse of the shutters that still needed to be hung straight. He'd been so busy trying to catch up since his assistant, Catherine, had left him in complete chaos at the office he'd neglected to go over and help Amanda with the larger repair jobs like he'd originally planned to do. There were a few borderline safety issues that needed immediate repair, like the loose railing Amanda had made an effort to fix and the lock on the back door that kept sticking, but the place needed a paint job besides. She'd been planning to do it—the paint cans stacked neatly just inside the front door told him that—but it was too big of a job for one person to tackle alone.

She might tell him she didn't want the help, but would it be so terrible to surprise her by getting a few things done for her so she had less to worry about? It would be a few weeks before he could get one of his crews on it, but the place was small and he had all weekend to get as much done as he could. Scott and his buddies would help out, too, if Joe tossed a couple of bills their way and bought lunch. The least he could do for his stubborn neighbor was to help her make the place look as presentable on the outside as it was on the inside.

To tell the truth, thinking about helping her was a welcome distraction from the mess his life had been thrown into with Catherine's defection to the dark side. He'd tried a few replacements, but none of them had worked out. Catherine had known her stuff, when everyone else seemed lacking. And seeing Amanda around, pretending she wasn't interested, lightened his perpetually dark mood and gave him the interruption he needed to forget about his work for a little while. A swim together would be good for both of them. Plus he'd get to see that cute body of hers in a swimsuit.

Now that was a bonus he'd been looking forward to for a long time.

છ૦૦૩

"What's the worst that can happen?" Amanda asked herself as she made her way down to the lake, towel clutched to her waist as if it could help her ward off the nerves fluttering in her stomach.

If it wasn't for the humidity in the air, it would be a beautiful day. The sun beat down from a nearly cloudless sky. The bright green grass was soft under her bare feet. The beauty of this place struck her every time she stepped outside the cottage, but today even the serenity of the nature around her couldn't calm her frazzled nerves.

She took a deep breath of pine- and sunshine-scented air and tried to force her stomach to stop doing flip-flops. It was just a swim in the lake with a man she might be able to consider a friend. Could it really be so terrible?

What a painfully easy question to answer. There was a lot that could happen, and none of it was good. She was way too attracted to Joe, and prancing around in front of him in her swimsuit could possibly be one of the worst ideas she'd ever had.

She shivered at the thought of him being attracted to her only because he'd come to the conclusion she was helpless. He might not see it, but she didn't need his help any more than she needed her family's help. She wasn't a damned charity case. She *could* handle things on her own. She *would* prove to everyone that she didn't need a man in her life to be okay. Her family, and her new neighbor, might not believe it, but she did and that was all that mattered.

She hoped.

"Hey. You look lost in thought."

She blinked and noticed Joe standing waist-deep in the water. She forced a smile and dropped her towel on the small beach nestled in the grass, tucking a strand of her hair behind her ear with her free hand. She'd been an idiot to accept his invitation.

"Amanda? You okay?"

She had to give herself a mental kick to recover her voice. Of course she was okay. Watching the water bead on his chest made her warm all over, but that didn't make her unstable.

Bad, bad line of thought, Amanda. Keep it friendly, but nothing more. Keep your distance, for God's sake. The man is pure trouble wrapped in a tanned, blond, blue-eyed package.

Keep her distance? Ha! As if that could ever happen. Every cell in her body was screaming for her to get closer to the guy, even as her mind warned that getting close to him would be a very bad idea.

"I'm fine. Just a little tired is all." Tired, stressed, in complete and total lust with the wrong man yet again, for the fifth time in her adult life...at this point, was there really any difference between the first and the last? From where she was standing, it didn't look like it. She was destined to make the same stupid mistakes, over and over again, and was hard-pressed to think of a way to break the horrible cycle.

Joe put his hands on his hips. Confusion lit his eyes, but when he spoke his tone was soft, almost coaxing. "Are you coming in the water or are you going to stand on the beach all day?"

Her best option would be to grab her towel, march back up to the cottage and slam and lock the door. Instead she just stood there, staring at him like some lovesick teenager, trying to get her frozen feet to move across the sand. When she couldn't get them to budge, she let out a sigh.

"Is it cold?"

One of his big shoulders lifted in a casual shrug. His smile widened. "Nah. It's been a hot summer. The water is great. Like bath water. Come on in. I have no idea what you're waiting for."

With that said, he turned and dove under the water.

Amanda edged toward the shoreline, dipping her toes into the water lapping gently against the sand. He hadn't lied to her. It wasn't cold. Actually, it was pretty refreshing. She waded further in until she was about waist-deep, and then looked around for Joe.

"Can you swim?" he asked from behind her. Right behind her. She jumped and spun around, arms crossed over her chest. Joe standing so close sent a ripple through her nerves and she swallowed hard. His lips were less than a foot from hers, and all she could think about was how he'd tasted when she'd kissed him. Pizza and iced tea and warm, sexy man. Her lips went tingly at the thought of kissing him again.

"Yes, I can swim. I need a little time to get used to the water first, though. I can't just jump right in."

A deep laugh rumbled in his chest. "There's nothing to get used to. The water is nearly as warm as the air. Plus..." He grabbed a sweat-dampened strand of her hair and twisted it between his thumb and forefinger before tucking it behind her ear. "You're all sweaty. The water will feel nice."

She bristled at the words, though she knew he hadn't meant them as an insult. "It's hot today. Has been all week. It's hot in the cottage."

"Do you need an air conditioner?"

Of course she did, but she wasn't going to get it from him. The more she leaned on him, the easier it would get, and pretty soon she'd be leaning on him for everything. Not an appealing prospect. "I'll be getting one when I get my next paycheck."

"Let me know when you're ready. I'll go to the hardware store with you to help you with the heavy lifting. The box will fit better in the back of my truck than it would in your car. I can install it in the window for you, too."

She barely restrained the urge to roll her eyes. A small unit would be light enough for her to be able to handle putting it in the window herself. No need to bother her neighbor with something so trivial.

"You don't have to do that. I can take care of it myself."

She ducked down into the water and started to swim away, but Joe grabbed her ankle and pulled her back toward him. Her face flaming, she fought against his hold, but he wouldn't let her go. His hands on her waist, he lifted her up. Once he had her settled on her feet again, he shook his head. "Why are you so resistant to my help?"

"It's my place. I can deal with it myself."

"Neighbors help each other around here. It comes with the territory, so you'd better damned well get used to it."

The concern in his gaze made a lump of anger rise in her throat. When was he going to get it? She couldn't prove to everyone—and to herself—that she could do it alone if he kept hounding her at every turn. Men were not in her revised grand plan, and Joe would just have to *get used* to *that*.

She raked her hair out of her eyes and shook her head. She didn't need this right now, on top of everything else in her life. Why did fate choose this moment, when she was finally on her way to getting what she really wanted in life, to throw such a huge wrench in her plans? A week ago it had been easy to pass off her interest in Joe as a simple case of lust, but now that she'd gotten to know him better, she understood it was more than that. She could see herself caring for him not far down the road, if things kept going the way they were. Kissing him had been a huge mistake.

"Listen, Joe. I think you're a great guy, but I'm just not interested in being taken care of right now. I moved away from my family for this reason. I really need to be on my own to do it all myself. Okay?"

He cocked his head to the side, hands on his hips, and studied her with an intensity that made her want to melt into the water and float away. There was something about that deep gaze that made her weak-kneed every time he turned it her way. And he knew it, too. She could see it in the slight curve of his lips.

Though he hadn't moved an inch, suddenly he was too close and she needed to get away. She took a step back, her hands in front of her in a gesture of surrender. "I don't think

I'm really in the mood for a swim, after all. I'm going to head back up to the house and take a cool bath instead."

"What's the matter? Scared?"

The challenge in his voice made her smile, despite the severity of her situation. She dropped her hands, swirling them in the lukewarm water. It felt so good and she really didn't want to leave, but if she stayed she might make yet another stupid, impulsive mistake in a long line of them. "No. I'm not scared. I'm just not...interested, either. Not in anything serious, at least. I thought you should know that so we could avoid any confusion in the future. One badly timed kiss doesn't mean I want to pursue things further with you."

"You're lying." He hadn't even hesitated. As soon as she'd finished speaking, the words had been out of his mouth, accompanied by his raised-eyebrow, amused gaze.

Her discomfort level skyrocketed. Could he really read her that well? Maybe she was more transparent than she thought.

"What makes you say that?"

"I just know you are. What I don't get is why you don't admit to it."

Because it's none of your business, anyway. How could she explain her mess of a life to him? It would take a lot more time than she had available, and even then, she doubted she'd be able to make him understand. "There's nothing to admit to."

"How about why you've been watching me, for starters. You could explain that to me."

As if he deserved an explanation. He'd been watching her, too, so he was just as guilty. "It was just this one time, and—"

"No, it was more than that."

She licked her lips. She was so busted. "You noticed?"

"Sweetheart, a woman like you stares at a man, he's bound to notice." He took a step closer to her, crowding her even though they were out in the open with nothing around them but water. He didn't touch her, but something in his gaze held her as effectively as if he had. "So we've established that you're interested. What I don't get is why you won't admit to it."

"I'm not looking for a man." The explanation ran from her mouth before she could stop it. Another side effect of the impulse-control issues she hadn't quite been able to get rid of.

Joe said nothing for a long time. When she thought he'd finally given up, he did something that caught her by surprise. He grabbed her hand, pulling her toward him until her toes bumped his under the water. "You know, I'm not really looking for anyone, either. And the last thing I want to do is push you into something you aren't ready for. But there's something about you that grabbed a hold of me on day one and hasn't been willing to let go since. I just think it deserves some exploration."

He said the words, possibly the sweetest and most contradictory she'd heard in a long time, just before he leaned down and kissed her.

The kiss was short—barely more than a brush of his firm lips against hers—but it was electric. Even as he backed away, she pressed her palms to his damp, cool chest and sucked in a breath. Wow. The man could kiss, she'd give him that. Part of her wanted to drag him closer for more.

"What'd you do that for?"

"It seemed like the right thing to do at the time." He let out a small laugh and shook his head, his hand coming to rest over hers and giving it a gentle squeeze. "Was I wrong?"

As much as she wanted to tell him he wasn't, that she wanted the contact as much as he did, she nodded. The man didn't need another unnecessary boost to his ego, and she apparently needed another reminder that she'd promised herself to keep her distance. "Yeah, I think you were."

She said the words, yet again, but the more she said them, the less she believed them. Now she was finally starting to see the truth. Whether she wanted it or not, getting involved with Joe was inevitable.

Joe seemed to sense her change of heart. Instead of backing off, he dropped his hand, cupped her face between his palms and leaned in again. This kiss was anything but brief, but just as electric as the first. His tongue probed at her lips and he slipped it in between to brush with hers. At the same time, he pressed his hand against her lower back and drew her up against him, catching her hand between their bodies. Her nipples pebbled at the feel of his hard chest so close to her breasts, and something inside her cried out for more.

Even knowing she could be sinking into trouble, she had no interest in moving away. She melted into it, melted against him, and dove into the kiss with everything she had. By the time he broke the kiss and stepped back, they were both breathless.

She brought her fingers to her lips and a little sigh escaped before she could stop it.

"Wow." Joe's whispered word echoed somewhere deep inside her. *Wow* was a very apt description of a kiss that was even more of a mistake than she'd first anticipated. So much for not getting involved. With that one contact she'd jumped in with both feet.

Still shaking off the remnants of the earth-moving kiss, Amanda turned away and started swirling her hands in circles just below the water's surface. "You're right, the water is really warm today."

Without another word, she swam out deeper, ignoring him when he tried to call her back.

She'd reached the float a few hundred feet from shore and settled onto the sun-warmed deck boards before he came after her. He joined her on the wooden float and flopped down next to her, arms tucked behind his head. "What are you running away from?"

You. Me. My life. Everything. Is that enough of an explanation? "Why does it matter?"

He turned his head to the side and regarded her through slitted lids for a few seconds before he answered. "Because you look like someone who needs to talk."

"How can you possibly make that assumption?"

One corner of his mouth rose in a sexy half-smile. "It's in your eyes. I see it every time you look at me. It's like you want to trust me, want to spend time with me, but you're holding yourself back. There's more to it than that, I think, but so far you aren't talking. What gives?"

Yeah, she was definitely transparent. "Am I that obvious?"

"I'd love to say no if it would put you at ease, but you are."

Just wonderful. Why was he interested in a woman who, at twenty-eight, had yet to manage to get her act together? Everything she'd learned about Joe so far showed her he was a great guy. He didn't deserve to get involved with a woman who changed husbands nearly as often as she changed the oil in her car. She started to turn away, but his next words stopped her.

"No, don't get upset. I'm just making an observation. It doesn't mean anything." He winked. "So...want to tell me what it is you're running away from?"

About as much as she wanted to have toothpicks shoved under her fingernails. She didn't make a habit of opening up to people, at least not on the level he wanted. The thought of confiding something so personal to a man she'd known for a matter of weeks made her stomach clench. "Not so much."

"Is it a man?"

She narrowed her eyes. It was like he could reach into her mind and pull out her most personal, private thoughts. "Maybe."

"You can trust me, you know. I'm a pretty good listener. For a guy, at least."

Once again, he'd known just the right thing to say to put her at ease. At a minimum, she owed the guy an explanation for her erratic behavior. If she told him about her marriages, his interest would most likely dissipate pretty fast, anyway. Most men didn't seem to want a woman who'd managed to go through three husbands before she even hit thirty.

"Okay, you're right. I'm running away from a man. No, not so much *a* man, but men in general. All of them. All of *you*."

He laughed as if he didn't believe her. "What do you have against men as a gender?"

"Nothing. That's the problem—and the reason I've been married three times. Almost four."

To her surprise, he didn't even blink. "Barry mentioned the three divorces."

"Don't forget the near miss shortly after my third divorce," she answered in a small voice, trying to calm the butterflies in her stomach. Generally, this was the time most nice guys would turn tail and run. She could practically tick off the seconds on her fingers. *One...two...three...*

"Three," Joe mumbled, shifting his back on the float. He closed his eyes, draped an arm over them and let out a long whistle. "When Barry first told me you'd been divorced three times, I thought he was joking."

"Unfortunately not." She didn't know whether to be put out by his comment or to find it amusing, so she just sat there and waited to see what he'd say next.

"What happened? If you've had so many marriages and a near-miss to boot, why are you still single?"

To explain that to him would be to give him the story of her life, which was something she wasn't ready to talk about. Instead she swiped a hand through her wet hair, forced a grin and lied through her teeth. "I like men. I like dating, too, I think. I mistook lust for love a few too many times, and then I got bored and got rid of them. No big deal."

His arm dropped from his eyes and his lids snapped open. Their gazes locked and Amanda had to take a breath. His expression warned that he didn't believe her, but he didn't dispute what she'd told him. A good thing, too, because she knew how it would go if she had to tell him the truth. It had happened too many times already. *See, Joe, I was diagnosed with leukemia when I was five...*and it would all go downhill from there. She'd *had* leukemia. Didn't have it now. Had been totally free and clear since she was fourteen, so long and drawn-out explanations would only dredge up years of pain she'd rather not relive. It would only make him uncomfortable. She brightened her smile and turned, resting on her stomach on the hot wood.

It seemed like forever that they lay there in silence before she couldn't stand it anymore. It was his turn to be uncomfortable now. *Let's see how you like being in the hot seat for a little while, Joe dear.* "What about you?"

"What about me?"

"How come you're single?"

"Haven't found the right woman yet." His tone told her there was more to the story, and since he'd prodded her, she figured it was her turn to pry a little into his life. An eye for an eye, so to speak.

"How old are you, Joe?"

"Thirty-eight."

"And you've never been married?"

"I didn't say that." He glanced at her out of the corner of his eye, a wary expression on his face. "I just said I'm single now because I haven't found the right woman. Never said I've been single all my life."

No, he hadn't, but the explanation was too simple, too basic. Too much like the glossy one she'd given him. "So...have you been married before?"

"Yep."

Now he decided to clam up? *Not happening, buddy.* A small part of her reveled in his discomfort. The man probably didn't have the tables turned on him very often. "Come on, Joe. Talk to me. You look like a man who needs to do a little talking."

"Throw my words back in my face, why don't you?"

She would have thought he was upset, if he hadn't started to laugh.

"You know," he continued, "I like you. You don't beat around the bush and play games like a lot of the women around here. You might not be willing to open up about your own life, but at least you don't jerk a man around and manipulate him to get what you want. You can ask anything you want to, if it makes you feel better about spending time with me. I'm an open book."

Her breath caught in her throat. He really had no idea what he was offering her. She didn't want him to be an open book. It would be so much easier to keep her distance if he stayed closed off. It had been easier to think of him as laid-back, without a care in the world, but his expression held a hint of bitterness and pain that gave her pause. He'd been through something that still bothered him. Maybe he'd understand her better than she'd first hoped.

She thought about it for a minute, considering leaving him alone on the float, but in the end decided she was too curious to walk away. The man was a study in contradictions, and it fascinated her. "When did you get divorced?"

"Five years ago."

"What happened?"

"My former business partner did."

She didn't know what to say to that, so for a while she said nothing. They lapsed into silence for a few minutes before Joe volunteered more information. "It's not as big of a deal as it sounds," he told her, though he gave her no reason to believe he was telling her the truth. "Laura and I...we didn't get married for the right reasons."

"No?"

"No, and we didn't stay together for them, either."

She understood that, though she'd never been through it herself. Her marriages had all ended well before the three-year mark. "Did you have kids together?"

"Yeah, two. Kelly and Scott. Great kids. Surprisingly well-adjusted, considering the mess our marriage was in."

That had to be tough on all of them. One thing she was glad for, with all her marriages, was that the subject of children had never come up. She couldn't imagine being a single mother right now, and none of her exes had really been the paternal type, anyway. "Do they live with their mother?"

"Yeah, pretty much." He didn't elaborate. "What about you? Have any kids?"

"No."

"Three marriages and no children?"

"I wouldn't make a very good mother."

"The jury's still out on that, but I bet you would. You're stubborn. That's a huge part of being a parent."

The last thing she needed was Joe, single father, thinking she would be a good parent. She wanted to tell him she wasn't looking to mother someone else's kids, even part-time, but she kept the bitter response to herself. It wouldn't be fair to him to make such a leap. He hadn't even mentioned the kids until she'd asked about them.

It wasn't that she didn't like kids. She did. In truth, she was afraid to have children. Though it was an irrational fear, she never wanted them to have to go through what she'd gone through as a child. It was too scary to even contemplate, and though she'd been reassured by many doctors that the odds of it happening were slim to none, it didn't change her decision or lighten the burden on her heart.

"Stubbornness aside, I just don't think motherhood is for me. It's too complicated to explain, but trust me, I have my reasons." Once her brothers and sister started having children, she'd be a wonderful aunt to them all, and as far as she was concerned, it would have to be enough. "Now tell me more about you. Barry said you're in real-estate development?"

"Not exactly. I'm a contractor by trade, and I do home restorations. I started out buying properties to fix up and rent, and I still do some of that, but my main business comes from people hiring me to restore old, run-down homes. That's what I love to do. To take a building that's falling apart and turn it into something spectacular."

"That sounds like a great job," she said, and meant it. That kind of job was fascinating for her, a woman with no discernable skills. "Do you like what you do?"

He let out a laugh that sounded almost...bitter. "I used to, but lately I've been questioning my decision."

"Why is that?"

"I told you before that my assistant walked out on me. It turns out I'm not as organized as I thought."

Poor guy. Here he thought she was the one in need, but it turned out things might actually be the other way around. "Are you still looking for help?"

"Actually, I think I'm all set in that department. I think I've finally managed to convince my daughter to come in and lend a hand when she's not in school."

He had to be kidding. He was going to use his child to do office work? "They have child labor laws for a reason, you know."

He stared at her for a long time before he spoke. "Kelly's nineteen."

"Oh. *Wow.*" Nineteen. Joe's daughter was nineteen, and Amanda was suddenly feeling very young. How had she not realized the man had an adult child?

He stood, shrugged and dove into the water. A few seconds later, he surfaced, very close to where she still lay. He crossed his arms over one another, resting them on the float. The expression on his face was uncertain, and his voice hesitant when he spoke. "I told you we got married for the wrong reasons. Scott is actually the reason. He'll be twenty-one in a few months. Does it bother you?"

She had to fight back a smile of admiration. His reason might not have been the right one, but it was a noble reason.

When so many men would run away and deny responsibility, Joe had stuck it out. Knowing that only made her like him more.

"No, it doesn't bother me. Why should it? I told you I'm not looking for any kind of commitment."

"Me either. But like I said, I like you. I'm kind of hoping you like me, too."

She smiled. Yeah, she liked him. Way more than she should. Instead of answering, she reached down and splashed lake water in his face.

He splashed her back, and as the tension started to seep out of the afternoon, she knew everything was going to work out fine. He could be a good friend to her, and lord knew she needed them around here.

Now she just had to keep reminding herself that she didn't want him as anything more than a friend, despite her body's insistence that she did.

Chapter Six

Amanda dragged herself into the cottage at a little after midnight. The late shift at work was always a difficult one, but the Friday night tips more than made up for the fatigue and the sore feet. Now she'd be able to afford the air conditioner she'd seen down at the hardware store.

The one that looked remarkably like the one humming away in the window next to the couch.

She froze midway between the door and the kitchen table, her breath stuck in her throat. What did that man do now?

Hadn't she told him she'd take care of it herself? Heat crept up her face and her blood pressure kicked up a notch or two. How many times did she have to tell him she didn't need his help before he actually believed her? And what in the world made him think it was okay to *break into* her house and install the damned thing?

A glance up toward his house told her he was still awake. She could see him sitting on the couch in his brightly lit living room, watching something on TV. Too ticked to think it was probably way too late to pay him a visit, she grabbed her keys and headed out the door, intent on berating him for his presumptuous attitude. Who did he think he was, anyway? He'd gone too far this time. Stepped over a line she'd clearly asked him not to cross. She might have tried to ignore his attempts at *helping* her in the past, but this was too big to ignore.

She stomped up the steps, pounded on the door and shifted from foot to foot while she waited for him to answer. After what seemed like an eternity, the door swung open to reveal an amused-looking Joe. "What can I do for you, kiddo?"

"First of all, don't call me that. I'm only ten years younger than you are. And second, there is something very important I need to talk to you about, and before you ask, no, it couldn't have waited until a decent hour." She pushed past him into the house.

Joe crossed his arms over a chest she'd just noticed was completely bare. "Didn't you want to yell at me for something?"

It took her mind a few seconds to process what he'd said. "Oh, yeah. The air conditioner."

"It makes it nice and cool in that little cottage, doesn't it? Amazing what a little window unit can do for a couple of small rooms."

Did he not even realize he'd overstepped his bounds in a major way? Of course he didn't. Men could be so dense sometimes. "Yes, I guess it does make it cool and all, but that's not why I'm here."

"Oh, no?"

She narrowed her eyes. He wasn't going to make this easy on her. Why must she spell it all out for him? "No. You can't just go buying me things and breaking into my house to put them in. That's rude and disrespectful, not to mention breaking the law."

He let out a harsh breath and shook his head. It seemed like an eternity before he responded, and when he did, his tone was contrite. "I'm sorry if I've upset you. I didn't break in, though. I used to take care of the place for the old owner whenever she had renters in and it needed work. I have a key— and before you ask, I'd completely forgotten I had it, or I would have given it back to you on day one."

A little of her anger dissipated, though she refused to let it show. "Thank you for being honest. I'd like the key, if you don't mind."

Joe nodded. "No problem. But I have to say, it might not be a bad idea to let me hang on to it, in case you get locked out sometime."

"Now that you've said that, it's probably going to happen tomorrow." She rolled her eyes, not ready to finish being angry with him. Who did he think he was, anyway? "I at least need to know how much I owe you for the unit."

"You're not buying it from me."

"Yes, I am. My place, my responsibility."

"It's not new. I used to use that one in my bedroom window before I had the central air installed. Consider it a loaner if you want, but you're not giving me a cent for the thing."

End of subject. He didn't say the words, but the way he walked into the kitchen and opened the fridge, his back to her, spoke volumes. He wasn't going to let her give him the money. Not without a fight.

She followed him into the kitchen space, on the opposite side of the curved stairway from the living room, stuffing her keys into the pocket of her black jeans. He was just trying to be nice. She understood that. But he shouldn't have been in her house without permission. "Well, thanks. But you still shouldn't have done it without at least asking me first."

"I'm sorry for going into your place without checking with you. I really am. I don't know why I did it. I really was just trying to help. I won't ever do it again." Joe turned to her, a bottle of beer in each hand. "Why do I think that thanking me was probably one of the hardest things you've ever had to say?"

He set the bottles on the counter, popped the tops and offered one to her. Beer wouldn't normally be her beverage of choice, but at the moment, with her emotions in turmoil and her legs ready to give out on her, she'd take what she could get. She accepted the bottle and drank down a sip of the liquid, letting it cool her parched throat. "Thanks. For the drink, I mean. And...thanks for the air conditioner. I really do appreciate it."

The last was said through gritted teeth. Joe raised a brow, one corner of his lip lifting in a half-smile.

"I do. I appreciate it," she repeated before swallowing against the sudden lump in her throat. "I'm...I'm glad you don't mind if I use it."

"Then why do you have such a hard time admitting you do?" He took a swig of his own beer before setting the bottle on the counter with a thump. "And better yet, why do you have such a hard time accepting help in the first place?"

She thought for a minute about blowing off his question, yet again, but in the end common sense prevailed. It made no sense not to tell him the truth. It wasn't like she had deep, dark secrets she was trying to hide. He'd bared his soul to her earlier in the day when he'd told her about his divorce and his children. The least she could do was return the favor.

"When I was younger, I was...sick. Everyone took care of me for so long, treated me like I was fragile. My mom and dad never outgrew it. I resented it, but at the same time, I got used to it. It carried over into my adult life, until recently when I decided I needed to move away. From everything."

"Sick? What do you mean? Like the flu or something?"

If only it had been so simple, she might not have turned out the way she did. Unable to be alone for more than a few months. Unable to feel complete without someone in her life to take care of her. "No. I had leukemia."

"Oh, wow. I'm sorry." He nodded, not saying anything for a long time. It took her about that long to realize tears were welling in her eyes. The look on his face turned to pity and he walked over to her, pulling her into a hug. "I am, you know. I'm really sorry you went through all that."

She tugged out of his grasp and put as much distance between them as she could, not stopping until she stood on the other side of the large kitchen table. It wasn't much of a shield, but the distance helped her get her thoughts in order. Pity had no place in her life anymore. She'd left that all behind for good when she'd moved away from her hometown and too many prying eyes who knew way too much about her. "I don't need your pity."

"Good, because I'm not offering it."

Her gaze snapped to his and the sincerity she found there struck her like a blow to the stomach. "You're not?"

"You said you were sick. Are you okay now?"

"Yeah. I have been for a long time. I was diagnosed when I was five, but by the time I was fourteen and I'd been in remission for five years they told me it was gone. I've been fine since then. At least physically." Mentally was another story. For way too long she'd let everyone treat her like fine china. Not anymore.

"That's really awful. It must have been so hard to live like that for so many years."

"Yeah, but it's in the past. I'm alive, and thankful, but at least now you understand why I don't want to be babied. I lived like that for so long, and I've had enough." And it was well past time to change the subject to take the focus off her. Enough talking about uncomfortable subjects for one night. Since the dinner they'd shared, she'd been curious about his house, but hadn't yet had the chance to ask. "This place is amazing. Did you do all the work yourself?"

"Yeah. It's been my pet project. I have a couple of crews to work on the other jobs, and I hire out whatever work they can't do because of either time or distance, but this one...I've done this one all myself, with my son's help." Pride shone in his eyes when he spoke. "The whole property was pretty run-down when I got it, so I got it dirt cheap, same way you got the cottage. At first I hadn't intended to live here. It was supposed to be another rental property to add a little extra income, but by the time I was finished, I knew it was where I belonged."

She understood that better than she could ever tell him. It was how she'd felt the first time she'd stepped into the run-down little cottage down the hill. There were no words to explain it. When she was there, she was...home.

ഇരു

Joe almost laughed at the way Amanda clung to the beer bottle for dear life. Like she expected him to attack her or something. He gave her hand a gentle squeeze, relishing in the feel of her skin against his for a second before he let go. "Relax, Amanda. It's just a house. It doesn't bite."

But he would. All she had to do was give him the signal.

And if she knew what he was thinking right then, she'd be out the door before he had a chance to take another breath. He hadn't been lying when he'd told her he liked her. He did. A lot. But he wouldn't push her into something she wasn't ready for, and he hadn't lied about that, either. The next move was hers to make.

No, he wouldn't push her, but he would have no problem reminding her every chance he got that he was interested...and that she was, too. Hell, she'd let him kiss her at the lake. Twice. Had even responded. That had to count for something.

It figured now he'd find a woman he could really get into, when the rest of his life was in such chaos. With Kelly filling in for Catherine things would soon be getting much more organized at the office, but there were still so many details that had to be hammered out for so many jobs. Business was booming, and though it was a good thing, it didn't leave him much time for a social life. He didn't have time to pursue anything real with the woman, but just the sight of her had him wanting to clear his schedule whenever she asked.

Chaos or not, he'd come to a decision down at the lake earlier that day, right about the time she'd tried to swim away from him. He wanted her in his life, to see where things went. To see if she could be the woman he was looking for to spend the rest of his life with. She was interested too, even though he had a feeling it would be a long time before she stopped denying it. At the moment, the heated look in her eyes when she glanced his way was enough for him.

"I know *the house* doesn't bite," she scoffed, dragging him out of his thoughts. "It's not the house I'm worried about."

"Me?" He blinked a few times, giving her his best wide-eyed innocent look. "You're worried that *I'll* bite?"

Though she fought it, the beginnings of a smile played at the corners of her mouth. Finally she broke down and giggled, and the sound washed over him like a caress. "Among other things."

"Well, then, let's get one thing straight before this goes any further," he said, walking toward the living room. "I wouldn't bite you. Not unless you wanted me to."

With that, he started down the hallway toward his home office, hoping she'd follow rather than turn tail and run.

Luckily, she did follow, and he hid a smile. She didn't want to want him, but she did. She chose to ignore his baiting comment, which really didn't surprise him. Instead of continuing along that line of conversation, he put his efforts into showing her his house. His pride and joy. Months had been put into fixing the place up, and by the look in her eyes, he could tell it showed.

"This is incredible." Amanda walked ahead of him up the stairs a few minutes later, caressing the railing with her palm. "You've got a talent for this."

"I wish I could say I did it all myself, but Catherine—my assistant—helped with some of the colors and a lot of the décor. She used to joke that I was colorblind, since I couldn't match to save my life. So she used to pick out color schemes on the places my company renovated, while I did the design work."

"She's talented."

A fact his biggest competitor hadn't failed to notice. Joe tightened his fist on the railing. "Which would be why the competition did everything he could to get a hold of her."

She spun so fast she almost knocked them both down the stairs. He had to put his hands on her waist to keep her from slamming into him. "I'm sorry. I didn't mean to dredge up sore feelings."

With her this close, just about pressed right up against him, he couldn't remember what sore feelings she thought she'd brought up. Man, he had it bad for this woman. *Real bad.*

Without thinking, he wrapped his hand around the back of her neck and pulled her lips down to his.

He'd expected her to back away, to reject him and recite a laundry list of the reasons why he needed to learn to keep his hands to himself, but she surprised him yet again. Her arms came around his shoulders and she moaned softly against his mouth. Taking that as a cue to continue, Joe tilted his head to deepen the angle of the kiss. The woman tasted incredible. His fingers itched to yank her flush up against him so she could feel how strongly she affected him, even with a simple kiss.

He put a hand on the railing and tightened again, trying to remind himself that she wouldn't appreciate a bold move like that. If and when she was ready for more than a kiss here and there, it would be up to her to let him know.

After a few minutes, Amanda stiffened against him and stepped back. She blinked, her face flushed, and seemed to force a smile. "You mentioned something about custom fixtures in the upstairs bathroom?"

He returned the smile, though he imagined it was probably a little strained at the edges. Nope, she wasn't ready to let him know yet. There was something between them, no matter how much the woman tried to deny it.

Bathroom fixtures. She wanted to see the bathroom. The thought should have been enough to cool his raging hormones, but all he could think about was Amanda naked in the jetted tub or soaping up under the rainfall showerhead. "Yeah, I did mention that, didn't I?"

She nodded and, without another word, turned to walk up the stairs ahead of him.

So much for things finally starting to go his way.

Chapter Seven

Amanda stood at the foot of Joe's bed, acutely aware of how uncomfortable being in his bedroom was making her. She shifted from foot to foot and avoided eye contact with the man standing in the doorway at all costs. The second she'd stepped into the room, dominated by a huge, four-poster bed, her voice had failed her and she'd been struck with the sudden urge to run away. Far away. Like into the next county.

Joe affected her in a way she wasn't entirely at ease with—and he knew it, too. And she'd followed him into his bedroom for his little "tour" without even thinking about what a bad idea that would be.

You wouldn't be here if you didn't want to be, a little voice in her head chided. She shrugged off the voice, even knowing it was right. Never in her life had she felt so conflicted over a man. Usually she jumped in with both feet and thought about the consequences later.

"You wanted to see the master bath, remember?" He gestured with his chin toward an open door across the room. "Custom fixtures and all?"

Had she wanted to see the bathroom? Right now, the bedroom was proving to be pretty interesting. The kiss on the stairs had been a taste of something forbidden. Something she'd promised herself she wouldn't indulge in but now, standing in the center of the room where the man slept, indulging in a little time between the sheets with him was at the forefront of her mind—right along with the warning that she needed to steer clear of any more contact with the man or risk getting involved in something she wasn't ready for.

"Amanda?" Joe asked when she remained silent.

"Huh?"

His laugh broke through her haze of fantasies and sent a frisson of heat down her spine. Even his laugh was low and rumbly and more sexy than it had a right to be. Of course she'd meet the man of her dreams now that she'd sworn off men completely.

Oh, no. Joe Baker was certainly not the man of her dreams. He couldn't be. The man of her fantasies, maybe, but in real life fantasies didn't amount to much. She'd learned that with her first three failed marriages and the ill-fated engagement. All of those men had been buff, handsome and charming. And the first three had been losers underneath. Ronny, fiancé number four, hadn't been a loser—but he'd told her he didn't love her when he left her at the altar.

Was it any wonder she was so screwed up when it came to relationships?

Joe walked into the room, stopping only a few feet from her. "The bathroom is that way."

He propped his hip against the footboard of the bed, hands in the pockets of his shorts, and just stared until she caught up. Bathroom. Across the room. *Come on, feet. Move.*

Finally she was able to break out of her daze and she walked across the floor, stepping into the marble-tiled bathroom. It was gorgeous, like the rest of the house, but the only thing holding her attention at the moment was the jetted corner tub. Every muscle in her work-tired body started screaming for a bath in the luxurious tub. "Wow. You really went all out with this place, huh?"

He stepped in behind her and she caught his expression in the huge mirror on the far wall right in front of the marble double sinks. "You like it?"

"Like it?" She ran a hand through her hair in a nervous gesture. Having him so close made her heart skip a whole bunch of beats. Being tired only added to the problem since it seemed to put a stopper on her willpower. "It's incredible."

"Yeah," he agreed, his voice even lower and deeper than usual. The tone made her glance up, and she realized he wasn't looking around the bathroom. His gaze was locked on her.

"I look terrible." She spun and backed away, further into the bathroom since he blocked her only exit. "I just got out of work a little while ago. I'm...wilted. I look like crap. And it's nearly one in the morning."

She snagged her lower lip with her teeth and bit down to remind herself that she really did need to walk away from him. Getting involved with him would be a bad idea, and at this point in her life, anything that happened between them would have to be casual. To expect more would be to set herself up for hurt she didn't have room in her heart for.

"When you bite your lip like that, it makes me think things I have no business thinking. Since you're not interested in me and all."

"Sorry." No point in denying what he said, because it would only lead to more trouble. He had to know she was lying, but she couldn't seem to stop herself. To admit interest would be to let herself go down a road she'd long since learned not to travel.

They stood suspended for a few beats before Joe walked out of the room back into the bedroom. "So...ah...that's the bathroom I was telling you about."

"You were right. I love it. I have to say, this whole house is incredible." Amanda stepped into the bedroom after Joe, her heart beating out of control. Disappointment clouded his gaze and it struck a chord somewhere within her. Why was she fighting this so hard? He wanted her. She wanted him. It was as simple as that, and suddenly it didn't seem like such a horrible idea after all. They could be just a friends with benefits sort of situation...she hoped.

"Joe?"

He didn't say anything, but he raised his eyebrows in question.

"I never said I wasn't interested."

"Actually, you said it quite a few times."

So maybe she had, but she hadn't really meant it. She'd been hooked the second she'd seen him, and it had taken her until this minute to admit defeat. She walked over to him and placed her hand in the center of his chest. "I meant I didn't want a commitment. Not that I didn't want you. I think what you said a while back is right. We should at least explore this...thing between us."

His hand came over hers and he pulled it away from his body. "You're sending me very mixed signals, Amanda. First you tell me you have no interest, and then this? What am I supposed to think?"

That it's been over a year since I've even been this close to a man? That sex, for the past year at least, hasn't even been a part of my vocabulary? No, this wasn't about sex. At least not entirely. She wanted him, true, but she actually *liked* the man. "Here's what you should think. That I'm interested in you, but I won't do anything about that interest unless things can be kept casual. I can't jump into anything serious right now. I need time to adjust, to think things through."

That was a novel idea, coming from a woman who'd made weddings a hobby. She was a first-class serial monogamist who'd never had a *casual* fling in her life, but hell, there was a first time for everything.

"Casual." He seemed to think about it for a minute before he nodded. The intensity in his gaze heated to the boiling point. "I can do casual."

He stepped closer, stopping when he was only inches from her. Her heart rate kicked into overdrive and she swallowed against her suddenly dry throat. Casual. Yeah, she could do that too. At least she hoped she could, because she'd set in motion something she didn't want to stop.

"Can you really?" she asked, trying to keep her emotions out of her voice. "Because if you can't promise me not to make this more than just...you know, I should go home now."

"Don't go," he said, walking closer. He cupped her cheek in his hand and stroked his thumb along her cheekbone, inciting a riot along her nerve endings. She leaned into the touch and closed her eyes.

"Unless you're not sure..." he continued.

Her eyes snapped open. She held up her hand to stop the question he'd already asked once. "I told you I'm sure. What more do you need, a written invitation?"

His eyes darkened to a stormy, midnight blue just before he reached for her and pulled her into his arms, sealing his lips over hers in a scorching kiss. A kiss that was different from the others they'd shared. There was nothing gentle about this one. It was a branding kiss, meant to shake her to her toes and all points in between.

Mission accomplished. Her legs were already protesting her weight and her fingers shook where she had them pressed into his shoulders. The heat of his body against her warmed her like the ninety-degree weather had been unable to do. She dug her fingers into his shoulders, trying to get even closer to the man who'd been starring in all her dreams since she'd first seen him.

He broke the kiss and trailed his lips down her neck until he reached her collarbone. He unbuttoned the first button of her three-button T-shirt and suckled the line of skin there. She arched into him, but he pulled back and stared down at her through lust-clouded eyes. He moved away, hands once again in the pockets of his shorts.

"You planning on finishing that beer?"

She swallowed hard. If it wasn't for his heated expression, she might be a little confused by his behavior. Was it just her, or had Joe suddenly gotten a case of cold feet?

"Um, actually, the beer was the last thing I was thinking about."

He smiled, but it looked strained at the edges.

"You okay, Joe?"

"Yeah. Fine." The look in his eyes warned he was anything but. "Don't you want to slow this down a little?"

"No. Not tonight."

There you go again, Mandy. Jumping in with both feet.

The fact should have bothered her, but it didn't. It was well past time she started going after what she wanted. She'd wanted Joe from the first time he'd walked into her house. There was nothing wrong with a casual fling. Men and women did it all the time, so why couldn't she do it, too? Chivalry had a time and a place, and this wasn't it. Gallantry wasn't what she was looking for tonight. Just the thought of going to bed with Joe made her feel powerful. Liberated.

She toed off her shoes and walked over to him, trying to fight a smile. He was going down tonight, whether he knew it or not. Tonight, she would finally be the one to take control.

She ran her hands up his chest. The impressive, full-on erection pressing against his zipper told her his feet were the only part of his body that were cold.

Joe let out a harsh breath. "What are you doing?"

Wanting to feel something, to do something crazy that, for once in my life, isn't going to lead to a wasted trip down the aisle. She put her hands on his hips and pulled him closer. She might not need his help, but there were other things she needed from him and she was sick of feigning indifference when what she felt was anything but. The guy turned her on. He wanted her, and was willing to keep it casual. What more could a girl want?

She could want the guy without expecting forever with him—though she hadn't realized it until just now.

"If you want me to stop, say it now, Joe."

"I'd be crazy to tell you to stop, but I don't want you doing something you aren't sure about."

She let out a frustrated sigh. He really was a gentleman.

The very *last* thing she wanted right now was a gentleman. "Do you have protection?"

He nodded.

"Then what is there to question?" She stripped off her top and let it fall to the floor, and by the time she'd unzipped her pants Joe pulled her toward him and helped her out of the rest of her clothes. Very quickly. It wasn't more than a minute before she stood naked in front of him.

She might have felt self-conscious if it hadn't been for the heat in his gaze as he looked her over slowly, taking in every inch of her bared flesh.

"Damn," was all he said, and it made her giggle. "What's so funny?" he asked without looking up.

"Nothing. It's just...it's been a while. And I know I'm not perfect." No matter what she did, those five extra pounds refused to leave her hips, and her breasts weren't much more than a handful. Joe didn't seem to mind. He skimmed his hands up her sides until he cupped them in his palms.

"Yeah, you are." He leaned in and sucked one of her nipples into the moist warmth of his mouth, and in that second she knew she was a goner. She'd never last more than a few minutes if he kept this up. Even now, her knees buckled at the feel of his tongue swirling over the hardened peak. Tiny jolts of pleasure shot from her nipples down to her sex, making her wriggle against him.

A moan caught in her throat when he moved across her skin to the other nipple, leaving a trail of damp heat in his wake. She tangled her hands in his hair in case he thought about stepping away. She wasn't ready for him to stop yet. Maybe she never would be. Why had she waited so long to let this happen?

Because she'd been an idiot. Had thought seeing someone would challenge her independence, but now she realized it wouldn't. It would reinforce it. She could see Joe on occasion, and not have to worry about falling for the guy since neither of them was looking for anything serious. It was a perfect situation for both of them.

Seeming to sense her need, he teased and tormented her body for what felt like an eternity before he laid her back on the bed and made quick work of his shorts. No underwear beneath them. How friggin' sexy was that? Generally, she liked a man in nice clothing, but Joe looked so much better in next to nothing. He even made a pair of faded denim shorts look good.

But naked...now that was a sight to behold. His erection was long and thick, and more than ready. Her sex grew even damper and she swallowed hard.

When she thought he'd fit himself between her legs, he surprised her by kneeling, lifting her hips and stroking his tongue along her folds. She almost came out of her skin. Her hands fisted in the navy blue comforter, her knees bending as she arched her hips off the bed, closer to his amazing mouth. He chuckled against her skin and a wave of intense sensation rocked her to her core. Her eyes rolled back in her head and she moaned.

"You like that?" Joe's laughter mixed with lust in his husky voice.

"Um, *yeah.*"

"Good." He stroked his tongue over her most sensitive part and her body exploded in an orgasm that nearly took her breath away. It had been so long, and he was *so* good. She slammed her eyes shut and let the sensations wash over her, enjoying the feel of his lips and tongue against her.

When she finally came back to herself, Joe knelt over her, the heat in his expression mirroring what she felt inside.

"You okay?" he asked, a little breathless. His shoulders were tense, like he was fighting to stay in control. Damn it, why couldn't the man give in to what he really wanted?

"I'm...wow. You're something else."

She leaned up on one elbow and reached out, circling his erection in her palm. She stroked and he shuddered, his eyes closing.

"Why don't you lie down and let me return the favor?" She gave his hard length a gentle squeeze.

"No."

The vehemence in his denial made her chuckle. He really was fighting so hard for his control. Too bad she was going to take it away from him in another few seconds.

"You said you have condoms. Where are they?"

He opened his eyes and looked down at her, letting out a long, loud breath. "Bathroom. Top drawer on the left."

"Good. Lay down. I'll be right back." She scooted off the bed and hurried into the bathroom, her body still shaky from the killer orgasm. It was a delicious sensation, one she planned to savor for a long time to come.

With a smile on her face, she opened the drawer and pulled out a box of condoms. New. Unopened. For some reason, the sight made her smile even wider. Maybe he'd been without someone for as long as she had.

And maybe not. A guy like Joe could get any woman he wanted, and probably did, but she wouldn't even allow herself to think about *that* at a time like this. She tore into the box, pulled out a condom and walked back into the bedroom, ripping open the wrapper as she went.

Joe lay on his back on the mattress, and Amanda's mouth watered at the sight. She'd never get sick of looking at him. There was something about a man whose muscles were honed from an honest day's work rather than hours a day on a weight bench that got to her. He reached his hand out, palm up, but instead of handing him the protection, she chose to roll it on for him. Slowly. In a way that had him gasping for breath by the time she was done.

She'd never been one to take control of sex, and now she realized what she'd been missing. It was a rush like nothing she'd ever experienced. To know he wanted her, but waited for her to make the next move, filled her with an incredible sense of power. She straddled his legs and lowered herself down the length of his erection.

His gaze more intense than she'd ever seen it, he grasped her hips, guiding her into a frenzied rhythm as he slammed his hips up to meet her. Finally, *finally* she'd managed to make him let go of his control, and the idea of it thrilled her. Her hands dropped to the mattress next to his shoulders, the breath sawing in and out of her lungs. He stretched her, filled her to bursting. Even now, the tingling of another orgasm started low in her belly and she moaned. Sex had been good before, but never like this. Never had she felt the sense of freedom and abandon she did with Joe.

The orgasm hit fast, pulling her along on a tide of sensation, threatening to drag her under with its intensity. She clutched the comforter, clinging to it as Joe continued to move inside her. Not long after, he tightened his grip on her hips, holding her in place as he took his own release. Their jagged breaths and panting filling the air around them, Amanda collapsed onto Joe's damp chest. He stroked her hair, whispering incoherent but soothing words that lulled her.

It felt like forever before she recovered enough to even move. She rolled onto her back, staring at the ceiling and trying to keep the giddy expression off her face.

"That was intense," Joe whispered.

"That's a huge understatement."

"Any regrets?" He asked the words as if he wasn't sure he wanted to hear the answer.

She thought about it for a few seconds, searching her mind for an answer that wouldn't hurt him, and in the end came to a startling revelation. She'd just had casual sex, for the first time in her life, and she'd *liked* it. A lot. No regrets for this girl.

"Definitely not. You?"

"No way."

Something in his tone made her glance his way. He was looking at her with that intense, searching gaze again and it made her swallow hard against a sudden lump forming in her throat. "This is casual, right? No strings, no commitments?"

"Yeah. You said that was what you wanted, and I agreed."

"Joe..." Her voice trailed off when she couldn't think of anything to say.

"Stay with me, Amanda." His gaze pleaded as much as his tone. "Not all night if you don't want to, but at least for a little while."

"I have an appointment in the morning. Later today," she amended when she looked at the clock. Staying the night would imply a commitment when that was what she was trying to avoid. She started to sit up, but Joe pressed a palm to the flat of her stomach and shook his head.

"Just because you want to keep it casual doesn't mean you have to be in a rush to leave afterward. Come on. Stay for a while. What are you afraid of?"

He thought she was afraid, did he? Ha! She'd show him. "Okay. I'll stay. But I can't promise you I'll be here when you wake up."

Finally he smiled. "I'm okay with that."

She'd just begun to doze off when he whispered in her ear. "Amanda?"

"Huh?"

"Will you let me paint your house?"

"Whatever you want."

Sometime later, her still mind in a haze, Amanda fell asleep in Joe's arms.

Chapter Eight

Joe woke up alone, but he really hadn't expected things to play out differently. He stood, stretched his arms overhead, and after a pit stop to the bathroom for a quick shower, he dressed and headed downstairs for breakfast.

His body still thrummed with contentment after his night with Amanda. She'd fallen asleep in his arms, and that had to count for something. She'd left before he'd woken up, but only just recently if the warmth on her side of the mattress meant anything.

A quick glance out the window told him he was right. She rushed down the walkway from her cottage toward her car, pulling her hair back into a messy ponytail as she went. So she'd left his bed not long ago, and was now running late for that appointment. For some reason, the thought gave him more than a little satisfaction.

He remembered her mentioning her meeting earlier in the week when they'd spoken. She had to meet with the college financial-aid counselor, and then run to the bookstore to buy her books while she was in town. He had plenty of time to take care of a few things that needed to be done. Once she started school, her days would be taken up with classes and her nights with work at Maggie's, and if he ever wanted her to have time for him again, he needed to make sure she kept her stress levels down. Helping her with household repairs seemed to be the simplest way to accomplish that.

Maybe it hadn't been right that he'd asked her if he could paint the cottage last night. She'd been half asleep and probably hadn't heard a word he'd said. But it brought a smile to his face anyway. She'd said yes, and he planned to take her up on it before she came home and realized what she'd agreed to.

A fast cup of coffee later, he was almost ready to get moving. If she didn't appreciate the air conditioner, she'd really hate what he had planned today. At least this morning he'd recruited a few accomplices in the form of his son and friends. That way, when she got mad, she'd have a few other choices to take her anger out on.

A knock sounded on the door just before Scott walked in with a couple of his old football buddies from high school. Joe recognized them—Ryan Sanders and Jake Reading. He used them on occasion when he needed backup crew for painting or laying tile. Between the four of them, they should be able to knock out the project in no time. Maybe even before Amanda got back from town.

"Hey, Dad."

"You guys are early. I haven't even had breakfast yet."

"It's after ten."

Surprised, Joe glanced at the clock. That couldn't be right. But it was. Well, shit. Time to get to work, so they could get as much done as possible before she returned home.

After another cup of coffee and a slice of dry toast, he and Scott and the other boys made it down the short walkway to Amanda's place to start the long-overdue paint job the place so desperately needed.

A half hour into the job, Scott sidled up to him. "You're whistling."

"Am I?" Joe chuckled. Though he wasn't surprised, he was a little shocked that he hadn't even noticed. Even the heat slowly making a return couldn't dampen his spirits today. "Hmm. Didn't notice."

"What's got you so happy?" Scott asked, waggling his eyebrows. "It wouldn't have anything to do with the fact that we're working on Amanda the sexy neighbor's house, would it?"

Joe shrugged and continued slathering the clapboard siding with sage green paint from the cans he'd found still stacked inside her front door. There was no way in hell she would appreciate his help, at least not at first, but the woman was stressed. He knew all the signs of a woman in trouble—first from watching Laura in the last few months of their marriage and later from Catherine before she left. He hadn't been able to recognize them then, and it had been too late to do any damage control, but he could see it in Amanda. Adding college classes into her hectic schedule just might put her over the edge, and she had yet to hire anyone to work on the railing that was still loose. She needed the help, even if she refused to admit it.

"Nah. It's just a good day. Your sister told me she'll fill in for Catherine until I find someone else, so on the work front, things are looking up."

"And what about on the social front? You look like a guy who's had very little sleep, if you know what I mean."

Joe could only shake his head. The last thing he wanted to discuss with his son was his love life. "I have no idea what you're talking about."

Scott raised his eyebrows in a way that reminded Joe of himself. "Give it a rest, Dad. Did you, or did you not, get lucky last night?"

Lucky? He was the luckiest man on the friggin' planet after his night with Amanda. The fact that she wanted casual niggled a little but he'd find a way to change her mind. "Yeah, okay. Maybe I did."

He glanced at Scott out of the corner of his eye, waiting for his reaction. Scott only smiled. "It's about damned time."

"Yes, it is, and that's all I'm going to say about it."

They painted in silence for a little longer before Scott chimed in again. "Are you happy with her?"

He should have known his son wouldn't keep his mouth shut long. He'd always been a talker. "It's not serious. She's a friend."

"A friend?" Scott smiled. "Friends don't usually sleep together."

Laughter reached them from the other side of the house. Joe glanced around to make sure his son's friends weren't listening before he continued. "She's been hurt before, and though she's not ready to admit it, she's afraid of being hurt again. So she wants to keep it casual."

"Okay, I can understand that," Scott said, nodding. He loaded the roller with more paint and moved further down the porch toward the far end of the front of the cottage. "But are *you* happy with that arrangement?"

Joe got to sleep with a beautiful, sexy, interesting woman who liked to take charge in the bedroom but didn't ask anything further from him than great sex. What wasn't there to be happy about? It was the perfect arrangement, most men's biggest fantasy, but something about it left him a little cold. He wasn't ready for forever with any woman, but Amanda intrigued him. She made him want more. Quiet dinners in fancy restaurants, walks around the lake, long conversations over morning coffee...yeah, he missed that part of being involved with a woman he cared about, and he wanted it back. Wanted to try it with Amanda to see if the connection between them extended to more than sex. But if he told her how he was feeling, she'd never speak to him again. He'd have to find a way to show her that a commitment with him wouldn't be as bad as she thought it would be. In fact, he had a feeling it would be pretty damned great.

"It's all I'm getting for now, so I'm going to have to be happy with it."

"You could try to talk to her, to explain you want more than a fling."

And run the risk of her moving out of the cottage and out of his life? No way in hell would he chase her away before he had a fair shot at getting what he wanted from her. "No. I'm not going to rush her. If she wants casual, fine. I'm all for it."

Between the painting and the conversation, Joe hadn't realized a few hours had passed until he glanced at his watch. Amanda's car pulled into the driveway and she jumped out, her expression stern. Her hands clenched into fists, she walked up the walkway and joined them on the porch.

"Hi," he said, bracing himself for her anger. It wouldn't be totally undeserved.

She blinked. "Hey. What's going on?"

So far so good, but that didn't mean it would stay that way. The woman was prone to mood swings he couldn't even begin to comprehend.

"I was just going to ask you the same thing. How did your appointment go?"

"Fine."

Just one word, spoken in a clipped tone that warned him she was about to let him have it. Fearing the worst, he decided to head her off before she had a chance to start. "I was going to surprise you with this, since I know how much you love my surprises. You did say I could do this last night, remember?"

She actually laughed, catching him off guard. "Thanks. I appreciate it. Sorry I got home early and ruined the surprise."

He swallowed hard. This had to be for Scott's benefit. She wouldn't get angry with him in front of a stranger. She'd wait until later, when she had a chance to get him alone, and then she'd let him know what she really thought. That was okay. He could handle her aggravation—and he could turn it around into something much more productive and enjoyable for both of them.

"If you hate it, go ahead and say it," he told her. "Scott won't mind. He's pretty much used to listening to me get yelled at, anyway."

Scott stepped around Joe and stuck out his paint-streaked hand. "Since my dad doesn't seem interested in introducing us, I'll do it for him. I'm Scott."

Amanda took his hand and shook it, shock written on her face. "Hi, Scott. I'm Amanda Storm. Your dad's neighbor."

Scott cleared his throat and Joe gave him a soft elbow to the ribs. Amanda glanced from Joe to Scott and back to Joe again before rolling her eyes. "When I saw you over here before," she said to Scott, "I thought you were Joe's brother."

"Nah." He clapped Joe on the back. "Good genes keep us Baker men looking young is all. We hear that a lot."

Luckily Scott didn't harp on the fact that Joe had been a very young father. Instead, he went back to his painting, mumbling something about leaving the lovebirds alone. Joe was going to have to kill him later.

He glanced at Amanda and found her face red and her lips tight. "Sorry about that. Kids."

211

"Yeah. Kids. You know, he's about the same age as my boss down at Maggie's."

She didn't comment on what Scott had said, and Joe would be eternally grateful for it. Still, he had to find out her state of mind. She had to be pissed that he'd taken what she referred to as "liberties" yet again with the cottage.

"Are you okay with this?"

"Do I have a choice?"

"You always have a choice."

She shook her head. "What are you going to do, strip the paint?"

His expression must have been horrified, because her eyes widened and she put her hand on his arm before standing on her tiptoes to plant a quick, surprising kiss on his lips. "I'm fine with it. Really. Well, mostly, at least. I think last night I realized something important."

"And what would that be?" He tried to grab her and pull her up against him, but she ducked away. He saw Scott watching the exchange out of the corner of his eye, but chose to ignore it. Let him think what he wanted. They were all adults here.

"That when you're trying to help, you're not doing it because you think I can't take care of myself."

Hadn't he been trying to tell her that all along?

He shook his head. If he had, he hadn't tried very hard, or she would have known. "I realize that. I'm glad you finally do, too."

"You're only helping me because you're a nice guy," she continued. "A gentleman. I would have recognized it sooner, had I ever met a true gentleman before."

Oh, man. Now she was going too far. His intentions had been kind, but he'd also been trying to get her right where he'd had her last night. In his bed. "Don't put me on a pedestal. I don't deserve to be there."

To that comment, she rolled her eyes. "No shit. I'm just trying to tell you I'm okay with you helping. Well, at least as far as the house goes. Just don't go thinking I need your help in other areas of my life, because I *so* don't."

Yeah, right. The woman needed help—help learning she didn't have to be alone to be happy, and she didn't have to settle for a man who wasn't right for her. "I never thought you did."

"Do you guys need an extra set of hands here?" she asked, glancing around at the house. "I have the rest of the day free and I don't mind pitching in."

"We've got it pretty well covered." He tucked a strand of her hair that had fallen loose from her ponytail behind her ear, letting his finger trail across her cheek on the way back. She leaned into the lingering touch. "My house is unlocked. Why don't you go up to my house and take a bath?"

Her eyes lit up at his suggestion. A huge smile broke out across her face and she shifted from foot to foot. "Really?"

"Sure. No one else is using the tub. You might as well give it a try."

"Thanks, Joe. I'll just get my stuff and head up." She kissed him again and turned, heading for the door. He grabbed her hand and pulled her back, crushing his lips down on hers for a harder, longer kiss. One that had his cock stirring to life. He broke away and slumped against the railing, hoping to hide his reaction to her. As much as he wanted to suggest joining her in the bathtub, if he did, the work around the cottage would never get finished.

"No problem." He watched her go, trying to calm his libido so he could get back to the task at hand, promising himself that tonight, if she'd let him, he would make up for all the time they'd lose today.

ᎮᏆᎦ

Amanda leaned back in the bathtub, letting the water cover every inch of her except her head. The jets in the tub hummed and whirred away, easing the tension in her work-weary muscles. Joe—and his bathtub—were life savers and he didn't realize it. His suggestion that she take a bath had kept her from doing some serious damage to the man. At least now she didn't feel like taking off the top of his head for starting the paint job on the outside of the cottage without warning her first.

Okay, he'd warned her. Gotten her permission, but he'd done it while she'd been half asleep. She would have agreed to anything at that point if he'd just stopped talking and let her fall asleep. She hadn't realized what she'd agreed to until she'd gotten home and seen what he was doing. Yes, she was upset—at first, but what she'd said to him had been the truth. He was trying to help because he was a nice guy. It wasn't his fault she had such an aversion to gentlemen.

She expelled a soft breath and sank even further into the water, letting it lap against her lower lip. The cottage only had a shower stall and the hotel bathtub had been a cramped, dingy four-foot job she'd barely wanted to step into to take a shower, so the luxury of the huge tub was something she hadn't dreamed of passing up when Joe had offered. Now this kind of help, she could get used to.

And she wasn't really *mad* about the paint job as much as she was surprised. There were some things she really needed to learn to let go of, and Joe doing work around the cottage was one of them. To ask him to stop helping would be stupid, now that she had a chance to think about it. Why do all the work herself when her neighbor, a contractor, wanted to do it for her? She'd pay him, of course, as soon as he told her how much she owed him for time and labor.

As for the air conditioner, she'd let it slide. Sleeping at night would be so much easier. Now that she wouldn't have to worry about having her clothes constantly plastered to her body, she could forgive him just about anything.

And then there was last night... A dreamy smile spread across her lips and she didn't have to look in the mirror to know she looked like a lust-sick fool. It had been incredible. Amazing. And so freeing. She'd been worried that, come morning, she'd wake up to thoughts of commitment and forever and the worst one yet—marriage. All the way to her appointment she'd been waiting for the thoughts to start, but they hadn't. The smile on her face grew. She'd finally broken the cycle. She could be happy seeing someone casually, having fun, and not worrying about rings and walks down the aisle and her mother's crazy wedding planning that only seemed to get more outlandish with every ceremony. If she ever did marry again, no way was she letting Miriam Storm plan her wedding.

The last wedding cake had been in the shape of a sun. Lemon-yellow frosting rays and all. And Rachel's southern-belle-style maid of honor dress had matched. Unfortunately for both Amanda and Rachel.

Instead of thoughts of commitment, a revelation had hit that morning on her way to town. Her incredibly insightful sister Rachel had it right all along. Who needed a man to be happy? Sure, being with someone could add to happiness, but if you couldn't be happy without a man in your life, there was a serious problem.

Her life had been one big problem until she'd moved to the little town of Ludlow, New Hampshire and found herself. She wasn't the woman she'd always thought she was, and that was the main cause of her unhappiness. Now she had a chance to change everything, and no way would she pass it up.

She washed her hair, worked in some conditioner and clipped the wet mass up on the top of her head. Feet resting on the edge of the tub, ankles crossed, she closed her eyes and let the water do its magic on the remnants of the tension she hadn't quite been able to get rid of since moving here and buying a house.

She owed Joe a favor for giving her this moment of pure, uninterrupted peace, and she knew just how she planned to repay him. The kiss he'd planted on her told her he wanted a repeat of the night before, and she was all too happy to oblige.

She'd found a man she enjoyed spending time with, enjoyed sleeping with even more, and she got to go back home to her own place every night she wanted to. Her life was finally exactly what she'd needed for so long, but hadn't known how to get.

Now she just had to figure out a way to keep things from changing. She'd had enough upset in her life and couldn't handle any more.

Chapter Nine

Amanda switched off the TV and pulled the woolen blanket up to her chin. Severe storm warnings tonight, the all-too-perky weather forecaster had said in a sing-song voice belying the news she was giving. Heavy rain, high winds and thunder. Amanda shivered. Anxiety settled into a cold ball in the pit of her stomach. This would be the first time she'd be truly alone during an electrical storm, and the thought really didn't thrill her all that much. She wasn't phobic, but storms didn't make her top ten list of things she enjoyed about the summer, either.

As if on cue, a flash of lightning brightened the room, followed by the harsh clap of thunder. She pushed up from the couch, fingers clutching the blanket around her, and walked to the window. She parted the curtains and looked across the wooded yard. A light burned in Joe's living-room window. He was still awake, but working according to what he'd told her earlier. He hadn't had time to see her tonight. They'd spent the past week together during every free moment they could manage to coordinate, but now he had a few things to catch up on.

For a few seconds, she thought about running across the lawn and knocking on his door, despite knowing he had more important things to do than calm an irrational twenty-eight-year-old with a mild fear of thunder, but nixed the idea almost as soon as it hit. She didn't need him, no matter what her scared brain might be telling her. She was almost thirty. It was well past time for her to learn to weather a thunderstorm all on her own.

After a brief hesitation, she let the curtain drop and was halfway to the kitchen for a glass of wine to help calm her frazzled nerves when another clap of thunder boomed through the room, sounding like it hit something right outside the cottage. She didn't even have time to think before an ear-splitting crash filled the room and the roof over the pull-out couch caved in.

Amanda screamed and jumped back, her heart pounding. Tree branches stuck into the room at odd angles, the dark green leaves glistening with water that dripped all over the beautiful hardwood floors. The thickest twisted limbs lay across the couch where she'd just been sitting, and through the open bedroom door she could see one had crushed the cabinet where she kept her clothes. The bedroom roof had caved in as well, and glass from broken windows lay strewn across the patchwork quilt on her bed.

A gasp caught in her throat, her mind having trouble wrapping around the concept of what she was seeing. The roof of her cottage was half gone, and a big gaping hole had taken its place. Her clothes and belongings scattered across the floor like trash in an alleyway and rain poured in, soaking everything in its path.

Another flash of lightning brightened the sky, and the resulting thunder made her heart all but stop. Tears of frustration, of anger, clouded her eyes. She pushed a hand through her hair. What was she supposed to do now? Her little cottage was ruined. Her car keys were in her purse, somewhere in the mess—along with not only her cell phone, but the single cordless landline phone.

She was still trying to figure out what to do when she heard pounding on her front door. She rushed to the door and yanked it open to find Joe standing on the porch, panting, shoulders hunched and hands balled into fists. Without a word, he pushed past her into the cottage, took one look at the tree on her mattress, and pulled her into his arms, crushing her against his chest.

For what seemed like an eternity he held her, stroking her hair and whispering calming things. She sank into his embrace, tears flowing freely for the first time in as long as she could remember. What had she done to deserve someone as caring and compassionate as him?

"I saw where the tree hit, and I thought something happened to you," he told her, still refusing to let go. "Damn it, Amanda. It scared the hell out of me. I don't think I've ever run so fast in my life."

She let his words wash over and comfort her. She held tight to him, drawing him closer, knowing that even if she could crawl inside his skin it wouldn't help get rid of the sudden desolation spiking through her. The life she'd built for herself was gone. Clothes, the school books she had just bought, and almost everything else she owned. She had nothing.

"Are you okay?" he asked, his tone tense. "Please talk to me and tell me you're okay."

"I think so. I'm not hurt, anyway. I was on my way to the kitchen when it happened. Not anywhere near the bed or the couch."

"Yeah, I can see you're fine. But how are you, really? That must have been awful to see. It would have scared the hell out of me, I'm sure."

She tried to tell him she was fine, that she could take care of herself and didn't need his sympathy, but the words clogged her throat. Her chest ached. So instead of moving out of his embrace, she sank further into it. She clung to him even more, her fingers digging into his shoulders, until he leaned down and sealed his lips over hers.

The kiss was brief, nothing more than a soft brush of lips, but it was enough. Her body hummed. She suddenly craved more. A lot more. Anything to help her forget. She reached for him, but he backed away and walked toward the tree. The only thing that let her know he was fighting something was the way his shoulders heaved with each of his breaths.

"You can't stay here tonight."

No shit. "I'll get a room at one of the hotels in town. I did it when I first moved here. What's a few more nights, really? I don't mind. But...can you give me a ride? I have no idea where my keys are."

She sucked in a shuddering breath at the thought of suddenly being so helpless, so dependent on another person, when all she'd wanted since her last failed relationship was to be on her own. Now she had no choice but to rely on Joe and whatever help he could and would give her.

"No," he said with a finality that echoed through the room. "You're not going into town."

"Why not? Do you think I can't—"

"It has nothing to do with what you can't do, Amanda. The road will be washed out. Always happens in storms like this. We're stuck up here for at least three days...after the rain stops."

"So you're saying I'm stuck? In this place, without a roof?" She sniffled and then started to cry in earnest, her tears mixing with the rain still pouring in through the ruined roof. Another crack of thunder tore through the air. "I might as well just sleep outside. There really isn't a difference, is there?"

"I won't let you do that. You'll have to salvage what you can and come stay with me."

She let out a sigh. What choice did she have? Her new life was in shambles and Joe was her only lifeline.

"I can see what you're thinking," Joe said, running a hand through his wet hair. "I wish there was something else I could do, but there isn't. We don't have much choice. Now we really need to get out of this rain. You're already soaked to the bone and I couldn't stand it if you got sick because of your stubbornness.

"Do you have anything to pack?" Joe asked when she said nothing, sounding impatient and a little unsure. He touched her cheek, glanced around the room and shook his head. "We're going to catch cold if we stand here much longer."

She started to protest out of habit, but in the end realized turning down his offer would be one of the stupidest things she'd ever done. He was offering to take care of her, and at the moment, her choices were limited. She went about taking a few minutes to pack what she could salvage, which, admittedly, wasn't a lot. The clothes were wet and dirty, and would have to be washed and dried before she could wear them, but her bathroom items were all fine so she stuffed them into a bag and met him back out in the main room. Her purse and keys would have to wait until morning, when the rain stopped and it was light enough to see as she searched the shambles.

"Don't worry about the clothes," Joe said, leading her toward the door. "I've got some shorts and T-shirts you can use. We'll deal with your stuff tomorrow. Come down and get it and wash it up at my place. For now, let's...let's just worry about all this tomorrow and for tonight be glad you weren't in bed when this happened."

Another look at the couch, and the tears started fresh again. Where was the fairness in all of this? She'd tried to better her life, tried to better herself, and where had it gotten her? Homeless, that was where. Once again relying on someone else for basic needs she should be able to provide for herself.

"Thanks." Defeated and downtrodden, she let him lead her out the door.

"I don't have an umbrella," he said as if it were a problem.

Amanda just shrugged. "Like that's even an issue right now. I don't think I could be more soaked if I jumped in the lake."

That earned a laugh out of him, albeit a small and hesitant one. "Okay, let's go, then. We can run and be to the front door in a couple of seconds."

He grabbed her hand and she had no choice but to run across the slippery stone path heading toward his house, lightning occasionally lighting the world around them. It really wasn't more than thirty seconds before they stomped up his front steps and burst through the door in a flurry of limbs and cold rainwater. Once inside, he closed the door behind them, took her bag from her hand and set it by the door. Then he put his arm around her shoulder and walked her upstairs toward the bathroom. Once there, he pulled a towel from the linen closet and handed it to her.

"Why don't you take a shower? I'll go get you some clean clothes and leave them here for you, and make some coffee so you can have something warm when you get out."

She nodded, taking the towel and closing the door after he walked out of the room. She turned the shower on, stripped off the wet clothing and stepped into the hot steam.

She washed her hair, soaped up and rinsed off under the spray, all the while feeling numb. It would be a long time before she came to terms with what had happened tonight. Already, she could feel her mind working hard to block the terrifying images from her memory. Another hour, and she would have been in bed. Would have been crushed by the tree trunk and ended up in the hospital. Or maybe worse.

Somewhere between rinsing her hair and turning off the water, her tears dried. No sense crying over something she couldn't change. There would be plenty of time to worry about it later, once she'd been able to absorb all that had happened. Joe had helped her, and she needed to remember that. He was right. They could deal with the mess in the morning if the storm cleared. Right now, she was lucky to be alive and concentrating on that would be better for her well-being than thinking of all she'd lost.

Her resolve strengthened once again, she climbed out of the shower, dried off and dressed in the clothes Joe had left hanging on the towel bar for her while she'd been washing up. When she finished, she brushed her hair in the mirror. It took a little while for her to figure out she was primping. For Joe. Now, of all times, in the middle of the second biggest crisis in her life.

Well, didn't that just bite the big one?

ဆာ○ఠ

Joe got the coffee started and leaned back against the counter, lost in thought. What was he supposed to do now? He had to let her stay, but she had no desire to be here. Sleeping with him was one thing, but he knew how her mind worked.

He should be thankful she wasn't looking to push him into marriage. He'd done the whole wife-and-family thing before, and it hadn't ended well. No way in hell was he going back to that place for a cute brunette with a killer smile and great eyes and an amazing body...

Stop, Joe. Not going there, remember?

Shit.

He was already in way too deep as it was. He needed to figure out some way to pull himself out, not a way to dig himself deeper into a place he didn't even want to be. If he didn't get out, *now*, he'd end up in big trouble.

Hell, it was way too late for that and he knew it. Had known it from the first time he'd sunk his cock into her welcoming heat. She was it. The woman he'd been looking for. At least he thought she was, but she wouldn't even give him the chance to find out. Physically, they'd gotten close since the first time they'd slept together a week ago. Emotionally, things were a little stickier. As far as friendship went, they were on solid ground, but mention anything beyond that and she acted like she'd developed a bad case of hives.

Great going, Joe. You've become the woman's fuck buddy, and you didn't even notice.

The coffee finished brewing and he poured himself a mug. He took a sip, black, and winced at the heat. It felt good, though. He needed the reminder to smarten up before he did something stupid, like get involved in a relationship that hadn't yet started but was already doomed to failure.

A few minutes later, Amanda walked into the room, looking better than she had a right to scrubbed clean of makeup and hair products and wearing his baggy shorts and T-shirt. She gave him a hesitant smile, and something in his chest stuttered.

"The coffee smells great."

"It's decaf. I hope you don't mind. I thought regular might keep you awake."

The smile grew and she padded across the floor, her bare feet whispering softly on the tile as she went. "Thanks. You're right."

She walked over to the cabinet, grabbed a mug and filled it with the dark brew. Unlike him, she added two heaping teaspoons of sugar from the canister on the counter and a large dollop of milk. After taking a few sips, she leaned against the counter, the stoneware mug cradled between her cupped palms.

"Thanks for everything, Joe. You've really been a good friend."

He shook his head. Too bad friendship was the last thing he wanted from her.

"Are you okay?" he asked after too long a silence. The air had changed, turning tense, and he just knew she was about to blow. *Bring it on, honey. Let it out so you can start to feel better.*

Amanda turned to face him, her hands on her hips and her expression murderous. "Am I okay? Let me ask you this, Mr. Perfect. Do I *look* okay?"

"You look...shaken."

"That's a huge understatement. I was finally able to move out on my own, and look at what happens to me." With her hand, she gestured toward the window facing her house, swinging her arm in a wild arc. "You wouldn't understand. You've got it all together. Not a thing out of place. You don't get what I've been going through, and why I want to change everything."

Now she'd gone too far. "I don't get it? Are you crazy? Sweetheart, I understand failure, and heartache."

"Yeah, right."

"I've been through divorce, too, remember? And my former business partner I was telling you about...when he left the business he took more than half the clients with him. His company is now twice the size of mine and growing, and sometimes he still feels the need to take things from me. It's been this way since we were in high school. Maybe even before that. Now I've lost my wife and my assistant to him, so don't tell me I have no idea what it's like to have my life torn apart."

She stilled, her lips parted, and cocked her head to the side. For a long while she just stared at him and it felt like almost an eternity before she spoke. "Why didn't you say something sooner? All these times I've complained to you about life and how it sucks, and you've just kept your mouth shut."

Wasn't that the question of the century? Joe raked a hand through his hair and turned away. She hadn't wanted to hear about his problems. She'd been too busy with her own. "It's no big deal."

"Apparently it is."

"It's really not." He'd only spent fifteen years of his life with the woman, had two children, to watch her get bored and walk away when the kids were nearly grown. But it was no big deal. Hadn't affected him at all.

Not one fucking bit.

He turned around, pressed his palms into the counter and let his head drop. Okay, so maybe it had affected him more than he'd been willing to admit.

He felt her hand on his back, right between his shoulder blades, and he sucked in a breath.

"Come on, Joe. Talk to me. You're a master at getting me to open up to you even when I don't want to. Now it's your turn to share."

No way in hell was he rehashing his past failure right now. She'd heard the story before, and there was no need to make her sit through another retelling. It wouldn't accomplish anything except to make him want some serious alone time, and it looked like it would be a long while before he got that. "I don't want to talk right now."

"Then what do you want to do?"

"I just want to..." Not knowing what to tell her, he spun around and kissed her.

The kiss was short, but scorching. No hesitancy from her, and that bolstered his spirits and drove the sudden, shocking need for her even higher. Tonight he didn't want to stop. He wanted to keep going until he lost himself in her.

He wanted to show her that letting someone else in wasn't a bad thing. They could be good for each other. She just needed to realize that, besides their differences, they really could be something to each other. She might not be looking for forever, but it didn't need to be that. It would be enough for him if she would cut the stubborn crap and promise to try.

He wound his fingers in her hair and held her close. Finally, he let her go and she stepped back. He braced himself for all her usual arguments, all her anger and aggravation, but got none of it. She launched herself into his arms instead.

He couldn't say how long the kiss went on, but it was enough to drive him near-mad. Soon they were tearing at each other's clothes. The urge to hold her, to make sure she was really okay was so strong it almost pulled him under. He leaned in, trailing his lips down the side of her neck, past her collarbone until he reached her breasts. He suckled one nipple and then the other. Tonight wouldn't be gentle. She had to know that. He just didn't have it in him. Amanda seemed to feel the same way, if the way she wriggled against him was any indication. Her fingers reached for his pants and she had them unzipped in record time. The air around him had a frantic edge that only pushed him to move faster.

He almost laughed, but then he caught the look in her eyes. She wanted him. *Cared* about him. That was there, plain as day. But she was scared of something, too. It made sense. She'd been hurt a few too many times. Sometimes when he touched her, even after all they'd shared, she shrank away. When she touched him first, she was fine. She needed to be in control, and he could give her that. Hell, he'd give her that forever if it made her happy. Didn't she know by now he'd do anything for her? She had him wrapped around her finger and the woman didn't even know it.

He stepped back and leaned against the counter, taking in the sight of her almost naked body. She only wore panties, ones she must have salvaged from the pile of clothes on the floor of the cottage, and it was the most incredible sight he'd ever seen.

He beckoned her with his finger and she walked over to him, an enticing mix of lust and insecurity on her face. It was endearing and he found it made him like her even more. But he wasn't supposed to like her. She didn't want him in that way.

He *had* to find a way to make her change her mind.

She brushed her lips across his chest and he shuddered. He was dangerously close to coming, but that made no sense. He wasn't a young man by any stretch of the imagination, but the adrenaline pumping through his system made waiting impossible and he didn't think he'd be able to hold back much longer. She scraped her nails over one of his nipples and he hissed out a breath.

"Are you okay?" she asked, her tone quiet. He would have thought she was nervous if he hadn't caught the coy look on her face.

"I'm fine," he ground out through clenched teeth.

"Yes, you are." She gave a small sigh and continued on her journey downward until she ended up on her knees in front of him. When she reached for his waistband again, he hauled her to her feet. "No."

"You wouldn't like it?"

Was she nuts? What man wouldn't want a beautiful woman on her knees in front of him? "I'd like it. Too much. I wouldn't last."

Amanda barely resisted the urge to put her hands on her hips and sigh. What was it with this guy? Here she was, willing to give him pleasure with no strings attached, and yet again he was turning her down? Not likely. In the past, she'd always let the man take the initiative when it came to sex. Joe didn't mind when she explored, and she planned to do just that. He was all hers for tonight, and he'd have to learn to deal with it. She broke free of his hold and spread the unzipped sides of the jeans he'd changed into when she was in the shower, pulling them down enough that she could free his erection from his boxers.

His fingers tangled in her hair and he moved her head away. "You really need to stop now."

"Why? Not having fun?"

"I need to get inside you. Like five minutes ago." He took her hand and started to lead her out of the kitchen, but she shook her head.

"Where do you think you're going?"

"We need to move this into the bedroom."

"What's wrong with right here?"

A stunned look passed across his face before he frowned. "In the middle of the kitchen?"

"Sure. Why not. The table looks pretty sturdy." She smiled, and he met the smile with a look that let her know she'd turned him on with her suggestion. A lot. It turned *her* on to think she could get him going with just a few words, even though he probably thought she was a total headcase.

Joe's throat worked as he swallowed. His chest sawed in and out with his heavy breaths. "Are you serious?"

She nodded.

"Awesome." He took a few seconds to sheathe himself with a condom he'd pulled out of the dresser drawer before he lifted her onto the table, wrapped her legs around his waist and slid inside.

He surprised her yet again by not moving. Instead, he leaned down and kissed her. It was a long, slow, thorough kiss that had her panting and clinging to him, desperate to get more. She'd never get enough of him. The man was sheer perfection. What she'd been searching for all her life. Too bad she'd been looking in the wrong places.

No. She had to stop that line of thinking. Sex was one thing. A girl had to have it every once in a while, so why not when a sexy guy was ready and more than willing? Getting involved on an emotional level was out of the question. Totally, completely, utterly out of the question. She shouldn't even be thinking of it. Now, for the first time in her life, she needed to be thinking of herself. If she let herself get close to Joe, she'd end up wanting to get married again, and look where that particular line of thinking had gotten her.

She blocked out all thoughts of emotion and just concentrated on what was important. The feel of him inside her. The crisp, masculine scent of him and his rain-dampened hair. The rough hairs of his chest against her nipples, making her want to scream out from the incredible pleasure of it all. The man was a walking sex god, and she finally had him right where she wanted him. Might as well enjoy the ride.

And what a ride it was. Joe stroked and thrust and wore her out. She'd come twice by the time he joined her, and by then she felt so limp and sated that she could just lay back and fall asleep. He picked her up and carried her to his bed, lay her down and climbed in next to her. By the time he covered them both with the sheet, she was half-asleep.

৪০০৪

Joe woke up disoriented the next day. He sat up, shook his head and coughed before realizing what was wrong. He hadn't gone to bed alone the night before. He wasn't alone now, either.

She'd stayed in bed with him all night? Now that was a switch. In the time they'd spent together, both at his house and at hers, she'd always managed to leave the bed sometime before he woke up. To have her there, finally, was the most incredible feeling in the world.

He glanced over his shoulder to see her tangled in his sheets, her long brown hair spread all around her. Her eyes were closed and the look on her face was nothing short of angelic.

She hadn't looked angelic the night before.

He smiled at the memory of her dropping to her knees in front of him, more than willing to give him what he'd wanted so badly. It shook him to think she was so open and free with herself, but it shook him more to think that he was going to get too deeply involved if he wasn't careful. She was dangerous to him. Something in the rational part of his mind reminded him of that even as his cock hardened from looking at her between his sheets. He should have walked away from her the night before. Should have slept on the couch. But he hadn't, and now he was in deep shit. Now he couldn't deny it, couldn't even try to pretend it didn't exist. He was falling in love with the woman and she just wanted to get laid. She wanted to be *friends,* too, but at the moment friendship didn't count for much.

She opened her eyes and smiled sleepily at him. "Good morning."

"Hey. How did you sleep?"

"You mean for the few hours you actually left me alone? Fine."

She hadn't been the only one who'd been insatiable the night before.

"Are you hungry?" he asked, looking to change the subject.

"A little, but I think we need to talk first."

Oh, boy. Here it came. The kiss of death for whatever was happening between them. Funny that he was the one wanting a commitment and she was the one running scared. He couldn't tell her what he wanted now, though. Not with the two of them trapped out in the middle of nowhere until the roads cleared.

He slid out of bed and pulled on a pair of sweatpants he found on the floor. "I'm not looking for anything permanent. Just in case that's what you're worried about."

She raised her eyebrows. "Good. Neither am I."

Something in his chest tightened. "Really? Are you sure?"

She laughed then, a soft sound that hit him low in the gut and made him even harder, sick bastard that he was. Here she was tearing his heart out, and he wanted her just the same. Better to think about what she did want rather than what she didn't. "Really."

Damn it. Even now that they'd started to get close, she was still denying wanting anything serious with him. What would it take to show the woman he was the right man for her? A freakin' miracle?

He turned away, glancing out the window at the dismal, rainy day. When he finally glanced back at her, he hoped he'd managed to school his expression before she realized what he really wanted. "Does that mean we get to go back to bed?"

"How typical is that?" She shook her head, sending waves of rich brown hair around her shoulders. She looked deliciously rumpled and he couldn't wait to get her under him again. If that was all he'd get for now, it wouldn't be difficult to live with.

"What a man you are, always thinking about sex," Amanda continued. "We'll get back in bed—but not quite yet. First I need something to eat. And some coffee. Not decaf this time, Joe. The real stuff."

"Yeah, okay. Let's head downstairs and see what we can manage." With a laugh on his lips, he made his way toward the kitchen in search of something to feed her. He had a feeling they'd end up back in bed sooner rather than later, and he wanted to make sure they both had plenty of energy. At least, while he was in bed with her, he didn't have to think about how the messy situation between them seemed to grow worse with every conversation they had.

Chapter Ten

"What are you doing?"

Joe glanced up to see Amanda standing in the doorway. He hadn't realized she'd woken up. Two nights had passed since she'd moved in with him, and in that time they'd worn each other out. If he hadn't had work to do, he would have stayed in bed a little longer himself.

He smiled and beckoned her into the office. "Getting caught up on a little work."

She stopped and ran a hand through her damp hair, her expression uncertain. "Sorry. I didn't mean to disturb you."

"You didn't. I wouldn't normally be behind on a weekend, but my daughter has to cut down on her hours due to schoolwork with the summer classes she's taking. Now I'm winging it while I try to find someone else. No takers so far. Again."

She surprised the hell out of him when she came over and sat in his lap, staring at the computer screen. "Need some help?"

"Do you know anything about interiors?"

"Not really, but most women have an eye for color. It comes with the territory, I guess."

She spent the next twenty minutes helping him go through paint and carpet colors, and he was surprised that she really did have an eye for it. He'd offer her Catherine's old job, but she wouldn't take it anyway. She'd already turned him down once, and he wouldn't offer again. She'd take it as a personal affront if he did.

By the time they finished, he had everything set the way he wanted it to be, thanks to Amanda's help.

"Thanks."

"No problem. Do you want me to make some lunch or anything? You must be getting hungry."

"Nah. We'll figure something out a little later." He set her off his lap, pushed out the chair and went into the kitchen. She'd cleaned up the house. He was surprised, to say the least. Not very domestic to begin with, he hadn't had time to clean anything as well as he would have liked to since Catherine had left him high and dry, and for the past few days things had sort of...piled up while he and Amanda had been busy doing other things. "What have you been up to? I thought you were sleeping."

"I've been awake for a few hours. You seemed so lost in thought I didn't want to disturb you. But then it started to get close to lunchtime and I figured you probably needed something to eat."

A small part of him shivered. Here she was, living with him for only a few days so far, and already they were playing house. He didn't think she liked it, but he had no problem with it. The roads would be out another few days, at least, and he still felt a little protective of her. There was nothing he could do but sit back and take it.

"Joe? Are you okay?"

"Yeah."

"I've upset you. I'm really sorry. I just...well...I'm going to be stuck here for a while, so I thought I'd make myself useful."

He sighed. She was reading him all wrong, and since he didn't want to spook her yet, he had to let her keep believing he was as nervous about the situation as she was. "It's okay."

"No, it isn't. I shouldn't have touched anything around here without asking. Want me to mess it up again?"

Her teasing tone had him laughing despite his misgivings. "No, it's fine. Really, Amanda. Sorry if I seemed upset. I'm not. I'm just used to doing things like that on my own."

"Now you're starting to sound like me."

He blinked, not sure what to say in response.

"Relax, Joe. It's no big deal. I was a housewife a few times before I learned I'm one of those people who isn't cut out for long-term commitment."

And he was just the opposite. He wanted a commitment out of life, but had settled for the wrong woman the first time out the gate. Though her case was a little more extreme than his, Amanda was in a similar situation. And he couldn't help but think of her as his. One way or another, no matter what it took, he'd show her they belonged together. His resolve was even more strengthened than ever. She could deny it all she wanted, but he saw it in her eyes.

Amanda Storm *would* be his. It was only a matter of time.

ഇരു

Sitting on the couch with Amanda curled in his arms, Joe couldn't think of a place he'd rather be. In the few weeks since she'd had to move in with him, the roads had cleared, her cottage was days away from being ready for her to move back in, and that was the last thing he wanted to happen. Having her with him, he'd been so...happy. Life couldn't get any more perfect. Though she wouldn't want to hear it, she had him thinking about marriage again. He couldn't tell her that. She'd run for sure.

Amanda snuggled closer to his side. "You're so quiet. What's wrong?"

"Nothing." *Everything.*

"Then what's on your mind?"

"You. Us."

He realized his mistake when she stiffened against him. If he hadn't had his arm around her, odds were she would have shot to the other side of the couch faster than he could blink. He let out a sigh and changed the direction of the conversation, hoping it wouldn't be too late. "You've got me so worn out."

She pinched his side. "It's probably just that you're getting old."

Or maybe that he wanted something he would never be able to have. A few weeks and he wasn't any closer to getting her to admit to her feelings than he'd been on the first night he dragged her in out of the storm.

They sat in silence for a little while before Amanda spoke. "Tell me about her. Your ex-wife."

He sighed. Of course she'd want to talk about Laura now. *Way to put a little distance between us, Amanda.* "There's not much to tell that you haven't heard before. We dated in high school. She got pregnant in our senior year and we got married. Stayed together way too long, and then one day she decided someone else could take care of her needs better than me. That was five years ago, after fifteen years of marriage."

"I'm sorry things didn't work out," Amanda said softly, settling back against his side.

"I'm not. I knew, almost from the start, that we weren't meant to be together. We both did. I just wish she'd come to me when she'd decided she wanted out rather than cheating."

"I can understand that."

"So tell me. What happened in your marriages?"

"Not much. As a good friend of mine back home was fond of putting it, I married bums. Men who couldn't take care of themselves let alone support a household or keep a marriage together. And the last guy...Ronny...he was a good guy. Wanted what was best for me, but he wasn't in love with me. He was just someone my mother had set me up with because she thought he'd finally be the one I stuck with and gave her grandkids."

"But you don't want kids."

"It's not that I don't want them. I just don't want them to have to go through what I did, being sick and helpless and all. It was a nightmare for everyone, especially with me being so young."

"I can imagine. I'm sorry you had to go through that, but there's probably a really slim chance any children you have would contract the same disease."

"Oh, believe me, I know that. At least the rational part of my mind does. But there's an emotional part, too. One that's afraid to ever have to go through something so horrific again."

"Is that what ended your marriages? The fact that you were afraid to have children?"

"It was probably a sticking point, but there were a lot of things." She sucked in a shuddering breath. "I was scared, Joe. Scared to be alone, but scared to get close to anyone at the same time. I was young, and I really didn't know what I wanted."

"What about now? Do you know what you want now?"

"Right now, right here, I'm happy. Probably happier than I've been in a long time."

He waited for her to finish, but wasn't really surprised when she didn't. Instead they sat there in comfortable silence, Joe stroking Amanda's back and wishing like hell she was willing to take the next step. At this rate, he didn't think she'd ever be and he wasn't sure if he'd ever be able to let her go.

ଓଔ

"What's a sweet girl like you doing in a place like this?"

Amanda set a glass in front of Charlie Reed, one of Maggie's regular customers. He was sweet, funny and the biggest flirt she'd ever met. "I don't know, Charlie. I keep asking myself that same question, but I have yet to come up with an answer."

Charlie winked at her and raised his glass in salute. "I know the answer."

"Oh, really?" She propped her free hand on her hip. "And what would that be?"

"Simple." He snatched her hand. "You work here so you can see me every night."

She laughed. His tone was teasing and light. He didn't mean what he said, and they both knew it. Charlie was sexy, in his own way, but he couldn't be more than twenty-two. Way too young for her, and the women he dated tended to look like runway models rather than almost-thirty-year-old future college students.

"Yeah, that's it." She looked him over, taking in his dark-haired good looks and charming smile. He'd make some woman very happy one day. Just not her. "I work here just to see you. It has nothing to do with paying the bills."

"Is everything okay?"

Amanda glanced up to see Joe standing a dozen feet away, fingers in the pockets of his jeans. She might have thought him calm and relaxed if she hadn't caught the irritated expression etching his features. She resisted the urge to roll her eyes. Barely. A few weeks of sex and now he felt like he owned her? What the hell? Wasn't it the woman who was supposed to feel clingy?

Though she had to admit she was starting to feel a little clingy herself. Not that she wanted to, but there it was. The days she'd spent with him had been the best sex she'd had in her life. Joe actually made her crave the sex rather than merely tolerate it. Her last two husbands hadn't been able to manage that. Only the first guy had come close. Joe was...special to her, though she'd only admit it under threat of torture.

"No problems, Joe. Why don't you go sit down and I'll be with you in a few minutes?"

He just raised his eyebrows.

"Joe, knock it off."

When he still said nothing, she shook her head, grabbed his arm and dragged him across the floor to the backroom. Once they were alone she fixed him with a glare. "What the hell do you think you're doing?"

"You're swearing now? I think I like it. It sounds good on you."

"Don't even go there." She started to protest more, but he didn't give her the chance. He pulled her flush against him, crushing her breasts to his chest, and kissed her.

The kiss was long, lingering, and made her tingle everywhere. She clung to him, holding him close as he continued the sensual assault. It was amazing, so good, and she still wanted more than she could rationalize. She'd known that getting involved with him would be a mistake, but she hadn't realized just how much of one it would be until this moment.

She tried to push him away, but instead ended up pulling him closer. Her fingers tangled in the hair at his nape. She parted her lips and his tongue thrust into her mouth, brushing hers. He backed her up until she was against the wall. His whole body pressed against hers, his hands cupping her rear. He squeezed gently, dragging her against him. The hardness of his erection against her belly made her let out a soft moan.

Joe chuckled against her lips. He murmured something she didn't understand and continued with the kiss.

It seemed like an eternity before he broke away, resting his forehead against hers. He chuckled again, his chest heaving with his breaths. "Why can't I keep my hands off you?"

"I was about to ask you the same question."

"Maybe it's something in the water."

She couldn't help but chuckle at the absurd explanation. "Yeah, that must be it."

Then she remembered how he'd acted around Charlie and she pushed at his chest. He stumbled back, shock written on his face. "What are you doing?"

"What were *you* doing? Back there at the table. That wasn't funny."

"You were flirting."

"So what?" she asked, trying to keep from raising her voice. "Charlie and I do that all the time. It doesn't mean anything."

"I don't like it."

"Why not?" Her hands plunked onto her hips. "You said it yourself. You don't want to get involved. You're happy with your stupid life the way it is, and no woman is going to come in and change that."

Joe's gaze darkened. He pushed a hand through his hair and paced the room. When he finally stopped and turned to face her, he looked ready to spit nails. "Don't twist my words around and throw them in my face. Maybe what I want has changed. Maybe you read more into the words than what I meant because you're so damned afraid of committing to me."

Something inside her jumped for joy at his words. It took a few seconds to realize it shouldn't make her happy.

"Nothing has changed, Joe. Neither of us wants this fling to turn into something more serious."

"Fling?" He spat the word back at her as if it left a bad taste in his mouth. "Is that all this is to you?"

The look in his eyes shocked her and she reeled from it. He was the one who had insisted he wanted nothing more than sex. He'd said he couldn't make promises he wouldn't be able to keep. She'd readily agreed, but Joe had been the one to instigate the conversation in the first place.

"Of course it is. We agreed to that after the first night together. Remember?"

His expression turned pained. "I've never wanted to get involved. Not since my divorce. But then I met you, and I don't know. I don't even know what I want anymore."

The look on his face told her he was lying, but she refused to call him on it. If she did, she'd have to admit she felt more, too, and that would be a huge problem for both of them.

"Then what is this all about?"

"Damned if I know."

"Well, we need to settle this."

He stared at her for a long time, seeming to be searching for something. After what felt like an eternity, he stepped back and leaned against the wall. "There's nothing to settle. Nothing has changed."

Yeah, right. Everything had changed in the past ten minutes, and now Amanda was afraid there was no going back. How could they, with so much standing in the way? "Are you sure about that?"

Joe lifted one shoulder. "Never been so sure about anything in my life." With a hard shake of his head he walked toward the door, turning to glance at her over his shoulder. "My crew will be out at the house tomorrow, like I promised you a couple days ago, to finish getting the place back in order. It should be another week, tops, before we get you settled back into your own place."

With those words, he'd managed to push her away. To shut her out. She'd expected it, maybe even asked for it, but at the same time he'd managed to tear her up inside. "Thank you. I appreciate it."

"No problem." He left, but after a second showed back up in the room. "Will I see you at home later?"

Something in his voice told her he'd be upset if she said no. But what could she do? She was already in a lot deeper than she wanted to get.

With a sigh and a small smile, she relented. "Sure. I'll be there when my shift is done."

"Good." With that, he walked away, leaving her standing alone in the backroom. She stalked over to the mirror, straightening her hair into a neater ponytail before she went back into the main room to finish her shift.

Charlie got her attention and she crossed the room to stand beside his table. "What's up?"

"You and Joe Baker have something going?"

She shrugged. "Not really."

Charlie looked at her for a long time before nodding. "Sure. Nothing much, huh?"

"Nope."

"Then I guess *that* doesn't bother you." He pointed to a table in the corner, where Joe had taken a seat. The woman Alex had pointed out to her last week—Claudia Marshall, Joe's old girlfriend—was sitting across from him, looking like she wanted to eat him alive.

Something snapped inside Amanda. Her stomach bottomed out. She swallowed hard and looked away from the scene. So he was having dinner with a friend. So what? Hadn't she just told him flirting was no big deal? He'd sworn to her over and over that he and Claudia had nothing going on anymore.

She tried to school her expression and returned her gaze to Charlie's. "He told me he's not involved with her. They're just friends."

Charlie raised his eyebrows. "That's not how she tells it."

"So I've heard."

"I just thought you should know she caught up with him after he came out of the backroom. She took his arm and he walked over to the table with her."

"He did?"

Charlie nodded.

Why now? She would have cried if she hadn't promised herself she'd never cry over a man again. Why here, of all places, where she worked? Did the morning they'd just spent in his bed mean nothing to him?

She glanced back toward Joe and Claudia, and the woman looked up and gave Amanda a smug smile.

That was it. Amanda was *so* done with Joe. Tonight, when her shift ended, she was going to pack what little she had left and move back into a hotel until her cottage was livable again. One closer to town, where she wouldn't have to worry about being stuck in the middle of nowhere with a man she never should have gotten involved with in the first place.

ಬಿೀಣ

Joe kept his eyes on Amanda for most of the night. She was pissed, and he didn't blame her. She had a right to her anger, but she was directing it at the wrong person. Hell, he was pissed, too. Claudia had damned near ambushed him. He'd been on his way back to his table after the conversation with Amanda when Claudia had grabbed his arm. He hadn't been able to get rid of her since.

He didn't want to be around her at all, let alone when Amanda was so close by. Amanda was still skittish, and since the storm, he'd been on edge, trying not to do or say anything that might chase her away. The roads were clear and the fact that she hadn't moved into a hotel yet bolstered his spirits. Maybe there was hope, after all.

Hope for what? Something she would reject as soon as he mentioned it?

Hell, he just wanted her home.

Home. Now that was a word he never expected to use as far as Amanda was concerned. In the past two weeks, he'd begun to think of his home as hers, too. Inevitable, given she'd been living with him, but still a touch on the shocking side. Of course the other shoe would drop. It had been too perfect. Too terrific to last. He should have known she'd eventually want to leave, and tonight he'd managed to do something stupid enough to push her over the edge. Next thing he knew, she'd be accusing him of somehow creating the lightning that took out the tree. He'd never imagined it would be his own words chasing her away.

"Why do you keep looking at her, Joe?" Claudia tapped her manicured nails on the table and let out an irritated huff. "Are you involved with that waitress?"

He threw her a glare. "Her name is Amanda."

Shock registered for about two seconds in her eyes before she masked it. "Fine. *Amanda.* Are you involved with *Amanda*?"

"I already told you she's living in the cottage next to me. The one your aunt used to own."

"The cottage that's ruined."

He nodded.

"And where is she staying while she waits for your crew to fix it?"

When he didn't answer, Claudia sneered. "In your house, Joe? In your bed?"

He still said nothing. There would be no point in arguing with the truth.

"You've got to be kidding me. I thought you'd given up on charity cases."

"Amanda isn't a charity case." Far from it.

"Yeah, she is. I know you. Once she gets on her feet, she's going to walk away."

Amanda had surprised him. With everything she had going on, he'd thought the same thing. But he hadn't counted on the fact that she was already on her feet and always had been. She was one of the strongest women he'd ever met, and she didn't even realize it.

"What I can't figure out," Claudia continued, "is what can that woman do for you that I can't?"

Everything. "She's..." Since he couldn't think of a way to explain it without using words Claudia wouldn't want to hear, he closed his mouth. Amanda was smart. Funny. Beautiful. Kind and caring.

His.

At least she had been, until he'd pulled the jealous caveman act and more than likely chased her away.

Joe couldn't get the woman out of his mind. He wanted more time with her. Maybe a lot more time. Now he just had to convince her it was the right thing for both of them. He'd been lying when he'd told her he didn't want something permanent. Giving her what he thought she wanted to hear. He didn't want to want it, but there it was.

"Joe?"

"What?" The word came out harsher than he'd meant and he groaned when he caught the crestfallen look on Claudia's face. He pushed away the feeling with a shake of his head. Claudia was a fake. Every one of her emotions was perfected for the sole purpose of catching a man. He would never be that man. Not for her.

"Are you in love with her?"

What a loaded question that was. He let out a sigh and shook his head. Hell yes, he was in love with the woman. How could he not be? "No, I'm not in love with her. I haven't known her that long."

"Long enough."

He glanced at Amanda, carrying a tray over to a table for four across the room, and his chest tightened. Yeah, sometimes that was all it took. And sometimes, on rare occasions, one look across a run-down little cottage and a guy was a goner. A few weeks of banter, a few weeks of sex and he could kiss his bachelorhood goodbye. The woman had gotten under his skin in a big way.

ಎಲಚ

Amanda was just getting off her shift when someone tapped her on the shoulder. She turned around to find Claudia Marshall standing behind her.

"He's not interested in marriage," she said without preamble, her acidic tone making Amanda's eyes narrow. "I just thought you should know you're wasting your time."

Amanda let out a sardonic sigh. "Like I didn't already know that before. As far as marriage goes, I'm not much for the hard stuff, either. Been there, done that, and three times is more than enough for a lifetime."

Claudia's expression faltered, but she stood her ground. "Why should I believe you?"

"I have no clue. You have no reason to doubt me. What stake would I have in lying to you?"

"I don't know, but what I do know is that you want him. You can't have him. He's mine."

So she kept saying, to everyone who would listen. Amanda wasn't buying it. But she didn't blame Claudia for wanting Joe. If Amanda had been looking, he would have been at the top of her list for prime boyfriend—or even husband—material.

"You have nothing to worry about, Claudia," Amanda assured her, grabbing her purse and keys out of her locker and heading for the door. "Joe and I aren't involved. At least not in the way you're thinking."

"He says different."

Amanda froze, her feet sticking to the floor and her tongue sticking to the roof of her mouth. The woman was lying. Had to be. Joe wouldn't have said something like that to her after he'd just told Amanda he wasn't looking for marriage or anything close. It was a full minute before she regained the power of speech.

"He's wrong. I don't want anything more than friendship from him." Aside from the mind-blowing sex, of course. The sex was something she was beginning to think she couldn't live without. Hell, who was she kidding? *Joe* was something she might not be able to live without, and that thought scared her most of all. "Seriously. I'm not looking to get involved. I have no need to justify myself and my actions to you. It's late, I'm tired, and I'm heading home now. Good night."

"Home? Don't you mean Joe's house?" Claudia huffed when Amanda said nothing. "Just by being here, you're a threat to what I've been working toward for so long. Understand this, Amanda. If you try to get in between Joe and I, I can make your life very miserable. I've spent *months* trying to get my relationship with Joe to the next level and I will not let some spoiled little child come in and ruin it."

Child? *Please.* "Fine. I get it. You're the one who seems to be having problems with understanding. Let me tell you this. What Joe and I have is just sex. Hot, incredible, sweaty, mind-blowing sex, but in the end, still just sex. Does that make you feel better?"

She stomped out of the building, got into her car and drove away. Her comment had been juvenile, but deserved. Amanda could only stand so much before she snapped.

She made the short drive out to Joe's and used her key to let herself into the house. As far as she knew, he was still at Maggie's. She hadn't noticed him leave. Perfect time for her to pack her things. She didn't need this kind of stress in her life.

The hotel back in town was calling her name. It would be a much better place than hanging around Joe, being in near-constant danger of going to a place she had no intention of ever visiting again.

ဆဝဖ

Amanda was gone.

Joe slammed the bedroom door and stomped down the stairs, through the house and onto the porch. He flopped into one of the wicker rockers and shoved a hand through his hair. He should have expected this. Had, on some basic level, but he'd held onto the hope that Amanda would still be there when he finally managed to ditch Claudia and head home.

His head ached. His chest ached. He should have seen this coming. He couldn't hold on to Amanda forever. Not when she didn't want to be held. Amanda, with the multitude of divorces leaving her gun-shy and unwilling to commit, was the woman he wanted to spend the rest of his life with. He'd fallen for her hard. And now, after he'd made a total ass out of himself with his jealousy, she'd gotten scared and run away.

He had a pretty good idea of where she'd gone. The hotel wasn't far away. He could chase her down, but what good would that do? If he went after her tonight, it would make her run even further. He had to give her time, let her think he accepted her decision before he went after her. And he *would* go after her. When he saw something he wanted, he got it. No exceptions. He'd give her the time she needed, but after that he would make no promises to keep his distance.

A car pulled up and a woman got out, but not the woman he wanted to see. Claudia.

"Hey, Joe." She walked up the steps and stood in front of him, hip propped on the railing.

"Little late for a visit, isn't it?"

"You never complained before."

Because he hadn't cared enough to complain. He hadn't realized Claudia had more on her mind than a casual fling until the idea of a commitment had snuck up on him. "I just saw you at Maggie's. Didn't we say all that needed to be said there?"

"Not even close. Where's your roommate? Did she move out already?"

Joe narrowed his eyes as he studied Claudia's expression. "What did you do?"

She shrugged. "I talked to her. She told me she isn't interested in a relationship with you."

He could practically feel her glee, and it made his eyes narrow. "No shit. Tell me something I don't know."

"So where is she?"

"I think I know, but I'm not certain. What do you care?"

"Did she really move out?"

He wouldn't dignify that question with a response. Of course Claudia knew Amanda had moved out. She wouldn't have come here if she'd thought differently.

"I'm so sorry, Joe."

"No, you aren't. You did something to chase her away." Even as he said the words, he recognized them for the lies they were. Whatever Claudia had done hadn't chased Amanda away. He'd already done that himself before Claudia had even gotten a hold of her.

He'd been the one to pull the jealousy shit. He should have known better, should have backed off or never started in the first place. Charlie Reed had been talking to her and he couldn't help himself. His brain had shut down and something far more basic had taken control. A knee-jerk reaction.

His reaction, obviously, had been the wrong choice.

Claudia clicked her tongue. "You're right. I'm not sorry. We have a good thing going here and she got in the way."

"We never made any promises to each other."

"I thought they were implied."

"No. You know they weren't. We've been through this a hundred times before. Dating once in a while doesn't equal long-term commitment. Even the dating is over now. Has been for a long time and you just refuse to let go. You knew from the beginning that it wasn't going anywhere."

"I was hoping I could get you to change your mind."

"Not gonna happen. You know what, Claudia? I think you need to leave."

She blinked, sputtering for a few seconds before she started to protest, as he'd known she would. The woman didn't know when to give up. "But, Joe—"

"No." He put his hand in the air to stop her protests. "This won't work. I'm sorry, but I'm not interested in you. We need to stop seeing each other. We won't work together the way you want us to."

She looked like she might argue, but he shook his head. "No, Claudia. Don't drag this out. It's over, though it was never really what you thought it was in the first place."

Without another word, Claudia stomped off and got into her car, peeling out of the driveway. Joe hadn't wanted to hurt her, but for months he'd been trying to shake her and nothing had worked. He'd had to do something drastic to make her understand. There was another woman in his life, and even though Amanda didn't know it yet, she'd taken him off the market. Someday he would make Amanda understand that. Someday.

With that thought firmly in his mind, he pushed out of the chair and went inside.

Chapter Eleven

"Amanda?"

Amanda turned around and found Joe's daughter, Kelly, hurrying toward her. She stopped and sighed, recognizing the younger woman from the pictures she'd seen at Joe's house when she'd been staying there. Just what she needed right now was a lecture from a woman trying to protect her father's feelings.

"Yes?" she asked, hoping she was doing a good job of feigning indifference.

"I'm Kelly Baker. I think you know my dad."

Amanda thought about denying it, but in the end decided against it. She couldn't lie about something they both knew was the truth. "I do. We're neighbors."

For the past month, since she'd moved back into her cottage, she'd done all she could to avoid running into Joe. Given her work schedule, and now college classes, it hadn't been all that difficult. The man seemed intent on giving her a wide berth, and though that should make her happy, it had only served to make her more miserable.

Kelly raised her eyebrows and at the moment she looked so much like a dark-haired version of her father that Amanda nearly laughed. "Is that all you are?"

"There wasn't much more than that. But now, yeah, we're just neighbors."

"Then why is he so upset over the fact that you left?"

Amanda frowned. Joe was upset? Kelly had to be mistaken, because when she'd moved back into the hotel he hadn't even bothered to chase her. Hadn't bothered to call save for the one time he'd phoned to let her know the cottage was back in move-in condition. The place looked amazing—exactly how she'd envisioned it—and she hadn't even had the guts yet to thank him.

He apparently hadn't had the guts to stop by with a bill for his services.

"I don't think he was upset over me. Maybe he got into a fight with Claudia."

Claudia, a woman who was closer to his age. A woman who had children the same age as Joe's. A woman he belonged with, *had* been with until Amanda had forced her way into the picture.

Kelly cocked her head to the side and stared at Amanda. She studied her for what felt like an eternity before she spoke. "You're denying the whole thing as much as he is."

"He's denying it?" For some reason, the idea of him ignoring what she'd been to him, if anything at all, made her fume. "I thought you said he was upset."

"He is. All he does is stomp around and slam things every time I visit. I've been trying to get out there to see him more since he seems lonely. Whenever I call, he's short-tempered and grumpy. That isn't like him at all. The way I see it, I figure the fact that you moved out on him has to have something to do with it."

"Moved out on him? I never lived with him."

"That's not what he said."

"Well, okay, I lived with him for a few weeks after that big storm wrecked the cottage. But it wasn't like *living* with him. We were roommates."

"Roommates generally don't share a bed."

Amanda narrowed her eyes. "Look, I don't need a lecture. There's nothing going on between your father and me, and it's that simple."

Kelly's expression softened. She tucked a strand of coffee-colored hair behind her ear and glanced around before she spoke, her voice low. "I'm not trying to give you a lecture. Believe me, I'm glad my dad is happy. Or, was happy, at least. My mom moved on years ago, and it's awesome to see him doing the same thing. Finally."

"What about Claudia?"

"She's been trying to get her hooks into him for years."

Kelly looked upset about that, and Amanda questioned her. "You don't want that to happen?"

"No. She's got four kids to support. She's just after the money she thinks my dad will provide and a man to warm her bed. She's such a snake that she's always alone."

"Your dad has money?"

"Yeah, he's not hurting for cash or anything. His business is doing really well. He doesn't advertise it, though. Plus he's got a whole bunch of rental properties that bring in a decent amount of income."

How had she not known that about him? During the time they'd been together, they'd spent many nights and many meals talking, and Joe had mentioned a rental property or two, but he'd glossed over the details of the business in favor of talking about her instead. "I had no idea the business was doing so well."

"You didn't?"

Amanda shook her head.

"That's a good thing. I'm glad you're not after him for what he can buy for you."

"I really mean it. I'm not after him at all."

"Yeah, okay." Kelly grinned. "The point is, he's miserable without you. I don't know what you did to him in that short amount of time, but he wants you back. Can't you at least go talk to him?"

"I don't think that's such a good idea. Besides, isn't he away for a few weeks? I thought he mentioned a business trip to check out a property."

"He's not leaving yet. You still have a good two days before he even heads to the airport."

Hope sparked inside Amanda and she smiled. She shouldn't, but he was miserable without her. And she was miserable without him, too. She needed him. It was as simple as that. And apparently, he needed her, too. "Are you sure he wants to see me?"

"Of course he does. You're the first woman to get to him since my mother moved out. That was five years ago, so that's got to say something." She smiled and started to walk away, turning back when she'd made it only a few steps. "Oh, and Amanda?"

"Yes?"

"I think you'd be good for him. He needs someone who isn't going to take any of his crap."

"I think I can handle him. And Kelly? Thanks."

"No problem. Just don't hurt him, okay?"

"I wouldn't dream of it." She just hoped Joe didn't hurt her. She couldn't handle one more failed relationship.

ഽഠരു

Twenty minutes later she was sitting in her car in Joe's driveway, her hands shaking and her forehead peppered with sweat. So much for having the nerve to make the first move. Now, faced with the crushing reality of what she planned to do, follow-through was looking less and less appealing with every second that ticked by. So here she sat like a sixteen-year-old stalking her crush, complete with clammy palms and a stomach full of killer butterflies.

Why now, of all times, did she have to lose her nerve?

Her cell phone rang and she brought it to her ear. "Hello?"

"Amanda?" Joe's voice reached her across the line. Her anxiety kicked into overdrive.

"Um, yeah. How are you?"

"I'm fine."

Humor laced his tone and she narrowed her eyes. "Are you laughing?"

"Yep," he said after a pause.

"Why?" What did he think was so funny? He was the one who had called her. "Care to let me in on the joke?"

"You've been sitting out in my driveway for ten minutes. Are you planning on coming inside?"

Busted. She let out a shaky sigh, raking a hand through her hair. If he hadn't thought she was nuts before, he was sure to think it now. "You knew I was here?"

"Yep. Heard you pull up."

"Why didn't you call sooner? Or better yet, come outside?"

"I was waiting to see what you'd do. But you did nothing and I got sick of waiting."

With a groan, she hung up the phone, got out of the car and marched up to his front door. He thought this was funny? She'd show him funny.

She'd just raised her hand to the knob when Joe opened the door, looking better than any man had a right to in boxers and nothing else. She didn't have time to comment on his lack of attire. He stepped forward, pulled her to him and kissed her soundly on the lips.

By the time he broke the kiss, she was breathless and could barely form a coherent sentence.

"Sorry if that was out of line." He moved back and leaned against the doorframe. "I've been waiting for way too long for you to make the first move, and I figure you showing up was close enough."

She couldn't help the nervous laugh that bubbled up in her throat. "You weren't out of line."

"Are you sure?"

She had a feeling he was talking about more than just the kiss. "Yes." The word came out as little more than a whisper, but the look in Joe's eyes told her he heard.

"You need to be sure, Amanda. I'm sure. Very sure, and I want to know we're on the same page here. I've been hurt before."

"Me, too."

"Are you willing to take the chance again?"

It was what she'd spent the past month figuring out. Did she have the courage to try again after so many missteps?

Yeah, she did. It was worth it. *He* was worth it.

"I am."

He was silent so long she was afraid he'd tell her he changed his mind. Finally, though, a smile spread across his face. "Would you be willing to make me a promise?"

"I'm not going to marry you," she blurted before she could stop herself.

"Not yet."

She wanted to tell him not ever, but she couldn't get the words to leave her mouth. She knew that with him, anything was possible. "Not yet. Maybe someday, but I won't make any promises regarding that."

"What I want you to promise me is that if you ever get freaked out like this again, you'll talk to me about it rather than push me away."

"I can do that."

"Good." He pulled her into his arms and tangled his fingers in her hair. "I have something to say to you, but you have to promise not to get upset about it."

"I promise." She had a feeling she already knew what he was going to say. It did scare her, just a little bit, but it excited her at the same time. "I'll be fine."

He waited for a few seconds, apparently judging her expression before he spoke. "I love you, Amanda. I didn't want to at first, tried to fight it, but there it is."

A giddy smile curled the corners of her mouth. She hadn't moved to Ludlow to find love, but now that she'd found it, she wouldn't trade it for anything. "I love you, too."

"You don't have to say it if you don't mean it."

"I do mean it. And I intend to spend a good, long time proving it to you." She'd do whatever it took. Joe had stuck by her, caring for her, showing her without words what she meant to him, and all the time she'd pushed him away and denied the truth she'd always known. Rachel had been right. It was just a matter of finding the right man rather than the nearest available one. "Now I think we have a lot of catching up to do."

Joe blinked at her for a few seconds before he threw his head back and laughed. "You know what? I think you're right."

About the Author

Born in Gloucester, Massachusetts, Elisa Adams has lived most of her life on the east coast. Formerly a nursing assistant and phlebotomist, writing has been a longtime hobby. Now a full time writer, she lives on the New Hampshire border with her three children.

To learn more about Elisa, please visit www.elisaadams.com. Send an email to Elisa at elisa@elisaadams.com or join her Yahoo! Newsletter group to keep up to date! http://groups.yahoo.com/group/ElisaAdams/

Look for these titles

Now Available

The Whole Shebang

Coming Soon:

Damage Control

GREAT
cheap
fun

Discover eBooks!

THE FASTEST WAY TO GET THE HOTTEST NAMES

Get your favorite authors on your favorite reader, long before they're
out in print! Ebooks from Samhain go wherever you go, and work with
whatever you carry—Palm, PDF, Mobi, and more.